Saving Grace

Also By Pamela Gossiaux

Horses and Hearts Inspirational Romance Series

Finding Hope

Healing Faith

Saving Grace

Russo Romantic Mystery Series

Mrs. Chartwell and the Cat Burglar (A Russo Romantic Mystery: Book 1)

Trusting the Cat Burglar (A Russo Romantic Mystery: Book 2)

Romancing the Cat Burglar (A Russo Romantic Mystery: Book 3)

A Cat Burglar Christmas (A Russo Romantic Mystery Novella)

Good Enough

Ordinary Girl

Why Is There a Lemon in My Fruit Salad? How to Stay Sweet When Life Turns Sour

A Kid at Heart: Becoming a Child of Our Heavenly Father

Praise for Pamela Gossiaux's Books

Finding Hope

"*Finding Hope* is a charming wonderfully told story of Hope, Love, Forgiveness, Romance and God. Anyone who has ever owned and loved a horse will relate deeply with Victoria Jones and her horse."
— William D. Curnutt,
Amazon Vine Voice, 5-stars

"Wow! This one is a keeper!"
— J. Barr,
Amazon Top 500 Reviewer, 5-stars

Mrs. Chartwell and the Cat Burglar

"A highly suspenseful, self-described romantic mystery that tugs at your heart and satisfies your intellect."
— John J. Kelly, ***Detroit Free Press***

"I highly recommend it! It has everything you could wish for: mystery, suspense, romance and a great adventure. I just couldn't put it down!"
— Susan Keefe, **Midwest Book Review**

Good Enough

"Richly meaningful while wildly entertaining, *GOOD ENOUGH* is a major new book by an exceptionally talented author"
— **San Francisco Review of Books**

Saving Grace

A Horses and Hearts Inspirational Romance

INTERNATIONAL BESTSELLING AUTHOR
PAMELA GOSSIAUX

Tri-Cat Publishing

Scripture quotations are taken from *The Holy Bible*, New International Version, copyright 1973, 1978, 1984 by International Bible Society.

Visit the author's website at: PamelaGossiaux.com

First Printing, September 2020
Library of Congress Control Number: 2020917792

ISBN: 978-1-7348968-4-8 (paperback)
ISBN: 978-1-7348968-3-1 (eBook)

Cover Design: Llewellen Designs
Formatter: Dallas Hodge, dalhodge56@gmail.com
Editor: Rachel Song, Songbird Editing
Author Photo: Vera Davis Photography

Published in the United States by Tri-Cat Publishing.
Chelsea, MI

Tri-Cat Publishing

To Duane.

You mend the fences, lift the heavy stuff, and don't complain about the hay in my hair or the mud on my boots.

I love you.

"For it is by grace you have been saved, through faith—and this is not from yourselves, it is the gift of God, not by works, so that no one can boast."
– Ephesians 2: 8-9

"Amazing grace, how sweet the sound,
That saved a wretch like me!
I once was lost, but now I'm found,
Was blind, but now I see."
– John Newton

Chapter One

Hannah Whitney rode the horse like she did everything else, as if her life depended on it. Leaning forward over the animal's neck, its black mane whipping her face, its hooves thundering under her, its muscles propelling her forward at a breakneck pace, twenty-four-year-old Hannah was running away from her life.

She wasn't supposed to gallop the horse. Grace was a very expensive pureblood Hanoverian, seventeen hands of warmblood sport horse. Her equine ancestors had been carefully bred over the generations to produce perfection in and out of the show ring. Purchased for Hannah by her father, Grace was *the* horse that would take her to the Olympics. "Guaranteed" was what her breeder had said. Hannah and Grace had trained together every day, *every single day*, for the past four years, and this was finally the year they would see if they qualified or not. Their qualifying show was in ten weeks.

But today she was running.

It wasn't Hannah's fault. Her dad had come out to the barn a few minutes ago, while they were training, and given her the bad news. *Really* bad news.

"Hans quit," he had said simply.

Marcus Whitney was a multi-million dollar pharmaceutical tycoon, whose offices spanned the entire United States. He stood there with his hands in the front pockets of his tailor-cut pants, the tails of his suit coat billowing in the breeze, looking quite lost for a man who could afford his own sports car collection.

"What?" Hannah had ridden Grace over to where he stood. The morning sun showed the creases around his eyes, more noticeable this past year, and the streaks of gray in his black hair. For a moment, she felt a pang of sadness at this little bit of vulnerability, as if he had been unmasked.

"He quit," her dad said again. He looked up at her, then lifted a hand to shield his eyes. "He says he can't take it anymore. You're difficult. You're rude. You're too driven. Those were his exact words."

Hannah frowned and ran her finger under the chin strap on her riding helmet. She felt a growing panic in the pit of her stomach.

"But he *can't* quit! The trials are in ten weeks. We don't have a program for Grace choreographed out yet. He was supposed to help me with that. I told him he was moving too slowly, that Grace and I need more time—" She heard her voice rising in volume. She did that when she was afraid. She had tried to break the habit of yelling when she was stressed out, for her own sake, for Hans's sake, but she couldn't.

"Hans is old. Seventy-five. He's been thinking of retiring for years," said her dad. "Since his wife has started to show signs of dementia, he thought now was a good time."

Hannah thought back to yesterday. Hans had gently suggested that there was more to life than winning, and she had yelled at him. She had accused him of not knowing anything, of not understanding what it was like to be *her*. Winning *was* everything! What did she have left if she didn't win?

"He called me last night," her dad said. He was watching her, like he did his investors, to see how she would react, to figure out which card to play next.

No. That wasn't it. He wasn't like that anymore. Her dad had changed not long ago. She still couldn't get used to the new, caring man he had become. He'd had a religious experience or something. It would all fall apart soon enough. She was sure of it. She only had to wait and her cold, business-first father would come back. *That* was a man she knew how to handle. This one threw her off her game.

"Last night?" Hannah said. "And you waited until *now* to tell me?"

Her anger flared again. It was fear, really. But she knew better than to show it.

Marcus Whitney shrugged. "I wanted you to get a good night's sleep."

A good night's sleep? She would never sleep well again. Not now.

"Besides, I wanted to reach out to someone else. Another trainer for you. He responded to me first thing this morning. Just a few minutes ago, actually. He came in person."

"I don't *want* a new trainer," Hannah said. Hans had been the best that money could buy. An Olympic-caliber dressage trainer, he had been a two-time gold medalist for Germany before coming to the

US to teach. His students regularly won medals in international competition.

"I want Hans back," she said. "I'll just call him and apologize."

"Too late," her dad said. "I hired this one already."

"*What?* Without me meeting him first?" There was that shrill voice again. She took a deep breath.

"I had actually reached out to him a few months ago, just in case."

Things had been rough with Hans for a while now. She had never really liked the old man. He was grouchy, cold, and yelled a lot.

"I knew Hans would quit," Hannah said. "You just can't count on people."

"Not if you drive them away," her dad said quietly.

Hannah straightened in her saddle and switched the riding crop and reins to one hand so she could rub Grace on the neck. Grace was her best friend. A pretty bay mare, her dark brown coat had caught Hannah's eye the moment she saw her. The mare had four big, white socks running up her legs, ending just below the knees. Her mane and tail were black. A white blaze ran down her face. White was unusual in Grace's breed, sometimes frowned upon. But Grace was so beautiful when she moved, so fluid, that the extra color made her exceptionally eye-catching.

"Who is he?" Hannah asked. "I should at least read up on him before I meet him."

"There's no time. As I said, he's here *now*," her dad said.

"Now?" Hannah looked around, startled. "Where?"

"I asked him to wait up at the house."

"Dad, why on earth…"

"Hannah, listen to me. You don't have much choice who we hire. You've run out of options. You've fired or lost the last four trainers. This is who is left. He's an Olympic winner himself."

"What's his name?"

Her dad hesitated. Then she saw him put on his game face—his jaw set, his chin raising a little as if daring her to defy what he was about to say. It was the same face he had used to tell her eight-year-old self that her mother had left them.

"Chase Livingston."

Her stomach dropped. "*What?* No. No way." She shook her head. Grace snorted and stomped her foot, as if to agree. Hannah rubbed the horse's neck. "You would let the world know that Chase Livingston is training Marcus Whitney's daughter? You really want *that* kind of publicity?"

Her dad's chin dropped a little. He ran his hand through his graying hair. "I just want you to be happy."

"Dad! No way! Are you trying to ruin my life?"

And that's when she'd run. The problem was, there was only so far she could go on the farm.

Fieldstone Farm and Dressage Center was a one-hundred-acre expanse of rolling green pastures lined in white fencing. The barn itself was a beautiful structure—a long stretch of white building with green shutters and black peaked roofs topped by cupolas. There was even a wrought-iron horse weather-vein atop the largest cupola.

Hannah pulled her horse up to a stop and jumped off. Both of them were panting. She had raced down the winding gravel path that led to the back of the property. There was a small pond here, surrounded by willow trees. It matched the pond up behind their large house. Only here, there was a white gazebo. She came here often for lunch. Or to hide.

She could barely see the house or barns from here, and it was the only place other than her bedroom that she could be truly alone.

She wrapped her arms around Grace's neck, and the mare bent her head down to nuzzle Hannah gently on the shoulder.

"Oh, Grace," she said. "I've messed up again. I'm so sorry."

Chase Livingston had won a gold medal in the Olympics in dressage when he was only eighteen, which put her at age twelve at the time. What had made him so famous was not only his young age, but the fact that he had trained his own horse and choreographed the freestyle competition *himself.* She remembered it like it was yesterday. She had attended with her nanny, and together they had watched his horse, Debonair Man, dance to Queen's "Under Pressure." He didn't lose points in anything, and his black horse had moved so gracefully that at times it looked like he was floating on air. They beat the Germans and Chase took home the gold.

She had never met Chase in person. He had gone on to win nearly every competition he entered, still with no trainer, which was unheard of. A prodigy, they called him. And then, four years later, at the next Olympic games, he had messed up. The mistake had cost him the medal, a lucrative sponsorship deal, and his career. Then he started spouting nonsense about finding religion, but critics teased that God certainly hadn't blessed his career. Chase had gone into hiding from the harsh media and hadn't been seen since. There was *no way* she'd be paired up with him. The embarrassment would be too much.

Hannah heard a motor and looked up. It was her dad in his bright yellow Jeep. There was a passenger beside him.

He slowed the vehicle down as he approached Hannah and stopped. He got out, looking once again spry and like the man-in-control she knew. Another man got out with him, who she knew was Chase Livingston. He was broadly built, around thirty years old now, not the slender eighteen-year-old she remembered from the Olympics. She put her hand up to block the sunlight. He had on sunglasses and a baseball cap.

The two men walked over to her.

"Hannah," her dad said. "Meet Chase Livingston."

For a moment, her heart stuttered. He had once been her hero. She had clipped photos of him from the *Sports Illustrated* and *Dressage Monthly* magazines and hung them up in her room. She had made a scrapbook of articles about him. She had followed his career, wanting to be like him someday.

Until he'd embarrassed himself. In a fit of fury that coincided with the day her nanny had quit, she had thrown the scrapbook out.

"Hello," she said quietly.

"Hi."

He reached out a hand for her to shake. She took it. His hand was warm. The muscles in his arms strained against his sleeves, and he had a broad chest under a tight t-shirt. He removed his sunglasses and looked at her with the same dark brown eyes that had stared out at her from her posters for years. She'd had a crush on him back them. Big time.

"It's really nice to meet you," he said. His voice was deep and warm. He stood about six-feet tall, just slightly taller than her dad. "So is this the horse we'll be working with?"

Hannah tore her eyes away from him to look at Grace. "Yes. This is Amazing Grace." She ran her hand along the horse's neck and was glad for her own sunglasses to hide behind. She glanced back at Chase and felt her heart patter again.

"We can start this afternoon," he said. "Or even now. I need to get an idea of what type of music you like, and what moves your horse does best, and I can start putting something together for you right away."

Hannah glanced at her dad. She wanted to be mad, but she hadn't expected Chase to have this effect on her. She had abandoned Chase along with the rest of the world when he had failed at the last Olympic games. She had been angry at him, a complete stranger, for messing up. For not winning.

But now that he was *here* in the flesh, well, she hadn't expected him to be so... *handsome*.

But how *good* was he? She frowned.

"Are you good at your job?" she said, trying to regain some of the momentum she felt she had lost. She had to come across as strong. Always. First impressions were important. She couldn't let him think she was weak.

"I am," he said. He met her eyes. A challenge.

"What have you been doing since you quit showing?"

There was a moment of silence. Chase cleared his throat. "Selling insurance."

"You're kidding, right?" Hannah said.

Marcus Whitney cleared his throat. "Hannah, I need to get to work," he said. "I'll drive Chase back to the barn. Why don't you meet us there and give him a tour? Then the two of you can decide when you want to begin."

Hannah glanced at Chase, then remembered she was angry with her dad. "I'm a little busy. Have Jonathon give him a tour." Jonathon was their barn manager.

"You're not *that* busy," her dad said. He used the same tone of voice he spoke in when closing deals at the office. *Don't mess with me*, it said.

Well, fine. She could give him a little tour. What could it hurt? And she knew better than to argue with her dad. She'd have to find another way to lose Chase.

She nodded at Chase. "I'll see you in a few minutes."

"Want a leg up?" Chase asked.

She glanced at her dad, then back at Chase.

"That would be nice, thank you."

He moved over to Grace's side and cupped his hands so she could put her foot in them. Then he gave her a boost up onto her horse. Once she was on, he took the stirrup and put it on her foot, his arm brushing her calf in the process. Her heart caught again.

What was *wrong* with her? She might have had a crush on him as a girl, but she was a grown woman now. This was ridiculous.

Remember how far he has fallen, Hannah, she reminded herself.

"You all set?" he asked.

From atop Grace, she looked down into his brown eyes. "Yes. Thank you," she said. He held her gaze for just a moment too long, then smiled. Gosh, he was gorgeous.

"Great. See you in a few minutes."

She watched as the two men walked back to the Jeep and climbed in. Then she nudged Grace with her legs, and her mare broke into a smooth canter. She raced past the Jeep and up the gravel trail ahead of them, beating them to the barn.

This was certainly going to be interesting.

Chapter Two

Chase watched Hannah Whitney gallop Grace past them and wondered what he had gotten himself into. "It's not worth it," his sister had said as soon as he told her that Marcus Whitney had offered him a job. "She's a spoiled brat."

That seemed to be everybody's opinion of Hannah. The brilliant and beautiful daughter of one of America's top pharmaceutical gurus, Hannah Whitney wasn't lacking in anything. And she was used to getting her way. He had watched her over the years from a distance, as she climbed her way to the top of the national finalists for the next Olympics. She was good, as was her horse, and he was pretty sure she'd be picked for the team despite her attitude. He had never seen her act out in public, but from the list of trainers she had gone through, and from word around the show world, Hannah Whitney was a piece of work.

And she was beautiful. He tore his eyes from her and her horse, all too aware that her father was riding in the Jeep beside him.

"You ready for this job?" Marcus asked, as if reading his mind.

"To work with Hannah? Yes. Of course." He kept his voice confident, neutral.

"She has a reputation." Marcus pulled the Jeep into the circular drive in front of the barn and shut the engine off.

"I heard. So do I."

"I heard."

The two men were silent for a moment. Then Chase felt Marcus's eyes on him.

"Do you know why I hired you, Chase?" he asked.

"Because I'm the only one left, sir?"

Marcus laughed. "I'm a rich man, son. I can find a trainer if I want one. No, I hired *you* because you're a Christian and my daughter is lost."

Of all the things that Marcus Whitney could possibly say to him, this wasn't even on Chase's radar. He turned to look at the man and took his sunglasses off.

"Pardon?"

Marcus removed his own sunglasses and smiled. Emotion lit up his blue eyes, which crinkled his face, giving him a softer, older look than his years. "You heard me."

"Um..." Chase wasn't sure how to respond to that. "Are you saying . . .?"

"When we were looking for Hannah's next horse, for Grace, we looked all over the world. She and I traveled to Germany twice, to France once, up to Canada, and to several farms here in the United States. We looked at a lot of horses. But then we found Grace, right here in the US. At the time, Grace had been in training with Ustaf Venuzelo, whom I'm sure you've heard of."

Chase nodded. Venuzelo was an Olympic gold medalist and trainer of the best.

"And the mare was beautiful. My daughter fell in love with her. Grace too, with Hannah, right away, like they were meant for each other. We had to have her. So I bought her, and I hired the best trainer I could find."

Chase wondered where this was going. He had done a bit of research on Grace after Marcus had first called him. The horse was well bred and hadn't been shown much before Hannah bought her. It was Venuzelo's tradition to keep horses at his farm until they were ready to win. Then he took them into the showring. It took most horses a good seven years of training before they were ready to complete at an Olympic-caliber level.

"Grace was owned by Julius Bloom, the online retailer. You're familiar with him?"

Chase nodded. Bloom owned the home shopping network that was worth its weight in gold.

"He came to the farm a little over a year ago to visit me."

Here, Marcus stopped talking. He turned forward and gazed out the windshield, watching his daughter, who seemed to be arguing with a stable hand.

"I was a terrible father," he said. "I was never home. I bought Hannah everything she wanted, but I was never there for her. Julius Bloom said he came by that day to check on Grace. He wanted to see how the horse was doing. But I think he came to check on me."

Out the windshield, Chase saw the stable hand nod his head to Hannah and disappear into the barn.

Hannah sighed, heaving her shoulders, then glanced in the direction of their Jeep.

"That day, I was busy as usual, on my way out the door to some meeting or the other," Marcus said. "I shook Julius's hand, and told him Hannah was in the barn. But he asked if I had a moment to talk. He looked serious, so I called my pilot and told him I'd be a few minutes late. We went into my study. Julius told me how he had worked hard to make it to the top, to be the best and the richest, and that yes, he had succeeded. But he had also been divorced three times and had grown children in different states whom he hardly ever saw. And they hated him. He told me that one day he realized that *everybody* hated him. His kids. His ex-wives. His employees. He was a driven man and expected everybody to work as hard as *he* did. He had no time for anybody, and all his 'friends' were simply yes-people, striving to please him just so they could move ahead.

"Then his daughter called to tell him she was getting married. She asked what the budget was for the wedding. He had never met her boyfriend or even known she was dating anyone, because he was that out of touch. So he asked a few questions about the groom. She said he was rich. He was successful. A partner in a law firm. She never mentioned love. It occurred to him that his daughter had grown to be just like him."

Marcus paused, still watching his own daughter out the windshield. Hannah had dismounted from Grace. Another young man came out to stand by her, and Hannah unbuckled the saddle and handed it to him.

"She always cools her own horse off," Marcus said. "She'll walk Grace until she's cool, then groom her. She never lets anybody else do it for her, even though we have the staff."

Chase watched as Hannah took Grace's bridle off and replaced it with a green and gold halter, the colors of the farm. She glanced at the Jeep again, saw they were still sitting in it, and began to walk Grace the length of the front pasture and back.

Marcus cleared his throat and looked over at Chase. "Julius decided then to kill himself. He had been miserable for months. He opened the door, stepped out onto the balcony of his twenty-second-floor office—"

"Wait!" Chase said. "Julius Bloom was going to commit suicide? *The* Julius Bloom? How come we never heard about that in the news?"

"Because he didn't jump," Marcus said, meeting his eyes. "Instead, he got a phone call right at that moment. On his cell. It was an unknown number, and he couldn't imagine who it could be. Curiosity got a hold of him, and he answered it. It changed his life."

There was a rap on the driver's side window of the Jeep. Both men jumped and turned to see Hannah. Marcus rolled down the window, and warm, humid air wafted in, breaking through the cold air conditioning. It was only 10 a.m., but it was already quite hot outside for a Michigan morning.

"I don't have all day," Hannah said. "Are you coming or not?"

She was looking at Chase.

"I was just filling him in on a few things," Marcus said. He turned to Chase. "Go. I need to get to a meeting anyway. We can finish our discussion later."

Chase nodded reluctantly, wishing Marcus would finish his story. He wanted to know about this mysterious phone call that Julius Bloom had received, and how it tied in with Grace and Hannah. He opened his mouth to say something, but Marcus gave a slight shake of his head. *No.*

"Okay," said Chase, glancing at Hannah. Then he opened the door and climbed out. "Thank you, Mr. Whitney."

"I'll see you both later," Marcus said. He leaned out the widow and kissed Hannah on the cheek, then drove up toward the house.

"Well," Hannah said. Her eyes met Chase's, then ran down his body and back up, stopping at his Chicago Cubs baseball cap. She frowned slightly, as if she didn't like what she saw. He wondered if it was him she disapproved of or the cap. "You want to see the place or not?"

Chase nodded and put his hands in the front pockets of his khakis.

Grace reached forward, snuffling at Chase's wrist. He took his hand out of his pocket and let her smell the back of his hand, then he reached up and rubbed her neck. "Hey, girl," he said. She was cool to the touch.

"I'll put her back in her stall first," Hannah said. She turned and motioned with her chin for him to follow. "Come on. You might as well start off by seeing where she stays."

16

He tried not to notice the curve of Hannah's hips in her tight riding breeches as she led her horse ahead of him. *She's a viper, Chase.* His sister's words rang in his head. *Be careful.*

To describe the stables as beautiful would be an understatement. Chase, as an Olympian, had trained at many nice places, so he wasn't given over to the sticker shock that would strike the average horse person. But even on the scale of opulence, Fieldstone Farm was incredible. The sheer beauty of the design was one thing, but the immaculate cleanliness was another. Everything was exceptionally tidy.

As they walked through the double green doors into the cool, cement walkway of the barn aisle and turned right, Chase didn't see any dirt on the ground. The stalls, made of a light-colored wood—probably pine—dipped low at the doors in a U-shape, so the horses could look over. Green wrought-iron bars ran from the front wall of the stalls upwards. Each horse had an individual cast-iron spicket inside their stall, with a bucket hanging underneath. One simply had to turn the faucet on to give them fresh water.

The barn smelled clean, of pine shavings and green hay.

Hannah glanced at him, as if to see his reaction. He kept his face neutral. He had to keep the upper hand, not let her think he was too impressed. He wanted her to know he was on the same level as her. He had been beaten down too many times over the past several years—ridiculed, belittled—and wasn't about to give this woman any ground. This was his one chance to get back into the world he loved, and he wasn't going to blow it.

He walked down the aisle beside Hannah and Grace, looking at the horses in the stalls, each probably worth tens of thousands of dollars. Or millions.

"How many boarders do you have?" he asked.

"Fifteen," Hannah said. "Most of them are Class A show horses, their riders pretty dominant in their sport. They're all hunter/jumper or dressage."

As they walked, none of the stable hands cleaning the stalls or emptying buckets met Hannah's gaze. No one said "hi" to her or asked how she was doing. Perhaps she had already talked to them all. Or maybe, like him, she didn't have any friends.

"Here we are," she said. Grace's stall was near the south end of the barn. A bronze nameplate with "Amazing Grace" was attached to her stall door. Hannah opened it and led her horse in. Grace lowered her head for Hannah to remove the halter. Hannah put her forehead briefly on Grace's, then petted her neck. "See you later, girl," she said quietly.

Grace moved over to drink from her water bucket, and Hannah slid the stall door closed.

"So this is the barn," she said.

"I see."

She walked briskly back toward the center where they had come in. "These here are tack rooms. Our boarders keep their riding equipment in here, but so do I." She opened a crisply painted green door into a room that was just as spotlessly clean as the rest of the barn. A young man was sitting on a bench, polishing a hunt seat saddle. Along one wall, saddles sat on arms attached along the wall, and above or next to them were the bridles for the horses. The metal bits shone, with not a hint of grass stains or horse slobber.

"Wow," Chase said. He couldn't help himself. He saw Hannah's lips tease upwards, like she was holding back a smile.

"Hello," he said to the young man who was polishing the saddle, and the man looked up, surprised. He nodded to Chase.

Hannah said nothing.

"Let's go." She turned abruptly and walked out.

"Hannah!" a deep, loud voice called to them from down the aisle as they exited the tack room. A blond-haired, blue-eyed man with a clean-shaven face walked over to them. He sauntered more than walked and was swinging a bridle from his hand. It was a Cordova bridle, Chase noticed. The most expensive brand money could buy. One that used to sponsor him.

"How are you today?" The man's eyes sparkled as he stopped and met Hannah's. He grinned, showing exceptionally white teeth, which reminded Chase of fangs.

"I'm well, Devon," Hannah said. "But I'm quite busy at the moment."

Devon's eyes traveled to Chase and narrowed. "Chase Livingston. Well, well, well. What cat dragged you in here?"

Chase didn't know this cocky man, but he didn't have time to form a reply. Hannah quickly spoke up.

"Chase is my new trainer."

Devon's eyes registered surprise, then he looked back at Hannah. "Ha ha. Funny."

"I'm serious." Her eyes met Devon's, never wavering, and her chin lifted a little, as if daring him to say anything else.

Devon glanced at Chase again, then looked back at Hannah. He stood about four inches taller than she did. "I like that new brooch," he said, and touched the golden pin on her collar with his index finger. The brooch was shaped like a horseshoe and was studded with what appeared to be real diamonds.

Hannah smiled sweetly. "Daddy gave it to me."

"Of course," Devon said.

"I really have to go," Hannah said, and sidled past Devon. "Chase, come on."

Chase and Devon locked eyes once more. Devon didn't move, and Chase had to push past him. Who *was* this character? Did Hannah actually *like* him? He couldn't tell if Devon's flirting was returned by Hannah or not. He certainly was arrogant. Chase used to be arrogant, too, until God had humbled him.

Hannah stopped midway up the aisle, across from the green double-doors they had entered. She motioned her hand to the right. "This is our indoor riding arena," she said. Chase saw two riders inside. One was mounted on a tall Hanoverian horse and was sitting the horse's smooth trot. They looked like they were floating. He watched the animal's long legs move swiftly back and forth in a two-beat gait. A second person, a man in his thirties, was working a horse on a long line around him.

"I'll show you the wash rack," Hannah said. She continued on down the aisle. Not far from the opening to the arena was an area with four wash stalls, two on each side of the aisle. The sides and floors were cement, with rubber matting on the floor. Each wash stall had a small shelf that held bottles of shampoo, brushes, and water scrapers, as well as nicely folded towels. A hose hung from the ceiling in each, and there was a handle on the wall.

"All of our water here is heated," Hannah said simply.

She showed him the outdoor arenas. There were several. Two of the jumping arenas had small training jumps, and a third had the massive Olympic-caliber jumps, some reaching seven feet in height. Then they came to the dressage arena. It was out behind the barns in a quiet area, a little bit away from the buildings.

"This is where I train," Hannah said.

The arena was surrounded in white fencing. Inside, lettered cubes marked off the areas where the horse would transition from walk to trot and so on, as dictated by the dressage pattern.

"We have two other dressage arenas," Hannah said, "but this one is mine."

"Only yours?" Chase asked.

"Yes."

The entire "tour" had been quick. Hannah walked fast, and she was clearly tense and tightly wound. She put him in mind of a tiger. She talked little and explained things quickly. He did his best to keep up. She hadn't met his eyes the entire time, but now she stopped and turned to face him.

"Any questions?"

Chase looked at her. She was probably about five-feet, six-inches tall, and he stood about five inches taller than her. Her piercing blue eyes didn't waver as he met them.

"No. Not now."

"Good. I'm going up to the house to get washed up."

"I believe you're supposed to show me the guesthouse."

She raised an eyebrow. "The guesthouse?"

"Yes. Your dad said the apartment above the barn was taken by your barn manager. So he said I was to stay in the guesthouse."

Hannah puffed and crossed her arms. She walked away from him, then turned quickly and walked back. "You're kidding me."

Chase shrugged.

"You're going to *live* here?"

"I'm from out of town. My home is near Chicago, which, you'll realize, would be a bit of a morning commute to Michigan."

Hannah shrugged. "Why don't you find a place to live in town?"

"In St. Ives?" Chase smiled. The small, tourist town was filled with bed and breakfasts and tidy little shops. "There aren't many apartments."

"I'm sure we can find you one."

He didn't want to tell her that Marcus had been insistent that Chase live on the farm. He wanted him near night and day, to train his daughter and her horse.

"You can ask your dad," he said.

Hannah frowned. "Fine. Come on." She walked over to a shed where she climbed into a golf cart. He climbed in beside her. She turned the cart on and sped out of the parking lot surrounding the barn. Chase grabbed the side bar to keep from falling out.

The guesthouse looked more like an upscale vacation rental. It was located some distance behind the barns, on the opposite side of Hannah's dressage arena. After exiting the parking lot behind the barns, one could drive down a paved path that ran in between two pastures lined in white fencing. Back behind the pastures was a little house surrounded by trees and a small lawn. It was a single-story building, sided in white, with green shutters and a green door that matched the barns. It was neat and clean on the outside, like the barns had been.

They got out, and Hannah walked up to the door and jiggled the handle. It was locked. She stood on her tiptoes and ran her hand along the top doorframe and grabbed a key.

The inside was just as clean. Off to their right was a small kitchen with oak cabinets and light beige granite countertops. An island separated it from a living room, which contained a plush couch and flat-screen TV.

"You have Wi-Fi back here," said Hannah. "I'm sure you probably have cable."

"I don't really watch much TV," Chase said, although he could imagine himself watching a few Cubs games, and, of course, the horse events on ESPN.

"Back there is the bedroom," Hannah said.

Chase walked in the direction she pointed. Behind the living room was a little hallway. Off to his left was a very neat and clean bathroom; off to his right was a bedroom. Someone had already brought his luggage in, and it was stacked on the floor next to the bed.

"Thanks," he said.

He turned to look at Hannah again.

"We can get started right away," he said.

"I've already worked Grace," she said.

"But you need me to choreograph for you, right?"

Hannah nodded. She had crossed her arms.

"So we can start by me getting a feel for what type of music you like. Then later, after Grace has rested, you can show me some of her moves."

"Have you ever done this before?" she asked.

"I won a gold medal for this," Chase said.

"Yeah, the wonder kid. I remember. But you've never done this for anybody else," Hannah said. Her tone was condescending.

They were both quiet for a moment, sizing each other up. He started to wonder if his sister has been right, and he should have turned down this job.

"No," he said quietly.

"Then how do you know you can do it for me and Grace?"

Chase didn't. It was a bet he was counting on. And praying about. He missed the dressage world—missed it terribly.

"Because I see things that others don't," he said. "When I see a horse work, the music just comes to me. The parts come together. In my head."

Hannah narrowed her eyes.

"Listen," she said. "We *have* to work together because I'm running out of time, and I need a trainer. But I'm not thrilled about it. You're..." She squinched her nose up.

"I'm what?" Chase said, challenging her.

She met his eyes. "You disappointed me," she said firmly.

"Me? When?"

"When you gave up. When you quit. You were so good."

He *had* been good. Until he wasn't.

Chase didn't want to talk about it. He glanced at his watch. "It's almost 11 a.m. Why don't you go home, and then we can meet after lunch. Say, around one?"

He saw Hannah sigh. Not a dramatic sigh, just a little sigh that looked like she had resigned herself to the situation. "Sure," she said. "Come up to the house. We'll work in the conservatory."

The conservatory? Sounded posh.

"Okay," Chase said.

Their eyes met again.

"Okay," Hannah said. Then she spun around on the heel of her expensive riding boot and let herself out.

This was going to be a wild ride.

Chapter Three

Hannah lay on her bed next to her gray cat, Pussy Willow. She had named him after a cat in one of her favorite childhood books. Her mother had read that book to her over and over again before bedtime when she was small.

She was laying on her side on the soft, white comforter, her face beside the cat. His big yellow eyes were watching her through half-closed lids. His purring comforted her.

Her hair was still damp from her shower, and although she had towel dried it, the dampness was soaking into her pillow.

She had a lot to think about before she met with Chase Livingston in an hour.

"What do *you* think?" she asked her cat. Pussy Willow watched her lazily. He didn't have an opinion about Chase, or life in general for that matter. He was simply enjoying being curled up next to his favorite person.

She was quite upset that her dad had hired a trainer without telling her. And what about Hans calling her dad last night and quitting? Didn't anyone think to include *her* in these decisions? After all, this *was* about *her.*

Hannah was tired. She was tired of trainers and tired of people in general. Sometimes, she simply wanted to ride Grace off into the sunset like people did in the movies, to be alone with her with no pressure, no people running her life, no decisions to make. But what would she have then? She'd have nothing.

"Maybe I should have gone to college," Hannah said to Pussy Willow. "Dad asked me several times if I wanted to go into the pharmaceutical business. Do you remember?"

She reached out and scratched him under the chin. He lifted his head so she could reach under better, and the purring grew louder. "But I'd go crazy in an office. Don't you think?"

Riding was her life. Grace was her best friend. She was only truly happy when she was on her horse, putting her through her paces.

"Pussy Willow," Hannah said. The cat pricked his ears at his name.

Hannah thought about the book he was named after. She had her mom's copy tucked safely in a box under her bed, along with a few photos of her mom and some other trinkets. The book was worn from wear.

"You weren't even born the last time she read me that book," Hannah said to the cat.

She remembered the night well. She had been eight years old, and her mom was tucking her into bed. Her dad was out late somewhere, probably at a business dinner. Hannah had a strict bedtime, and usually her mom wouldn't read to her past 9 p.m., but that night, when she asked for the book a second time, her mom obliged. Then she had tucked her in, sung 'You are my Sunshine', and kissed her good night. Had Hannah known why she was getting all the special attention, she could have maybe stopped what happened next.

She had awoken the next morning for school to the little Tinkerbell alarm clock her parents had given her. It played Disney tunes, and she had set the alarm to play "When You Wish Upon a Star." She used the bathroom, then wandered downstairs to the kitchen where her mom was usually getting her breakfast ready. But she didn't see her mom.

"Mom?" she had called. "Mom?"

The house was quiet, her dad having left for work very early, as usual.

She walked back upstairs and looked in her mom's bedroom. It was empty, but the bed was made. She walked through the house calling for her but didn't find her.

"Mom?" She decided to go downstairs and look outside. At the time, they had lived in a subdivision, and the yard was a pretty good size, but not so big that she wouldn't be able to see her mom. It was November, and too cold outside for her mom to be in the garden.

She had felt a growing fear in her stomach as she came back inside and looked in the attached garage. Her mom's car was gone.

She stared at the empty space for a few minutes.

Maybe there had been an emergency.

She closed the door and ran back into the kitchen, nearly slipping on the tile flooring. Her mom always left notes on the kitchen table if she needed to tell them anything. Sure enough, there was a note with her dad's name on it, written on yellow notebook paper and folded in half. Hannah grabbed it and unfolded it.

Dear Marcus,
    I can't go on like this. You can have everything. Don't look for me.

Eva

Hannah read it over three times. What did it mean?

She ran upstairs and tried to call her dad, but his secretary said he was in a business meeting. She tried his cell phone, but it went to voicemail. She tried her mom's cell phone, but she heard it ringing up in the bedroom. Her mom had left it.

Her mom would be back soon, surely, because Hannah had to get to school. The note was obviously for her *dad*, not for her.

She went upstairs and got dressed. She brushed her teeth, combed her hair, and packed her book bag. Then she came downstairs and got herself a granola bar. She sat at the kitchen table, eating it, and staring out the window into the yard. The snow had covered her mom's flowerbeds. She wondered what the roses did in the cold. Did they sleep? Were they aware that the world was dead around them?

She waited.

It was past 8 a.m. now. Her classes were about to start. She went to a private school, so there was no bus to pick her up like there was for her friend down the street. She found a brown paper bag. She put an apple inside along with a peanut butter and strawberry jam sandwich and a juice box. She hated the school lunches, so her mom always packed her one from home.

Hannah put on her shoes and her coat, and sat on the living room couch where she could watch the driveway and the road out front. She wanted to be sure to see her mom when she got home. Her book bag and lunch were beside her, so she'd be ready.

At the time, they didn't have a nanny, and the housekeeper only came on Thursdays. Today was Tuesday. So Hannah was alone.

She sat there all day. She remembered getting hungry at some point and eating her lunch. But she was still sitting there when her dad came home at 8 p.m. that night and found her sweating a little bit in her winter coat.

Hannah's phone alarm went off, signaling that Chase would be here soon. She had no desire to talk with him, but it didn't seem like she had a choice if she wanted to be ready for the Olympic trials.

"I've gotta go, handsome boy," she said to Pussy Willow. He had fallen asleep but cracked open an eye when she spoke.

She went into the private bathroom that was part of her bedroom suite and blow-dried her blonde hair.

It was thick and full, and looked good around her shoulders. She swept mascara onto her eyelashes and put some light pink color on her lips, then added a little blush.

Her dad had always said that part of having the advantage in a meeting was looking top notch. She was wearing her designer blue jeans and a tight-fitting, black, scoop-neck t-shirt that said "Boss Lady" on the front. She left her feet bare, since she was staying in the house. Last night, she had painted her toenails pink.

She took one last look at herself in the mirror. She was ready.

But she had butterflies in her stomach.

Hannah wasn't usually intimidated by people, but Chase was complicated. While she had never met him in person before today, she had followed his career so closely as a teen that she *felt* like she knew him. She thought of the scrapbook full of newspaper and magazine article clippings she had pieced together and then later thrown out.

He had let her down. Just like everyone else in her life, Chase Livingston had let her down.

She sighed and walked down the stairs, just as the doorbell rang.

"Hello." She heard Anastasia, their housekeeper, say.

"I'm Chase Livingston, Hannah's new trainer. I'm here to meet with her."

"It's okay, Anastasia, I'm expecting him," Hannah said. She stopped on the third step from the bottom so that she was looking down at him when he came inside. He looked up at her briefly, then thanked

Anastasia. The housekeeper disappeared to go off and do whatever it was she did during the day.

Hannah walked down the last few steps. "Let's go into the study," she said.

"I thought you said the conservatory," Chase said.

"I changed my mind." The truth was, she had left her music out, and she wasn't ready to let Chase Livingston know that she could play the piano. She wanted to size up his own musical abilities first. *Know your enemy*, her dad used to say.

The study was on the east side of the house, and the east wall had glass windows that spanned the wall's length and up to the ceiling. Hannah loved this room in the mornings when the sun was just rising. The golden color came in and washed over the burgundy leather desk chairs that surrounded a cherry wood table and formed a little conference area in the middle of the room.

Hannah sat in one of the chairs and twirled it back and forth.

Chase took a seat across from her. He laid his iPhone flat on the desk in front of him and unzipped a small, black shoulder bag. He pulled out an iPad and a notebook and pen and laid them all down next to the phone.

"The most important thing is that you and Grace are happy and confident with what we pick," Chase said.

"The most important thing is that we *win*," Hannah said. Their eyes met. They hadn't started with hello, or how are you. He had jumped right in.

The musical freestyle dressage competition was Hannah's favorite competition and had been since she was little. She remembered watching her first dressage show on TV. She had been enthralled as the horses seemed to effortlessly dance to the rhythm of the music. A lot like the freestyle events in ice skating or gymnastics, freestyle dressage was about creating a pattern that show-cased the horse's strengths, while setting the horse up in the best way possible to execute its weaker elements. The event was all done to music, and the rider was supposed to appear effortless, not showing cues or speaking to the horse.

Chase flipped open his iPad. "Here's a list of the required elements," he said.

The rider couldn't do whatever he or she wanted, of course. The horse and rider had to execute all of the chosen elements, and points were given or subtracted for each success or error.

Hannah kept her eyes on Chase. "I know what they want," she said. She glanced at his tablet and scanned over the list of elements. "Where's my joker line?"

"There's no room for a joker line."

Hannah looked up. The joker line was a safety net that every rider wanted. It was a free moment put at the end of the program in which a rider could repeat an element they might have missed earlier in order to capture the point and nullify the error.

She raised an eyebrow.

"You don't need one," Chase said. "I never used one."

"What if we make an error?"

"Don't make any errors."

This surprised Hannah. From what she knew of him publicly, he had turned into a disgrace to the

33

dressage world. A coward. He had lost is nerve in the ring. Wuss Livingston, is what they called him.

"Tell me about your incident," she said suddenly.

His face clouded over. "I'm sure you've seen it on television. If not, it's on YouTube."

She had.

"I saw you fall off your horse during the Olympic games. You *had* the gold! You had it, and then in the last moment...what? What on earth happened?"

They had said a bee stung the horse. Or that it startled from a child in the crowd who clapped his hands.

Chase put the iPad down.

"Fine. Let's get this out of the way then," he said. He leaned back in his chair and folded his arms across his chest. Hannah noticed again how well built he was. He certainly must spend some time in the weight room.

"What happened?" she asked again.

"My horse spooked."

"I kind of noticed. The whole *world* noticed," said Hannah. "But why?"

"I forgot the pattern," Chase said. "I got off course, I got jittery, and Manny got upset."

Hannah had seen the horse's tail twitching agitatedly in the videos she had watched.

"Then a cameraman moved too close to the arena, and my horse caught him out of the corner of his eye, I guess. He spooked. I felt off. That's it."

It had been a team competition. They were leading, and he got them all disqualified. He lost the gold for them all.

She kept her eyes on him. "That wasn't all."

Chase took in a slow, deep breath and let it out before he spoke. "No. That wasn't all. Why don't you finish the story since you seem to know the details?"

"Your team kept you on and gave you a second chance even though you lost the entire Olympic gold for them. And you froze. You actually rode into the arena at the next competition and froze. Who does that?"

She still remembered seeing it, Chase and his horse entering the ring, moving into a canter, and then staying in the canter for not one, not two, but three times around the arena before Chase came into the center. The judge had rung the bell, disqualifying him.

Hannah kept her eyes on Chase, not letting him off the hook.

He shrugged. "Seems like you know the story well."

Too well, Hannah thought. He had been her idol, her *hero*. She had watched the films over and over, trying to figure out what had happened.

"But what you did next was worse," she said.

"Worse than losing the gold for my teammates?"

"You *quit*," Hannah practically spat out the word. "You just gave up. Most athletes would get back in the saddle, literally, figure out what their problem was, and get back into action. You not only let yourself and your horse down, but you let your teammates down, and your fans."

He was watching her closely now, and his eyes narrowed. The same dark, brown eyes that had stared at her from the poster she used to have hanging in her room.

"Are we ready to get started? You only have ten weeks before your qualifying program."

"With *you?* You still haven't told me why you froze out there."

Chase touched his iPad, waking it up.

"How do I know you won't fail me?" Hannah said.

He looked across the table at her. "From what I hear, you're lucky to have me."

"What do you mean?"

"What number trainer am I? How many have quit on you?"

Hannah was quiet. After a moment, he looked back at his iPad.

"We want to make sure the music really suits Grace," Chase said, ending the discussion. "We want her to appear graceful, like her name, but also powerful and balanced, effortless." He looked up to see if she was following.

As much as she hated to admit it, he was right. He was all she had. She nodded.

Chase opened up an application titled "Song Maker."

"The first thing we need to do is pick your beat," Chase said. "What do you want? Sassy? Energetic and fiery? Soothing and mellow?"

"Do I look soothing and mellow to you?" Hannah said.

Chase laughed. "No." He deleted that category.

"I want something powerful," Hannah said. "Something that says, 'Don't mess with me. I'm here to win.'"

Chase typed in a few song titles and played about ten seconds of each.

"No," Hannah said. "That's not it. Hans used to say Grace and I were *dynamisch.*"

"Dynamic," Chase said. "I can see that."

Hannah dropped her eyes and pretended to examine her nails. She suddenly felt like crying. She missed Hans and felt too tired to begin all of this again. At least with Hans, she knew what to expect. As much as he yelled at her, he had felt like a father figure. He was always there for her. Always. Unlike her own dad had been.

And she didn't want Chase training her. People would laugh, and she wasn't sure she'd have the energy to defend herself. Again. She picked at her thumbnail while she tried to regain her composure. What was wrong with her?

"Hannah?" She heard Chase's voice but didn't look up.

"What?" Her nails needed a fresh coat of paint. The polish she had on was starting to peel, which was a constant problem since she was always using her bare hands to scrub horses and cinch up saddles.

"Why don't you get on Grace and show me some of her moves. That will give me a better idea of what we're looking for. You ready for that?"

Hannah looked up. "Yes. Sure."

She stood. She was always ready to ride. In the saddle was where she felt the most confident. That was right where she needed to be at the moment.

Chapter Four

Chase dropped his electronics off at the guesthouse, then made his way to the barn. Hannah had already saddled Grace when he arrived. He noticed she hadn't changed into her riding clothes but was still wearing the same jeans and her "Boss Lady" t-shirt. He smiled at the wording on the t-shirt. She certainly was something.

She did have her tall, black riding boots on and had pulled her hair into a ponytail under her riding cap.

"Ready?" she asked him.

He nodded, and she led Grace out back to her riding arena. The afternoon was warm, but not overly so, and the farm was quieter than it had been that morning. Most people had worked their horses and gone on to their homes, or offices, or wherever it was they had to be on a Tuesday morning.

There was a mounting box near the entrance to the arena, and Hannah was leading Grace over to it so she could climb up onto her horse. Grace was about seventeen hands tall. The term "hands" came from an old English measuring system, when people used the width of their hand to determine a horse's height. A hand was four inches in width, and the horse was measured from their back, down to the ground. At seventeen hands tall, Grace's back stood at sixty-eight inches tall, or five feet, seven inches, about an inch taller than Hannah's head. She wouldn't be able to reach the stirrup.

"Want a boost up?" Chase offered.

Hannah glanced at him. "Sure."

He walked over and cupped his palms. She stepped into them, and he boosted her up. She was light and graceful.

He slid her stirrup onto her foot, then went around to make sure her foot was in the other stirrup as well.

"Hans couldn't do that," Hannah said. "I always had to use the box to mount."

"Hans is like...what? Eighty years old?" Chase said.

"Close."

"Just walk her around on a free rein," Chase said. "I want to see how she moves."

Hannah entered the arena and let the reins slide through her finger, so her horse's head was loose and relaxed. Grace had a long stride, and she carried herself in an easy manner. He watched them move once around the arena.

"Let's see a trot," he said. "Just something nice and easy."

Hannah gathered her reins, and Grace moved into a smooth trot, her two-beat gait eating up the ground in long strides.

"Give me a few figure eights."

Hannah's hands and body never showed any movement, her cues seeming nonexistent as the horse circled first to the right then to the left in perfect circles. It was as if Grace was reading her rider's mind. That was how dressage was supposed to be.

"Nice," Chase said. "Now show me some leg yields."

Grace began to move forward and sideways at the same time, her front and back legs crossing over each other. She moved diagonally halfway across the arena, then the other way coming back. She was really an incredible horse, and Hannah moved as if she were one with the animal.

"Now show me something fancy."

Hannah put Grace into a smooth canter, her three-beat gait faster and smoother than her trot. Grace's ears eagerly perked up, and her tail started to swish excitedly back and forth as she anticipated more to come. She was clearly enjoying this.

When a horse canters in a circle, it always leads with the inside leg. This was called, appropriately enough, a "lead." Hannah asked Grace to canter a straight line, and changed leads first at every two strides, then at every one stride, a very advanced move which required precise control of both the horse's body and the rider's balance.

He watched them for about twenty minutes as Hannah put Grace through her various paces. Grace was beautiful, with her four white legs moving so effortlessly, and her eyes bright. She was eager to please Hannah, and he could tell the horse loved to perform. Finally, Hannah rode her into the center of the ring, where Chase was standing, and stopped her, asking Grace to trot in place for a moment before coming to a halt and bending into a bow by outstretching her right front leg and coming down on one knee.

When they were done, Hannah petted Grace on the neck.

"Beautiful," Chase said.

Hannah smiled, the first smile he had seen. Their eyes met briefly, and he could swear she blushed.

"Thanks," she said quietly. She actually seemed happy.

Riding was Hannah's element. As it was his, as well. Or used to be.

He pushed past his own memories. "I have some ideas for music now that I've seen more of Grace's personality. I'm excited to see what we can come up with for the two of you."

"At least there's less shouting," Hannah said, sounding a little wistful. "Hans used to shout at me all the time."

"Do you miss him?" Chase squinted up at her.

She shrugged. "He's only been gone a day. But yeah, I guess. We've worked together for two years. Pretty nearly every single day."

Hannah swung her leg over and hopped down.

"Let's go cool her off, and then I'll show you some of the song ideas I have," Chase said.

They led Grace into the barn. A stable boy was cleaning out the stalls, and they had to make their way around a wheelbarrow. A young woman was washing her horse off in the rack when they got there, and Devon was standing beside her.

Hannah turned and whispered to Chase. "Be nice to him, no matter what. I'll explain later."

"Hello, beautiful Hannah," Devon said.

41

Hannah smiled politely at him. "Hello, Devon."

Devon's eyes traveled to Chase. "I see you have your fancy new trainer with you."

Hannah pulled Grace into the wash stall next to them and started to hose her off.

"We're working on coming up with some music," Hannah said, keeping her eyes on her horse.

"Tiffany and I are just finishing up as well," Devon said.

"Devon is Tiffany's trainer," Hannah explained to Chase.

"I see."

Chase didn't like this man. For one thing, he seemed obnoxious.

"Devon is working with me on jumping today," Tiffany said. She turned the hose off and started to brush the water off her horse. She looked to be about sixteen. "We're going to Nationals this fall in three-day eventing. We qualified!"

"Congratulations," Chase said.

"So, Hannah," Devon said. "I'm having a cookout tonight at my place. Want to come?"

"Chase and I have work to do."

"Surely not that late."

"Why not work late?" Hannah said. "He's at the guesthouse. My father expects us to work round the clock."

Hannah's eyes flicked at Devon, then back to her horse. Chase wondered what was going on here.

Devon walked into the wash stall, picked up a brush, and stroked some of the water off of Grace.

"I'm sure if I asked your dad, he'd make an exception."

Hannah peeked under Grace's neck at Devon. The hose moved with her and squirted Devon right in the crotch.

"Oh my goodness, I'm so sorry!" Hannah said.

Devon jumped back, swearing. Then, he recovered himself. "No worries. It's fine." He grabbed a towel and wiped at the front of his khakis. When he was finished, he turned his attention on Chase. There was something hard in his eyes.

"So you think Wuss Livingston here can get you to the top?" he said to Hannah.

"Chase can, I'm sure of it," Hannah said. She turned the water off and started drying Grace.

Devon stepped closer, just out of Chase's reach.

"The guesthouse, huh? That's where he puts people who are only temporary."

Chase felt the heat rise to his face.

Hannah tossed the brush into the bucket and turned Grace around.

"Devon here is one of our farm's best trainers," she said lightly. "He'll take Tiffany to the top, I'm sure." She looked at Chase. "Come on."

Reluctantly, Chase stepped away from Devon and followed Hannah. When they got to Grace's stall, he asked, "So why isn't he training you, then?"

"Because he's not *that* good," Hannah said.

"What's going on with the two of you?"

"Nothing."

"That hose accident wasn't a mistake."

He saw the corners of Hannah's lips lift as she tried to hide a smile. "I have no idea what you're talking about." She put Grace into her stall and closed the door.

"He seems obnoxious. Why do you put up with him?"

She hung Grace's halter on the peg on the stall door and turned to face Chase. He could smell soap and shampoo, just under the light sweat on her body. "He's on the voting committee for the Olympic board," she whispered.

"Oh." That explained a lot.

"He has a thing for me."

"I noticed."

"He thinks I have a thing for him."

"Do you?"

Suddenly, it seemed to matter. He had no idea why.

Hannah frowned. "That's none of your business. But no. I don't have time for that, anyway. I just try to be *nice* to him. If I rub him the wrong way, there go my chances."

Chase sighed. The horse show world was just like the rest of the world, and everything was political. How well he had found that out.

Chapter Five

They were back in the study with Chase's iPad. Hannah listened as Chase suggested some songs.

"Grace exemplifies exactly what her name implies, that she's graceful," Chase said. "I've seen you work before, and Hans has usually chosen something classical for you. But I want—"

"Wait," Hannah leaned forward in her chair. "You've seen me work before?"

Chase nodded. "You think I don't follow the dressage world anymore?"

She hadn't thought about it, really. He had left, disappeared, gone into hiding. She just assumed he didn't care.

"I don't know," she said, shrugging. She sat back in her chair.

"I've seen you perform. Your music doesn't fit you, or your horse."

"But we win."

"You do. But I think you want to do more than win. I think you want to make a statement."

This was interesting.

"Like what?"

"I've heard riders use Katie Perry's song 'Firework' or Queen's 'We are the Champions.'"

Hannah thought about that. Hans had never let her step out of classical music before. He said you didn't need song lyrics messing with people's heads when they were trying to watch the horse. He was an old-school German. Bach. Brahms.

"I don't know..." Hannah said. Devon often used some of the more contemporary songs with his students. Maybe that was a thing now.

"I actually thought of a song last night," Chase said.

"What?.

"Katy Willis's 'I Am More.'"

Hannah frowned. She loved that song, but the words, well, they hit a bit close to home. "Why?"

Chase shrugged. "Let's listen to it."

Chase went to his music app and turned it on.

I am brave, I'm a star, I shine bright.
I try hard, I'm the best that I can be.
Look at me. Look at me. What do you see?

Hannah looked at Chase across the table. He was tapping his fingers, lost in thought.

You see the power, you see the strength, you see it all,
I have all the answers, I am tough, I will not fail.
But look at me. Look at me. What do you see?
I cry for the world, to see, to see me.

Hannah lowered her eyes. Did this man see through her?

Deep inside, I am more than I show.
I'm the girl that I don't let anybody know.
I am brave, I'm a star, I am free.
I am more. I am more. I am me.

She looked up and saw that he was watching her.

I am more. I am more. I am more!

The song ended, and Chase raised his eyebrows in question. Hannah nodded. She hated to admit it, but he had scored. "The song's okay," she said, shrugging her shoulders. She didn't want to admit how perfect it really was. The tempo was right on target, and the music had an unmistakable power to it.

He smiled. "So, let's get started."

Hannah's phone dinged with a text. She looked at it. It was Devon, asking her to come to the barbecue again. She turned her phone over.

Chase had the list of dressage moves in front of him. He was reviewing them and scribbling in his notebook. She watched him as he worked, wondering about this man that she used to idolize. He was still handsome. Maybe more so. His thick, brown hair was wavy, curling a little bit around his ears and at the nape of his neck. His fingers were long and his hands looked strong. He looked up, and she quickly looked away, not wanting him to know that she had been staring at him.

"I'll do most of this on my own, and then come back with a pattern," he said. "Unless you want to help me choreograph?"

Hannah shook her head. "That's what you're getting paid for."

Her phone dinged again. She turned it over to look. Devon. She turned her phone on vibrate.

Chase was back to work, now scrolling through his music app.

"In just a minute, I'll have a few questions for you about the elements, and then I'll let you get back to your life," Chase said.

His attention was on his tablet, so she looked at him again. Chase Livingston had been her first crush. From far away, sure, but still, her first love. She had watched him perform effortlessly for years with his horse Debonair Man, the two of them like one. She saw the love he had for his animal, the bond the two of them shared.

He had loved his dog too. He'd had a small, Jack Russell terrier who traveled with him and who Hannah had seen in photos. The dog had been given to him by his mom on his eighteenth birthday to keep him company on the road. Snazzy, her name had been. What had happened to her?

He also had a sister, Hannah remembered. Anna? Amelia? She couldn't remember the sister's name.

Hannah had spent many nights laying in her bed, wondering about Chase. She wanted to marry a man like him, a man who loved animals so much. A man who loved winning, who loved the same sport she did.

And then, he had quit. He had fallen apart, and she had seen through the perfect persona to the man he really was. And she hadn't liked what she saw.

"Tell me why you froze in the arena," she said to Chase.

He looked up and was silent for a moment. "It's none of your business."

"Yes, it is," Hannah said. "if we're going to work this closely together, we need to be honest with each other. If you think I'm going to trust you to just change my whole brand and move on to different music and trust you with my future, I need to know."

He leaned forward. "First, tell me why Hans quit."

"He's old and his wife has dementia."

"No, I want to know why he *really* quit."

Hannah was silent. She wasn't a liar. If anything, she believed in integrity to a fault. After what her mother had done, she swore she'd never, ever waiver on her integrity. After all, her mom had promised to love her dad until "death do us part." Ha.

"Hmm," Chase said when she didn't answer and turned back to his tablet.

"Hmm? What does *that* mean?" Hannah said. She was suddenly angry. Who was *he* to think he was better than her?

"Just, hmm."

"Hey," she said. She waited until he looked up. "Don't give me attitude. Trainers are a dime a dozen. My father can fire you in an instant."

Chase laughed. He actually *laughed*. Not a hardy laugh, as if making fun of her, but a chuckle. Just enough to let her know she wasn't getting under his skin.

This frustrated her.

"He can and he will," she added. No one was going to get the best of her. She needed to let him know right away who was in charge here.

"Trainers might be a dime a dozen, but not for *you*," he said. He leaned back in his chair and met her eyes. "Do you want to tell me why, before Hans, that you lost Kerry Wellington and Bobby Snell as well? What about Mara Furoke?"

Hannah felt her face redden slightly. That was the problem with her fair complexion. It show-cased her emotions.

She held his eyes. He *knew*. He knew perfectly well why they had quit.

Although Kerry hadn't really been her fault. He was hard to work with from the start. Driven and a perfectionist, every time she made a slight error he was on her, giving her extra work as an "incentive" not to mess up again. He had worn her out. The day she had thrown the bucket of water on him, she had been exhausted, humiliated, and in tears. But when he left, he took the Oldenburg mare she had been leasing from him. Which is why they had had to look for another horse. She often wondered if he hadn't quit whether she'd still be riding that mare (who had captured a few national titles, by the way) or if she would have still gotten Grace. She couldn't imagine life without Grace. Sometimes, maybe fate played a role.

"You said you've been following my career, so I assume you know why they quit," Hannah said. She tried to keep her voice aloof, like it didn't matter. But she found that she was ashamed of her past behavior.

"I *do* know," Chase said. His voice softened. "Look, Hannah. We don't have to get along. We don't even have to like each other. But in order for this to work, you have to trust me."

"How can I trust you? You haven't trained anybody else, *ever*. And you're like...a hundred years younger than all of my other trainers. You're nearly the same age as me, which doesn't give you much in the way of wisdom."

"So it's my *age* that's bothering you?"

"Oh, not just your age. There are so many other things that are bothering me." She crossed her arms. At this point, most people she argued with gave up. Grew quiet. Even Hans only argued with her so far, eager to keep his job. Her dad paid well. She wondered how much he was paying Chase.

"Like what?" Chase asked.

"Answer my questions. You froze. And your horse didn't like it. He felt confused, unsure. That's why he spooked and threw you. You're good, and I can't imagine why you would freeze. I think something happened that had nothing to do with dressage at all."

As soon as she said it, she realized it was true. She had never thought of it that way before. When she was in the ring, she was always so focused. The rest of the world disappeared, and it was just her and her horse. She got caught up in the moment and didn't know anything else until she was finished with her routine.

Chase had been like that too. She could see it when she watched him perform. Nothing else mattered. But that day, something else had.

She searched his eyes, but he was like a closed door to her. He didn't give any indication that she was right.

When he spoke, his voice was soft. "We only have ten weeks," he said. "Ten weeks for me to write you a freestyle program, and for you and Grace to memorize it before your performance. *The* performance that will determine if you get chosen for the United States Dressage Team and if you go to the Olympics. Can we focus on that right now?"

Hannah's phone vibrated.

"Yes," she said. She flipped her phone back over, ready to reply to Devon that she was busy. Then she had a thought. What better way to get inside somebody's head than to see them in a social situation? Maybe Chase would go from trainer mode to friend mode, have a beer or two, and tell her what she wanted to know. If she took Chase with her, it would irritate Devon, give her a chance to get to know Chase better, and provide her with the opportunity to get the upper hand again. It was perfect! She knew just the dress she'd wear.

"Do you want to go to a barbecue with me tonight at Devon's?"

Chase shook his head. "No. No way. Not with that guy."

"But I *need* to go. And I don't want to go alone." She tried her best to look sweet.

Chase shook his head. "Don't play me, Hannah."

She sighed. "Look. I'll be straight with you. Devon *likes* me. A lot. I want to go and mingle, because it's a great way to learn about who's doing what in the showring next, to size up the competition. But if I go alone, Devon will think I'm his date. If I bring you, you can act as a buffer."

"A buffer?"

Hannah nodded. "Please?"

"I can't date you. I work for your dad."

"It's not a date. I'm bringing you as my trainer. And technically, you work for *me*."

"No. I don't. Let's get that straight from the start."

Geez, he was difficult. "Whatever. I promise to be good." She smiled.

Chase was silent for a moment, watching her. "Fine. But you can't stay out late. We have an early day tomorrow. I want to start at 8 a.m."

"Now you sound like my father."

"No, I sound like your trainer."

Hannah had no intention of listening to his rules. But she wasn't about to tell him that.

"Okay," she said, "it's set. Why don't you go back and get cleaned up, and I'll see you in an hour. You can drive me in your SUV. That is yours, right? The one parked outside your house?"

Chase nodded. "You're a real piece of work."

Hannah laughed. "I'm not as bad as you might think."

"We'll see."

Chapter Six

Chase didn't want to be at the barbecue, but Hannah had insisted. And he had to admit, he was a little curious about where Devon lived. He had read about him through the years in news articles as he climbed his way to the top in the training world. He was young, like Chase, for a trainer in the sport, and cocky. At thirty, he was just getting started with pupils, and had hired on at Fieldstone Farm just two years ago.

It turned out that Devon's house was fairly nice. Not Fieldstone Farm nice, but he wasn't hurting in the financial department. A two-story in an upscale neighborhood, the house boasted an inground pool that about thirty people were making use of this evening, as well as a cabana with a flat-screen TV. A wet bar sat at the back of the cabana, and two bikini-clad ladies sat on barstools, twirling little umbrellas in their sugary margaritas.

The night was on the cool side. The sun was nearly gone at 8 p.m., but there were enough rays left to keep the warmth of the day around.

"Welcome to hell," Hannah muttered when they stepped through Devon's back gate.

"And there's the devil," Chase said.

"Hannah! I was so glad when you said you were coming!" Devon said, swooping over to see them. He had a tall glass in his hand filled with an iced drink. He was dressed in white swim trunks and a Hawaiian shirt, open down the front and showing a slight six-pack. He took off his Ray Ban sunglasses.

"Chase," he said, nodding.

Chase nodded back.

"Would you like a drink?" Devon directed the question to Hannah.

"Something non-alcoholic," Hannah said. "No sugar."

"Hannah doesn't drink," Devon explained to Chase. "She's a health nut."

"Nor should you," Hannah said to Devon. "We're athletes. Your body is your temple."

Devon cracked a smile. "Yours certainly is," he said, running his eyes over her. Then he winked and went off to get her something to drink without offering Chase anything.

Hannah was wearing a soft, white cotton sundress with straps at the shoulders. She had on sandals. She had told Chase that they weren't planning on swimming, so not to wear his swimsuit. He hated that she *told* him instead of asked what he wanted to do, but it sounded good to him so he didn't argue. He left his swim shorts in his suitcase and wore khaki shorts and a polo. He had on the gold chain he had bought himself last year, tucked under his shirt like he always wore it.

"Are you going to let him treat you like that?" Chase asked. "Like...you're the next course for dinner?" He himself had trouble not staring at her.

She had her blonde hair in a loose ponytail, and some of it had escaped the band and fell in wispy curls around her face. She wore a gold necklace with a shell that hung down inside her neckline someplace where he wasn't about to look.

"I can handle him," she said.

Chase was about to comment when Devon returned with a glass of sugar-free lemonade and handed it to Hannah.

"Oh, Chase, I'm sorry," he said with fake sincerity. "Would you like anything?"

"I'll get it myself," Chase said. He left them and walked over toward the cabana. If Hannah wanted to handle Devon, he'd let her.

"Hello," said one of the bikini-clad women. She had long, dark hair and bright red lipstick on which was leaving a stain on her glass. She smiled at Chase. "You're new here."

"I'm with Hannah," he said. Then he ordered a cola from the bartender.

"Ooooooh, Hannah has moved up in the world," she said to her girlfriend, a brown-skinned woman with short hair, and the two women giggled. The brunette looked at Chase's biceps and traced her finger down his right arm. "Nice."

"I didn't think Hannah dated," said the other woman. "She's all work, no play."

"I have no idea," Chase said, moving out of reach.

"You'll find out, honey," said the brunette. "And when you do, if you get bored, I'd be happy to entertain you."

Chase took his drink from the bartender with some relief and walked away. He had been here less than five minutes and already been insulted by the host and hit on by the guests. Life in the fast lane.

There was a time when he would have welcomed the woman's advances, maybe even gone home with her. That was before he accepted Jesus. He was different now.

Hannah appeared at his elbow. "Why did you leave me?" she hissed under her breath so no one could hear.

"I thought you could 'handle Devon'," he said.

"I can. But the whole reason I brought you was to be a buffer."

"So you're using me?"

"No."

"Yes."

He stopped walking and turned to look at her.

"I told you I'm here because I want to score points with people," Hannah said quietly. "See that couple over there? No! Don't look. But the man in the white shirt and the woman in the one-piece next to him? They have a lot of clout with the Olympic committee, and it certainly won't hurt my chances to get on the team if they like me. And so far they do. So we have to chat with them before we leave."

Chase waited a moment, then slid his eyes in their direction. He didn't recognize them, but he had been out of the sport for a while. His knowledge was limited to who he could see on TV or in news articles.

"And that woman in the far corner with the lap dog, that's Angela Raspindle. She's definitely going to be on the team."

Chase knew that name well. The middle-aged woman had been in the same circles when he showed. She would know him, and she didn't like him. Now he *really* wanted to leave.

"So let's go chat with the couple and then we can go home," he said.

Hannah raised her eyebrows. "Why are you in a hurry?"

"Because, to start out with, your boyfriend is a jerk."

"Devon is *not* my boyfriend," she said.

"So this whole thing is political, huh?"

Hannah shrugged. "Is there any other reason to party?"

Chase laughed a little at that. "I guess not." He noticed a few people were staring at him. "I didn't realize there were going to be so many people here from the sport," he said. "I thought this was just a few local friends."

"Devon always invites the biggest names he can find."

They made their way over to the couple, and Hannah introduced Chase.

"This is my new trainer," she said, without mentioning his name. If the couple recognized him, they didn't say anything.

Hannah made small talk while she sipped her drink. She was smooth and conversational and laughed in all the right places.

"Oh, there's Angela!" she said, pretending to have just seen the woman. "Excuse us while we go and say 'hi'."

She turned and started walking toward Angela. Chase touched her arm. "Hannah, I'm going to wait over by"—He glanced at the cabana and the brunette smiled at him—"by the gate."

"What? No. You have to come with me."

"She'll recognize me."

Hannah froze at that, hesitating. Then she said, "So? You can bet Devon has told the world. Everybody knows by now that you're my trainer. What's the big deal?"

"She was one of my teammates."

Hannah stopped walking. She hovered by his elbow, and he wished he could see behind her designer sunglasses to see what she was thinking. Whatever it was, he was certain he didn't want to talk to Angela.

"Well, we're probably going to run into a lot of your old teammates," Hannah said. "We're both going to have to get used to that, aren't we?"

"No," Chase said. "I don't have to get used to anything. She hates me."

"She probably hates me, too. Everyone else does. It's something you learn to live with."

Hannah turned and walked over to Angela. Chase reluctantly followed. Had he known this was going to be a gathering of Olympic-caliber equestrian athletes he would have stayed home.

"Hannah!" Angela exclaimed, waking up the little mop of a dog on her lap. It yawned and eyed the two of them from under its shaggy hair. "So good to see you!"

"Angela!" Hannah said. "How are you?"

"I'm fine." But Angela's eyes were now on Chase. "Why is he here?" Her voice turned icy.

"Chase?" Hannah said. "He's my new trainer."

Angela raised an eyebrow. "You train now?" she asked. "What are you going to teach her? How to quit?"

"Maybe I wouldn't have failed if I had more support from my teammates," he said, hearing the edge in his voice.

"It was over the minute you entered the ring. I could see it on your face," Angela said.

"He's fine now," Hannah said smoothly. "Do you think my dad would have hired him otherwise? I have great confidence in him."

"Well, you're the only one," Angela muttered. "If you want to throw your career in the toilet, that's up to you."

Hannah pulled her phone out of the small purse she was carrying. "I need to take this. Chase, come on." She put the phone to her ear and said "hello" as they walked away.

Chase was angry, and he could feel the blood pounding in his ears. They had all loved him when he was the "wonder kid," winning everything in sight and carrying his team. But as soon as he had failed, they had turned on him like rabid dogs.

"I told you this was a bad idea," he muttered.

Hannah held her phone to her ear until they reached a garden area, out of sight of Angela, then she snapped it shut.

"So is this how it's going to be?" she said.

"I didn't know this was going to be a hang out of the equestrian elite."

"I didn't know it would be a problem."

"How could you not?"

Just when he thought it couldn't get any worse, Devon stopped in front of them.

"Are you leaving?" Devon said. "You just got here."

"Yes, I got a call," Hannah said smoothly, putting her phone away. "Devon, it was so good of you to invite us."

"Hannah, stay for burgers. Just another half hour. Please." Devon took hold of her free hand. Chase saw him rub his fingers over the top of her knuckles. "Wanda will want to talk with you. She's been asking about you."

Wanda was another probable pick for the upcoming Olympic team, Chase knew. Hannah swallowed and gently pulled her hand away. She glanced at Chase. "Just one burger," she said. "Then we really do have to go."

Devon shot Chase a triumphant look. "Good," he said. "I think they're done. I can smell the meat."

"I'll wait in the car," Chase said after Devon left.

"No. Come with me." Hannah grabbed his hand and led him over to the grilling area. She got two plates and handed him one. Chase filled his plate, then took his and wandered over to a table where he sat alone. Hannah stood and ate, talking to Wanda and several others who joined them. He saw her glance in his direction a few times as the people she was with must have asked about them. He looked away and saw that the bikini-clad brunette at the cabana bar was still making eyes at him. He ignored her and was glad when Hannah came over about ten minutes later and said she was ready to go. Chase stood up, threw his trash out, and together they walked through the gate. He didn't exhale until they got in the SUV and drove off.

Chapter Seven

Hannah hadn't expected there to be so much of a backlash. A bit of embarrassment that she had lowered herself to working with Chase Livingston, sure. But *animosity?* People seemed angry that she had hired him, as if there was some silent agreement that this former Olympic gold medalist was no longer allowed in the sport. Was she to be shunned now because she was working with Chase Livingston?

They were silent as he drove her home and dropped her off. Chase said he expected her bright and early in the morning, at 8 a.m. in the ring. She frowned and told him nine. He disagreed, and she didn't say anything since he already had had a rough night. He'd learn. She wasn't about to take orders from him, especially since he was nearly the same age as her. Her other trainers had all been much older, more mentor-like.

Her dad was in his study when she came in the front door.

"Hannah? Is that you?"

"Yes, Dad," she said. She went in his study, and he rose from his office chair to give her a kiss on the cheek. "I missed you at dinner."

"Devon had a barbecue. We ate there."

"We?"

"I invited Chase. It was terrible. Oh, Dad, why on earth did you hire *him*? I'll take *anybody* else, even some kid's 4-H dressage teacher."

Her dad smiled. She loved how it traveled up to his eyes.

"Do you really think a 4-H trainer could choreograph an Olympic-level dressage freestyle routine in ten weeks? Or at all?"

Hannah returned his smile. "No. But there has to be somebody else."

"There's always Devon."

Hannah shook her head. "You know he's just a hunter-jumper trainer. We discussed this." But Hannah knew the real reason her dad didn't push Devon on her was that he didn't like him. Devon was an excellent trainer who brought a lot of riders into their stable and kept things running. He was also part of the nominating committee and had the ears of the people who would nominate Hannah for the team. As a savvy businessman, her dad knew it was best to tolerate him until Hannah made the team.

"Then I'm afraid Chase is all you have," her dad said. He changed the subject. "I had lunch with Marion, and she asked me to give you these." He handed her a box.

They were chocolates from Hannah's favorite baker in town. Homemade. Last week, while she was enduring a brunch with her dad and his girlfriend, Hannah had casually mentioned how much she liked these chocolates. Marion must have been paying attention.

She wrinkled her nose but took the box.

"Be nice," her dad said. "Marion is trying."

"She's not my mom."

"She's not trying to be." Marcus paused. A year ago, he would have pressed her, forced her to like Marion. But he was different now. She watched him change the subject again.

"How *is* Chase working out? Did you get anywhere today with your routine?"

Wrong subject.

"Dad, I really don't want to work with him," Hannah said. "I mean...he's nice enough. But do you have any idea how humiliating it is to be trained by him? He's not even a *trainer*! He's...he's...he's a has-been!" The anger Hannah had been feeling all day flared up. She had a temper, and she was trying hard these days to quell it, ever since her final run-in with Hans. But this was too much.

"I went to Devon's party, and Chase's old teammate was there. Angela. I didn't realize...I had forgotten she'd done dressage with him." *Stupid,* Hannah thought. How could she space off something like that? "Anyway, she hates him. And Devon makes fun of him. What if having him here affects my chances to be on the team simply because I'm associated with him?"

Marcus listened carefully, then folded his hands behind his back and walked over to the big east windows. It was dark out, and she could see his reflection in the glass. With his back to her, he let his smile fade, and she noticed again how much older he looked.

"He didn't really do anything that awful," her dad said. "He froze in an Olympic game. His horse threw him. It happens."

"Not to him. Not to the wonder kid. Plus, he let his entire team down."

"Winning isn't everything," her dad said quietly. He had been saying that a lot lately. What happened to the man who would buy, sell, and trade companies and stocks with no qualms about what it did to his employees?

"And then, in the next competition, he froze *again.* He couldn't ever pull it together. And then he *quit!*"

"Or was he driven out?" her dad asked.

"What do you mean?"

"He was in a team sport. He competed individually, yes, but if I remember right, he was driven out. There were other factors, I think."

Marcus turned to look at his daughter. "Hannah, I want you to give him a chance," he said gently. "I don't know how to say this, but you don't have any other choice. He's the only one willing to work with you."

"There are plenty of other trainers out there."

Marcus raised an eyebrow. "Like?"

"I'll call them. I'll find one. I just don't want *him.* Dad, I have a reputation to uphold. I am good, I am Olympic-bound, and I don't want some inexperienced has-been training me!"

Hannah realized her voice had risen. She lowered it. The ability to maintain the upper hand and to be taken seriously was a direct result of looking like you were in charge. She had read that in a book somewhere.

"That's not nice," her dad said.

He was right. She had become "not-nice" a lot these days.

"I'm sorry. I'm tired." She looked at the time on her phone. "It's late. I'm going to bed. Good night, Daddy." She kissed her dad on the cheek and headed upstairs.

"Good night. I love you!" her dad called behind her.

"I love you too," Hannah called back. That was another thing about him that had changed. He said the "L" word a lot now. After a lifetime of never hearing it, it was awkward for her to get used to. She had always *known* he loved her; he was just never one to say it out loud.

Pussy Willow heard her come upstairs and wandered into her bedroom. "Hey fellow," she said, scratching him behind the ears. He purred loudly.

Then she closed her bedroom door and sat down on the floor. She dug under her bed and pulled out the tattered old cardboard coat box and opened it. Inside was the cat book her mom used to read to her. She paused to look at one of the photos of her mom that she kept in the box.

Eva had had beautiful blonde hair, like Hannah's, and she wore it just below her shoulders. In this photo, she was smiling and holding five-year-old Hannah's hand. They were dressed up, wearing matching navy-blue dresses that had tiny white polka dots all over them. Her mom had found a tie in the same color and pattern and given it to Marcus to wear. Hannah remembered how much she loved that they all matched. Her dad had taken this photo right before they left for Easter dinner at her aunt's house. Hannah and her mom had gone on ahead to wait for Marcus. Her dad had had a business meeting that day and never showed up for dinner.

She put the photo aside. She wasn't here to reminisce. She dug a little deeper and found what she was looking for. She unrolled the poster, now crinkled and a little yellowed. It was a photo of 18-year-old Chase Livingston astride Debonair Man, holding the Olympic gold Medal. He was smiling. She picked up a second poster and unrolled it. A head shot of Chase, smiling and holding a Cordova dressage saddle.

His brown eyes stared out at her from under thick, dark hair. His smile radiated from the paper. So young. This had been four years before his debacle. He'd gone on from there to receive several more sponsorships, one from Nike. His young age and his story made him one of America's favorite athletes. He'd even made the cover of *Sports Illustrated*. She had a copy of that someplace.

Hannah wondered if her nanny had actually thrown the scrapbook away when she'd found it in the garbage. Where else would it have gone? Hannah thought how fun it would be to look through it again, but she'd be mortified if Chase ever saw it. She had never seen it again, after that day she tossed it out in a fit of anger.

Pussy Willow was rubbing his head against her knee, begging to be petted.

"I hate that he's my trainer," she said. She remembered again how disappointed she had been when he quit the sport. How angry.

Hannah put everything back in the box and shoved it under her bed. Then she climbed onto her soft white comforter and propped her pillows up against the brass headboard. She leaned up against them and took out her phone.

She typed Randall Thompson's name into the search bar. He was a good trainer. Maybe he'd take her on. Before she could change her mind, she dialed his number. It was 10 p.m. here, but he was on the west coast.

"Randall, this is Hannah Whitney," she said when he answered.

He seemed pleased to hear from her, and they exchanged pleasantries.

"I'm looking for a trainer," she said.

"Ah, I heard that Hans quit," Randall said.

That was the problem with the equestrian world. Word traveled fast.

"His wife has some health issues," Hannah said.

"Hmm. So you want me to ask around?"

Hannah tapped her fingers on her knee. It was a trick Hans had taught her to quell her nerves. Tapping.

"No," she said. "Actually, I was wondering if *you* would train me."

There was a pause. "No, I'm pretty booked. And you're all the way in Michigan. That's quite a commute from California."

"We can pay," Hannah said. "Dad would make it worth your while. We have a guesthouse you can stay in."

"I'm sure he would," Randall said. "But the answer has to be no. Hannah, I wish you the best of luck. I need to grab this call."

And he hung up.

Hannah typed another name into the search bar of her phone's browser. Jonathon Reichert. She got the same answer and tried three more trainers. Two of them were distantly polite, the third one actually said, "Heck, no." She glanced at the clock. It was 10:30 p.m. now. Probably too late to call anybody local. But finally, hesitantly, she called Rita Smith. Rita lived only about an hour south of St. Ives.

"Rita, this is Hannah Whitney," she said.

"Hannah," Rita said. She sounded like she had been woken.

"I'm sorry to call so late, but I have an emergency. I need a trainer."

She quickly explained that Hans had quit.

"I spoke with Devon earlier," Rita said. "He said your dad hired Chase Livingston."

Hannah sighed inwardly. "Yes. But it's only temporary."

Rita laughed. Hannah had never really liked Rita. "I should hope so! Oh honey, you really *have* hit rock bottom if you have him on your staff," she said. "But I'm sorry. I can't help you. Nor would I if I could. I don't need your drama. You tell your daddy to keep his money, and I'll see you in the show ring." She hung up.

Hannah sat there, holding the phone in her hand. She really was out of options now.

Maybe she could write her own program, like Chase had.

She wouldn't know where to start. She had never paid attention when her other trainers handed her the programs. They were always something she just *did.* She had input about which moves she wanted, but she had never put those moves to music.

Pussy Willow pressed up against her. She absently petted his thick gray fur.

"It's only ten weeks, right?" she said to him. "I can endure that." She looked up at the motivational poster up on the wall across from her bed. It was the first thing she saw every morning when she woke up and the last thing she saw at night before she went to bed.

> *Don't wish for success.*
> *Make it happen.*

Then she got off the bed and went to brush her teeth. Morning came early.

Chapter Eight

Chase was at the barn bright and early. The stable hands had fed Grace, and she was ready to work. He put on her halter and led her out of her stall.

"Do you need help, Mr. Livingston?" asked a timid young man.

"No, I can do it."

"Umm...Miss Whitney doesn't usually like anyone touching her horse. We always let her handle Grace. Did she specifically ask you to?"

"I'm her trainer," Chase said. "It's okay."

He got Grace ready, put her saddle on, and cinched it up. The mare was calm and easy to handle. He led her out into the arena promptly at 8 a.m. and waited for Hannah.

It was a beautiful morning, the sun warming up the green pastures around him and a mist rising from the pond up behind the house. There were a few boarders working their horses. Thankfully, he hadn't seen Devon yet. If that man was a trainer here, he'd be around a lot. Chase didn't want to think about that.

He looked at his watch. It was 8:10 a.m. Hannah was late. He'd give her five more minute and then text her.

To his right, he saw someone jogging up the paved path that came from the back of the farm and curved up past the arena he was in. As the person came closer, he saw that it was Hannah. She was wearing black spandex running shorts, a gray t-shirt, and a pink headband around her forehead. Her hair bounced behind her in a ponytail. What on earth was she doing?

She saw him and turned to jog over to the arena. "What on earth are you doing?" she said, echoing his thoughts. She stopped and put her hands on her hips. She was breathing hard.

"What are *you* doing? We have a lesson now. When I dropped you off last night, I told you to be here at 8 a.m."

"And I told *you* I don't start until nine."

"I'm your *trainer!*" Chase said. "I make the rules!"

"We pay you. *We* make the rules," Hannah said.

"Your *dad* pays me. Let's ask him."

"You have no right to touch my horse. *Nobody* but me touches Grace, is that understood?"

"Why?" Chase was flabbergasted. Most riders *wanted* their horse ready. He figured that especially this spoiled, rich girl would want her horse handed over to her all tacked up. He should have listened to the stable boy's warning. He also vaguely remembered Mr. Whitney saying that nobody but Hannah cooled the horse off. Maybe nobody but Hannah got the horse ready, either.

"Give her to me," Hannah said. She started to open the gate to come into the arena.

"Hold on!" Chase said. "Since you're here, and I'm up and showered and ready to work, go get your riding helmet on and we can start."

"I'm busy right now," Hannah said. "I always start my morning with cardio."

"Well, things are changing. You didn't tell me you jogged."

"I don't jog. I *run*."

Chase took a deep breath and exhaled slowly. He remembered his sister's words and, for the second time in twenty-four hours, he regretted taking this job. But he needed the money.

"Hannah," he said quietly. "Since you're already"—he searched for a word—"*sweaty*, go ahead and finish your run. *Today*, I'll put Grace back in her stall, and I'll see you at nine."

Hannah hesitated, her eyes on her horse. Then she nodded. "*This* time," she said. "But don't ever touch her again, or I'll have you fired."

"You keep threatening that," he said.

She turned on her heel and continued jogging around the curve and up the long driveway that wound past the front of the house.

Devon came out of the barn then and walked over to where Chase was standing. He shook his head, watching Hannah's shape grow smaller as she ran toward the house.

"Mmm, *mmm*," he said. "She's something." He turned to Chase. "Keep your hands and eyes off of her cowboy," he said. "She's mine."

Chase glared at him, remembering Hannah's words to tolerate Devon until she got on the team. "You might want to treat her with a little more respect then," he said evenly.

"She likes it," Devon said. "She's hot, and she knows it." Devon started to walk back toward the barn but turned and raised his finger, wagging it. "Don't ever touch Grace," he said. "Hannah hates that. I'd hate to see you get fired."

Chase took another deep breath. Ten weeks. *Ten weeks* and then he'd have enough money to pay off his sister's debts and start on his own savings. If Hannah made it to the Olympics, then he'd just not go as her trainer. She'd have plenty of other offers, he was sure of it.

Ten weeks. He could do it. He knew he could.

After Chase put Grace back in her stall, he texted Hannah and told her to text him back when she was ready. He'd meet her at the arena when she had Grace tacked up and was prepared to begin.

He received a short text back saying, **9 a.m. Be prompt.**

He frowned. Maybe he *wouldn't* last ten weeks.

He had a half hour to kill, so he walked back to the guesthouse and sat down on the front porch swing. The wrap-around porch was a nice addition to the small house. He thought about going inside and making more coffee, but it was so pleasant on the porch that he changed his mind.

From here, he could see the barns through the trees. They were about a tenth of a mile up the long blacktop drive. There was some activity around them, but all he could hear were the birds and the rustling of the maple leaves around the guesthouse.

He took a deep breath and tried to shake off his anger from interacting with Devon and Hannah this morning. Those two were definitely made for each other!

He heard the sound of tires and saw a sporty blue car slowly coming up the road toward his bungalow. The driver stopped once to let two geese cross the road. A Corvette. Nice. The sun was creating a glare on the windshield, but when the car pulled up in front of Chase's guesthouse under the trees, he saw that the driver was Marcus Whitney.

Marcus got out and waved. He was wearing a wheat-colored suit with a white shirt underneath.

"Hello," Chase said, and stood.

"Take a seat," Marcus said, waving his hand. "I just came by to chat for a moment."

He came up on the porch and sat on one end of the swing, to Chase's right. Chase sat back down on the other end. The swing fit three people, but it still seemed strange to be sitting here, swinging with his boss.

"I know you're supposed to meet Hannah at nine," Marcus said, looking at his watch. "I won't keep you long. I told Hannah that you might be late because I wanted to stop by."

"Sure," Chase said, wondering what this visit was about.

"How's it going?" Marcus turned to look at Chase. He removed his sunglasses so Chase could see his blue eyes.

"It's going well," Chase said. What else could he say? *Your daughter is a brat, and Devon, your other trainer, is worse?*

Marcus smiled. "Are you sure about that?"

Chase shrugged, uncertain where this was going.

"I know my daughter well," Marcus said. "She's not easy to deal with."

He paused, waiting for Chase to speak.

Chase searched for words. Should he agree with the man? Or deny what they both knew was true? "She's a little bit—" He stopped.

"Pushy." Marcus said. "Stubborn. Used to getting her way."

Chase laughed. There was nothing pretentious about this man. "True."

"That's why I'm paying you so well." Marcus chuckled. He glanced out over the front yard. A robin was trying to pull a worm out of the ground. "I wanted to finish the conversation we started yesterday."

"Okay." Chase was eager to hear what had happened to home shopping guru Julius Bloom.

"As I was telling you, Bloom was about to jump off his balcony and end his life. But then he got that phone call. Fortunately, he answered it." Marcus looked off into the distance. "I would have done the same thing. Curiosity. You can't go off into the great blue yonder wondering who was calling."

He smiled again. He seemed to be a cheery man, at peace with the world, despite his busy lifestyle and socioeconomic status.

"The phone call was from a woman he didn't know. 'Julius?' she said. And Julius said, 'Yes. Who is this?' She said she had a message for him. She had been sitting in a coffee shop, reading her Bible, when someone turned the TV to his home shopping channel. A commercial with Julius came on, and she saw him sitting there, selling these 'Magic Brooms' that were supposed to make cleaning your floor easier, and thought 'This man needs God.' And then, clear as day, she said she felt that God said, 'He does. Call Julius Bloom and tell him about Me.'"

"So she called him?" Chase asked.

Marcus nodded. "She did. His cell phone was private, unlisted. So he asked how she got his number. She told him that she looked it up in the public phone directory."

"Did she?" Chase asked, surprised.

"Well, she got it someplace. But when he checked later, it wasn't listed. She asked him if there was a hole in his heart, an empty space that he couldn't seem to fill. Julius said he started crying then, and said that yes, there was. He was so empty inside. Remember, he was ready to jump. So she told him about Jesus, and it changed his life."

Marcus was quiet for a moment while Chase thought about the story. One phone call. On time. When needed. It sounded like a God thing to him.

"Did he find out who the woman was?" Chase asked.

Marcus shook his head. "Nope. He tried to do a reverse phone number look up, but her number didn't exist. He asked the telephone carrier to trace it. The woman never gave him a name, and he never found her. He's convinced she was an angel."

An angel. "Wow. That's quite a story," Chase said.

Marcus nodded and looked at Chase. "Yes, it is. You're familiar with angels."

Chase sidestepped that comment. "You said Julius came to visit you?"

"Yes. As I said, he was Grace's previous owner, so he had been watching Grace and Hannah perform. He was curious, you know, about how they were doing. He loved that horse too. And he said that one day God told him that Hannah and I needed Jesus. So he came to tell me the good news."

Marcus grew quiet again, contemplative. His smile disappeared. He turned to look at Chase again. "I've made a lot of mistakes in my day. I lost my wife because of it. I lost a lot of friends and family, and I'm afraid I've been a terrible father to Hannah. Last year, after Julius left, it was like my eyes were opened. I started giving back. I started being kinder to my employees and giving them time off and not driving them so hard. And most of all, I started trying to love Hannah better, and to make up for all the lost years. But she's hurt, and that has made her hard. I can't get through to her. She thinks I'm going through some kind of phase and is waiting for it to pass. Last week she asked me when I was going to stop being a Jesus freak. I'm sure you can relate to that."

Chase nodded. How many times had he himself been called that in the news?

"So she's probably not too happy about that, either," Chase said. "Me being a 'Jesus freak.' You know she doesn't want to work with me?"

"I know. She put up a fight about it. But she likes you."

"She *likes* me?"

Marcus nodded.

"What gives you that idea?"

But Marcus didn't answer. "I'm hoping that you can share Jesus with her. She'll never hear it from me; she won't let me talk about it. I was praying about how to reach her, and one day I saw an old dressage magazine with you on the cover. 'Wonder Kid Speaks to Angels: Did He Hit His Head Too Hard?' was the title."

"Oh yeah. That one."

Marcus smiled again, briefly.

"And I knew, then. I *knew* that you were the trainer for Hannah."

"Because I'm crazy?" Chase asked, smiling.

Marcus looked at him again, his eyes turning serious. "No. Because you have your priorities in the right place."

A silence fell between the men as Chase contemplated what Marcus was asking of him.

"I've only known Hannah for one day. She already doesn't listen to me, and I can tell you, she's not going to listen to me *at all* if I start talking about Jesus," Chase said.

"Don't talk about it. Just *show* her. Lead by example. Hannah has never known unconditional love. Who else is a better person to show the sustaining love of God than the one man who the whole world turned against?"

Chase swallowed. There was such conviction in Marcus's words, such trust, that Chase felt tears sting his eyes. He turned his head and blinked them away.

The whole world had indeed turned against him. At least that's how it had felt at the time.

Marcus looked at his watch, then slapped his knees with the palms of his hands. He stood. "I need to get to work, and you have a lesson to get to. Good luck. And I will pray for you. You're gonna need it." He winked.

Chase sat there and watched as Marcus got in his car, turned around in the driveway, and made his way back to the house.

Ten weeks to train Hannah and Grace for the trials, and ten weeks to lead her to Christ. Not too tall an order.

But Chase smiled. Suddenly, he didn't feel so alone. Maybe his gut feeling to take this job had been right. God had a plan after all.

Chapter Nine

Hannah was sitting on her horse, watching Chase walk up the road toward the arena. It was only about five minutes past their 9 a.m. time. She had waved at her dad as he drove past and wondered what the two men had talked about.

Her dad, as a CEO, liked to keep up with his employees. He often held meetings, paid short visits, and made phone calls just to see where people were on things. He had gotten more into personal, one-on-one meetings in this past year after his "change."

That's how she thought of it. His "change." Some men bought fancy sports cars or had affairs when having a mid-life crisis. Her dad had found Jesus. He already had plenty of sports cars.

Hannah sighed and looked at her watch as Chase approached. He smiled in return. It irked her how unperturbed he was. He had a radio in his hand.

"Let's get started," she said crisply when he entered the arena.

"Hello, Grace," Chase said, coming up and putting his hand on the horse's neck. Grace turned to nuzzle him in return. So the horse was on his side too?

"What's that ancient thing?" Hannah pointed to the hand-held radio. "Is that how you listen to music?"

Chase smiled. "This is my mom's 1980s-era boombox," he said. "It has a CD player in it, and it's loud enough so that you'll be able to hear it."

"You know we have a stereo system here," Hannah said. She dipped her chin in the direction of the speakers, which were mounted on poles around her arena.

"Well, this is the way *I* used to do it," Chase said.

There was a seating area on the side of the arena for observation, but instead of going there, he set the boombox down on the fence post and turned it on. "This has your previous music in it. I found the CD," he said. "Run through your last freestyle routine for me."

"My last one? What good will that do?"

"It'll show me what your strengths and weaknesses are."

"You can watch it on YouTube."

"I'd like to watch it live."

She stared hard at him for a minute, then gave a dramatic sigh. Actually, she loved this routine. They had won big time with it.

"Fine," she said, and took Grace out of the arena so they could enter with a flourish.

Chase waited until she signaled, then he turned it on. The music flowed out strongly over the arena. Grace pricked her ears forward, recognizing the music, and Hannah felt her horse's muscles tense in anticipation.

It was a classical piece, a German sonata that Hans had picked out. It started out slowly, allowing Grace to showcase her effortless trot; then the music built up into a crescendo, and Grace really got to move out.

Like always, Hannah got caught up in the movement. She forgot about Chase, about her dad, about her life, and for five brief minutes, Hannah was carried away in her favorite world, becoming one with her horse.

As the music ended, she stopped in the center of the arena and asked Grace to bow. The horse stretched her right front leg out and came to her knee on the left. She arched her neck, bowing her head, before she came back up to stand squarely on all fours.

Chase clapped his hands together slowly. "Wow," he said. "I've watched that routine on TV, but I've never seen it in person before. I have goosebumps." He held his arm up for her to see. "Thank you."

Hannah smiled. It felt good to have gone through the familiar routine. For a moment, she briefly missed Hans again.

"I saw a few things I want to be sure to highlight in your new routine, and I have some ideas for some new things I'd like you to try," Chase said.

He had that darn notebook with him again. He came over and started drawing patterns on it.

As he sketched, she couldn't help but notice how muscular his arms were. He was right next to her⌐⌐— below her really—his shoulders just about even with Grace's back. From here, she could smell his shampoo, or aftershave, she wasn't sure which. It was a light, clean smell, and reminded her of a favorite soap she had used as a little girl. She didn't like strong scents, so was pleased he didn't wear cologne.

Devon always wore too much cologne. She had told him over and over that it upset the horses' delicate noses. And hers, but she didn't mention that. Never show weakness.

"What do you think?" Chase asked. He looked up at her.

She realized she hadn't been paying attention.

"It looks great," she said.

Chase started at her for a moment. "No. I asked you a specific question."

"Oh." Hannah felt her cheeks coloring again. What was *wrong* with her? "Can you repeat it?"

"Sure. Do you want to do the piaffe or the pirouette? I think both are strong but . . ."

"The pirouette." She just picked one, eager to look like she was on top of things.

But he didn't write it down. Instead he was watching her closely. "Why?"

"Why? Because."

"Because why?"

She didn't owe him an explanation! "What does it matter? It's what I prefer."

"It matters a great deal. Why don't you explain the technical differences of each to me."

"The technical differences?" Hannah was flustered.

"Unless you don't know."

Of course she knew the technical differences! She had studied dressage her entire life!

"Oh my gosh," she said, and exhaled loudly to show him she was annoyed. He just cocked an eyebrow. "Fine. Grace is good at the piaffe, and collects her haunches under her really well, so we can easily accomplish that kind of movement. Plus, her white feet look pretty when she trots." Hannah smiled. Chase waited for her to continue.

"*But...*" she said, emphasizing the word. "The pirouette..." She glanced at the diagram he had drawn on the notebook. The pirouette required the horse to really work from its haunches, something Grace had trouble with, and it was more difficult to work into the routine where he was pointing. She *should* have picked the piaffe for this particular section. She should have been paying attention. She defiantly decided to continue on, feigning confidence even though she suspected her choice was wrong. "The pirouette will give us more points. It's a more difficult move. Our goal is to win."

She stopped. She expected Chase to criticize her, belittle her, so she was thinking up a sharp retort. But instead, he spoke in a non-condescending tone.

"That's what I originally thought too," he said. "Manny's strong suit was the piaffe. But riders who consistently did the pirouette scored better. So I started to work on that with him until he got it. The problem is, here," he tapped at the notebook, "is not a good place to execute it. She's too close to the corner and won't have room to do the turning very well. This area is a better place for Grace to do the piaffe, and we can save the pirouette for here." He tapped at another place on the notebook.

"Oh," Hannah said.

"So let's try it."

He said it so simply, so easily. *Let's try it.* She was so used to getting yelled at that she had no idea how to react.

"Okay," she said. She did what he asked. They executed the piaffe in the corner, then moved forward to the next phase. Grace flicked her ears, trying to understand what it was her rider wanted. Hannah explained the best she could, using soft hands on the reins and light, barely perceptible leg pressure. Her horse did what was asked. The pirouette was not Grace's strong point, but she tried her best.

"That was quite good," Chase said. "Let's do it again."

Hannah did. Chase asked her to repeat it four more times, then called her over.

"I think Grace can handle it. I'm going to write it in as one of the more pronounced elements of her routine."

"Really?" Hans would have never let her do that. *Don't take chances that disadvantage you,* he had always said.

"Why not?" Chase said. "As we get closer to the trials, if she hasn't mastered it, I'll write it out."

"You can do that? I mean...then I'll—*we*"—she rubbed Grace's neck—"will have to memorize the routine all over again."

"I'm pretty confident that Grace can handle it," Chase said.

"Okay."

Hannah got back to work. She spent two hours riding, with Chase asking her to repeat some of the more difficult dressage moves over and over. He took notes on his yellow notebook. Finally, he folded it shut and looked at his watch.

"Let's be done for now," he said.

Hannah nodded. The sun had really heated up the air, and Grace had a lathered sweat on her. Hannah's own hair was damp around her neck. She needed another shower.

"I'm going to get some lunch," Chase said. "Then I'm going to spend the afternoon working up a routine for you. Are you available to meet this evening?"

"I think so," Hannah said. "I'll check my schedule when I get back to my phone." She had nothing going on, nothing at all. But she didn't want him to know that.

"Sounds good." Chase walked over to them and patted Grace on the neck. Then he looked up, his brown eyes meeting Hannah's blue ones. "You did a really great job today," he said. "I know I'm not Hans, or like your other trainers. I'm young, and yes, I've never done this for somebody else before. But I've done it for *me*. And it got me to the Olympics *twice*. Give me a chance, Hannah. I'll do the best I can for you."

She nodded, again taken aback by his demeanor. He seemed so *nice*. And she had been anything but nice to him so far.

She switched her crop over to her other hand so she could dismount and accidentally dropped it. Chase bent down to pick it up, and when he straightened up, she saw that his gold chain had slipped out of his shirt.

"Here," he said.

"Thanks." But her eyes were on the gold chain. It had a cross on it. She remembered then, that he was a Jesus freak too, just like her dad.

She dismounted from her horse.

"See you tonight," she said, dismissing him. The last thing she needed was another man in her life who had gone through "the change." She had forgotten about the media blitz about *that*. At that point in his career, she had already given up on him and quit watching the news footage.

She avoided Chase's eyes as he said goodbye and walked back toward the guesthouse.

"Grace, he's certainly different," Hannah said. Her legs were tired. The three-mile run and the two hours of riding had left her with a relaxed, stress-free feeling from the mix of endorphins and fatigue. She loved how she felt after a good ride, with much accomplished before the day was even half over.

Grace walked into the barn beside her on a loose rein, also relaxed from their workout. Hannah took her saddle and bridle off and led her over to the wash racks. After Grace was washed off, she put her back in her stall and gave her a flake of hay to munch on.

"You're a good girl," she said. "I'll see you later."

She slid the door closed and latched it. When she turned around, Devon was standing there.

She jumped, startled. He was wearing that cologne she hated. How had she not smelled him approaching?

"Hey, Hannah," he said, showing his whitened teeth in what she supposed he thought was a smile.

"Hey," she said. She turned and hung the lead rope up, taking her time with it, hoping he'd leave.

"I'm glad you came last night. You looked great in that dress you were wearing."

"Thanks," Hannah said. She had finished hanging up the lead rope, so had no choice but to turn back around. "I need a shower now. I'll see you later."

She brushed by him, but he took hold of her wrist.

"I came to ask you to lunch. After you shower. I am meeting with some of the Olympic Council, and I thought you'd want to come along. You know, make some good marks." He winked. She hated when he did that.

"I'll save my good marks for the show ring," she said, pulling her arm out of his grip.

She brushed past him, heading down the aisleway.

"Hannah, wait!" he said. He trotted to catch up with her. "Look, I know you're still angry with me. I apologized about ten times. I don't know what else I can do?"

Hannah took a small, deep breath, suppressing the huge sigh she wanted to let out. She stopped, just outside of the barn, and turned to him.

"Devon, I know you're sorry. But we aren't together anymore, okay?"

"But we were so *good* together," he said. "I don't understand what happened."

"It's not appropriate for us to be together since you're on the committee." Hannah gave him the practiced smile she had learned to use on her father while growing up. *Everything is okay, Dad. Really.* "Everything's fine, Devon. I need to go shower."

"So no lunch?"

"Not today. Maybe next time."

She leaned forward and gave him a peck on the cheek. It kept him happy and played into the delicate balance she walked every day between angering 'Devon of the Olympic Nominating Committee' and keeping her dignity.

"Okay?" She looked at him with big eyes and saw the smile that meant he believed her.

"Sure," he said. "Lunch next time. I'll put in a good word for you today."

"Thanks. I really appreciate it. I do need to go shower. I probably smell!"

She laughed and walked off before he could say anything else. She couldn't wait to get in the shower and wash all the dirt off her. Especially now that she could smell the lingering scent of his cologne on her hair.

Chapter Ten

There was a weight room in the basement of the little bungalow, so Chase lifted before he showered. Then he unpacked the rest of his stuff. By the time he was finished, it was midafternoon, and he was starving. He had picked up some groceries yesterday morning on his way to the farm, so he had a few things in the house already.

He made himself a sandwich, and just as he was sitting down at the kitchen table, his cell phone rang. It was his sister.

"Hey, bro, how's it going?" she said. Anika's voice was perky. She was always so upbeat, despite the hand life had dealt her.

"It's going about as you predicted," Chase said. "But this place is beautiful, and her dad is great. So that's something."

He told her about the guesthouse and the layout of the farm.

"You haven't gone mad yet?" she asked.

Chase smiled. "Not yet."

There was a pause, and Chase took a bite out of his sandwich. He heard Anika sigh.

"I just wanted to tell you, again, that you don't need to do this," Anika said. "I really appreciate it and all but—"

"Anika, I'm not just doing this for you," Chase said. "I like being back in the horse world."

"It's not too...weird? People aren't treating you awful?"

"Not at all." Chase thought of Devon and of Angela at the party. "Not anything I can't handle. And Hannah has no choice but to put up with me. No one else will train her."

"She's that much of a pain?"

Chase laughed. "She's okay. How's Taylor?"

Taylor was Anika's eight-year-old son. Her boyfriend had left her when Taylor was six. Anika had never finished college because of the pregnancy, and they had never married. He had cheated on her several times, drank too much, and finally left. Chase figured it was good riddance, but his absence had left Anika without a paycheck.

"Taylor's fine. He's still staying with the neighbor while I work." She was a waitress at the corner grill in her town. "I'm getting the bills paid."

But she would never pay off the debt by herself. Anika had had a brief stint with online gambling after her ex left. It had started as a way to try to make ends meet but soon became an addiction. She'd sought help and hadn't gambled in over a year. That he knew.

"I'll send what I can," Chase said. He had insisted on transparency, and she was supposed to send him documents to prove she was paying off her debts. She had so far, and he was certain she was serious about turning her life around.

"I really don't need your help," she said.

He knew she meant it. Anika was independent. But Taylor had to make do with clothes from the thrift store and peanut butter and jelly sandwiches for both lunch and dinner. When Chase had been visiting one day and saw Anika come home with underwear from the thrift store, he knew something had to be done.

"It's washed," she had said, defensively, when he mentioned it.

"No boy wants to be seen in faded underwear in the locker room," Chase said. He knew all too well what it felt like to be bullied. He had skipped that humiliation in school but made up for it as an adult.

He and Anika had grown up in a small home on the outskirts of Chicago. They'd attended a very poor school district. Their parents had (and were) both loving, which went a long way toward a good life, but they were far from rich. Their dad was a failing laser printer salesman, and their mother a piano teacher who saw students in their small home. Chase had shown an early interest in horses and had read every horse book he could get his hands on.

One day, his father had surprised him with tickets to a horse show. They'd attended, and Chase was fascinated by the horses, especially the dressage events. When he was twelve, he'd managed to get a job on a horse farm just outside of town. He'd take the bus to the closest stop every day after school, then walk the extra two miles out into the country. Hank Solomon had taken him under his wing, and his riding career had begun.

"Mom's teaching Taylor piano," Anika said. "He loves it."

Both Chase and Anika knew how to play. Chase figured his early introduction to music had something to do with his ability to choreograph dressage moves.

"That's great!" he said. "I haven't played in a while."

He suddenly missed home. His little apartment in the Chicago suburbs seemed so far away.

"I hope you make it big as a trainer," Anika said. "Actually, I know you will! And maybe you can find your horse."

"I haven't really lost him," Chase said. "I know exactly where he is."

"But he needs to come home."

Chase sighed. "Yes. That would be nice."

Manny's owner would never sell, at least not at a price that Chase could afford.

"Hey, I've got to go," Anika said. "I was on my break and just thought I'd call and check in. Don't let the she-viper get you down."

"Hannah's not quite a viper," he said, laughing. "But I'll take those words to heart."

Chase hung up the phone and finished his lunch. Then he poured himself a second glass of iced tea and sat down at the kitchen table to work on Hannah's routine.

He thought she'd be better off with a pirouette at this particular point in the routine. It had surprised her. He wondered if she had been allowed to make any choices at all through the years when it came to her sport. Although, he couldn't imagine Hannah Whitney ever giving way to someone else's authority.

He made a few notes on his paper, then lifted his pencil. He thought about Devon's attitude when he was with Hannah and about what he had heard about Hans. Perhaps her defiant attitude was merely a defense mechanism to protect herself. Like it had been with his horse, Manny.

He suddenly wondered if Hannah's attitude *was* more than just "spoiled brat." She certainly *was* defensive and not about to trust anyone. He knew her mother had left her when she was eight. That would mess anybody up.

He had seen her look at the gold chain when it fell out of his shirt. Suddenly, her demeanor had changed. Defiance. Why trust God when you don't trust *anybody?* Her dad's charge to tell Hannah about Jesus was not going to be an easy task. But then again, all he had to do was share his own experiences and let God handle the rest. He'd have to think of a way to ask Hannah about her dad and his conversion. That might open up the conversation to Jesus.

Chase shook his head to clear the thoughts. He needed to get to work. They only had ten weeks. Minus one day now.

He pulled out his iPad, and by dinner time, he had what he felt was a great routine mapped out for her.

Chase was out on the front porch, sitting on the swing, when Hannah arrived at 8 p.m. for their discussion on her routine. She drove down the lane in a red Mustang convertible. The top was down, and she put it up before she got out.

She smiled as she walked toward the porch where he was sitting. She was wearing a yellow skirt that just showed her knees, and a white tank top. She had a light blue sweater in her hand, probably in case it got cold. She had worn her hair down. She didn't have sunglasses on this late, and her eyes were a startling, deep blue.

Chase felt his stomach flutter a little bit. Suddenly feeling awkward, he wondered where he had put his iPad and his notes.

He took a deep breath and exhaled slowly, calming his heart.

She was distracting in so many ways. Smart, stubborn, and talented, but she was also breathtakingly beautiful. He had noticed that right away, the moment they had met. After all, he *was* a man. And she could be a model on the cover of a fashion magazine.

She didn't seem to have a boyfriend. He wondered, again, if there was anything between her and Devon.

"Hi," he said, standing as she walked up the steps. "Can I get you something to drink? I have iced tea and water. That's about it. I haven't had a chance to do much grocery shopping yet."

"Hi," she said. "A bottle of water would be fantastic."

"I'll be right back. Go ahead and have a seat."

She looked around the porch and chose the cushioned wicker chair near the table.

Chase went inside and found two bottles of water. He grabbed his iPad and notebook, and suddenly wondered if she would like the routine he had mapped out.

He had never done this for anyone else before. It's what he would do if it were *his* horse. But Grace wasn't his horse. What did he know? He felt a prick of uncertainty. What was he was doing here, and how was he going to pull this off?

She'd kill him if it didn't work out.

And he'd never be able to prove himself to the dressage show world, something he wanted so badly it hurt.

He took a deep breath to steady himself. *It's all in God's hands.*

Then he pushed open the screen door and went out onto the porch.

Chapter Eleven

Hannah noticed that Chase still had the cross necklace on. He wore it all the time, but she hadn't given it much thought at first, because it was hidden beneath his shirt. Tonight, the chain was tucked inside his light blue collared polo. He was wearing loose cargo shorts and was barefoot. She kicked off her sandals and tucked her feet up in the chair under her.

"How was your day?" Chase asked as he opened his iPad and pulled out the yellow notebook. The guy sure liked to take notes.

"It was fine," she said. She had ordered some new clothes online. Brushed Grace twice. Played with her cat. Her dad had come home for dinner, like he always did these days. She was still getting used to family dinner. But that had pretty much been her day.

She tried to see the notebook, which was upside down since he was across from her. There was a pattern on it.

"This is what I have so far," Chase said. He turned the notebook around, then pointed out some of the moves in the routine. After he took her through it once, he punched in a song on his iPad and played it quietly.

He traced the routine with his pencil as the music played.

She liked it. It had energy and felt motivating. She could picture Grace doing her extended trot during the faster rhythms of the music, and the ending was perfect for their bow.

The words resonated as well: *I am more. I am more. Look at me!*

She nodded.

"It's good," she said.

Chase was quiet. She glanced up and saw that he was watching her.

"Just good?" he asked. "I want you to be floored by it."

"I'm rarely floored by anything," Hannah said. In truth, she *was* a bit floored, not only at how quickly he had worked, but at how well he seemed to know what she wanted and needed after just watching her ride for one day.

"I kind of noticed," he said. He leaned back in his chair. "So it's good to go?"

She was also a bit floored by him. He watched her intently with those deep, brown eyes and didn't look away like other men she knew. Not many people could hold eye contact. It was like he really wanted to know her, to know what she was thinking. It was like he actually cared.

"Yes," she said. "It's good to go."

"Hmm."

He crossed his arms over his chest and glanced down at the notebook. "Well, okay. That was easy." He didn't sound convinced.

"I like it," she said again. "I mean, I actually do. I had no idea you'd be done."

"It's a work in progress," he said. "We'll make changes as we go through it."

The sun was nearly gone behind the trees, and the first fireflies were coming out. The woods around them sparkled like jewels. The air was getting cooler, and she put her sweater on.

It was getting too dark to work.

"You want to go inside?" Chase asked.

Hannah shook her head. It felt so peaceful, sitting here, with the evening sounds around them. It was almost like they were friends.

He reached for his glass of tea, and the setting sun glinted off the gold chain around his neck.

"Tell me how He changed you," she said.

"How what?" Chase put his glass down. "Who?"

Hannah nodded toward his chain. "Jesus. Isn't that why you wear a cross?"

She remembered the harsh media criticism about his conversion.

Chase paused. She had caught him off guard.

"Are you genuinely interested or are you here to poke fun?" he said.

She frowned. "I don't poke fun. If I made fun of you, I'd be making fun of my dad. He's a Jesus freak too." She said the words before she realized it. "I mean..."

"Jesus freak?" Chase said. "Is that what you think of me?"

That and other things.

"No," Hannah said. "I'm sorry. It's just been weird, with my dad. I can't get used to him the way he is." She laughed a little bit, trying to brush it aside.

For some reason, suddenly, she really wanted Chase to like her. She rarely felt that way about anybody. She had given up caring years ago.

"I just figure that your...faith?...must be powerful. After all, you gave up a lot because of it."

He sat there a moment, searching her eyes. "I did," he said finally.

At first, they had ridiculed him because he had frozen in the ring—twice. But then, she remembered now, as reporters asked him how he was coping with his losses, he had said he had his faith now and that the rest of it was all secondary. He trusted God to take care of him.

The headlines had then turned from "Wonder Kid Loses His Focus in the Showring" to "Ex-Dressage Wonder Clings to God for Healing" and "Has-Been Horseman Sees Angels—He Really *Has* Lost His Mind!"

Hannah had quit reading them after that.

"You saw an angel," she said.

A smile tugged at the corner of Chase's lips. "You really want to start there?" he asked.

"Why not?

"How about I tell the story my way and start at the beginning?"

Hannah shrugged.

The night had grown darker, and she could barely see his eyes across the table. The fireflies were brighter now. She took a sip of her iced tea. The ice cubes had melted, and it was watered down. The condensation on the glass made her hand damp, and she wiped her palm on her skirt.

She remembered her scrapbook and thought about it laying there in the trash, all her memories of Chase gone, destroyed, along with his career.

"Well, after my Olympic dressage debacle," he said, "and then my subsequent failures, I was taken off my horse. I leased him, as you probably know. Manny was never mine. He belonged to Hank Solomon, a man who had discovered I had a little bit of talent when I went to clean stalls for him at the age of twelve. He put me up on a horse and let me take riding lessons in exchange for barn work. He was a very kind man. He died shortly after I won the gold on Manny. His son took over and wasn't so understanding when I started to lose, taking his horse, and the good name of his stables, down with me."

"Do you miss him?"

"My horse? Of course I miss him." Chase's voice grew quiet, and he ran his finger across the side of his glass, leaving a trail in the condensation. "Of course I do."

He was silent for a moment, and Hannah thought he wasn't going to continue. Then he looked up. "So there I was, without a horse. Then Cordova, the big tack company I was advertising for, pulled their sponsorship, followed by the horse feed and horse shampoo companies that were throwing money my way. I was still okay, as I had a few sponsors left in my pocket. Enough to survive. I had one more show in which to prove myself. I got in the ring, and for the third time, my mind went blank. When I came out, Solomon's son took my horse and told me I was finished."

Hannah couldn't imagine not riding. What else would she do?

"So that evening, I lost the other two sponsors. I went home to my condo, my nice condo not too far from the farm, which I could now no longer afford to keep. I stayed in bed for two days. Then one morning, I woke up, and despite the fact that I had just lost everything, I decided I wasn't going to stay down. I went back to the farm where Manny was kept and asked if I could go back to cleaning stalls, polishing leather, or *anything*, just to be around Manny. Solomon's son laughed at me. He said he'd never have an embarrassment like me set foot in his barn. He told me to get off his property. Then he stormed out of the barn, leaving me alone.

"I stood there for a moment, in shock. Manny had his head hanging over his stall door, and I sat down on a bale of straw right under him. I felt him nuzzling my hair, and I started to cry."

Chase glanced over at Hannah. "Don't make fun. I did. Me. A grown man, crying over his horse."

Hannah smiled, but she was touched. He had really loved his horse. She knew that, from the articles she had read on him, and from just watching the two of them together in the ring.

"I get it," she said.

Chase continued. "Then this woman appeared. There was no one else in the barn, and she just walked up to me and called me by my name. I had worked there for years and had never seen her before, so I asked her what her name was.

"She didn't answer. She just told me that everything would be okay. She said God had a greater plan for me, and that I wasn't to be troubled. And then she left and walked out of the barn. I had this incredible feeling of peace come over me. I can't explain it. The next day was a Sunday, so I went to church and started seeking out God. After that, everything became clearer." Chase shrugged. "The rest is history."

"So you think this woman was an angel?"

"I called the barn the next day to ask about her. No one had ever heard of a woman who matched her description. And the weird thing..." Chase paused, as if weighing how much to say. "She was kind of glowing." Hannah could see his sheepish grin.

"Glowing?"

"Yeah. I thought it was the sun behind her, but her head, her hair, there was like a halo around it. Some sort of light—an aura—was behind her."

Hannah raised an eyebrow. He *was* crazy.

"You asked," Chase said.

"I did indeed."

They were quiet for a moment, then Chase spoke again.

"You wanted to know how Jesus changed me. The things that mattered to me *before*—wealth, winning, popularity—stopped mattering so much. My focus changed from what I could get, to what I could give. I still miss showing. I miss my horse. I miss my friends, or the people who I thought were my friends until they deserted me. I definitely miss the money. But in a way, I'm more content now than I have ever been in my life. I'd even go so far as to say I'm happy."

105

Hannah looked out over the grassy front yard and into the trees across the road. Her Mustang sat there on the curb, with her personalized plate HORSGRL. She thought about what he had said.

"There's nothing wrong with winning," she said finally.

"No. There's absolutely nothing wrong with winning. Just as long as it's not your main goal in life."

Hannah glanced at him, then back to the trees. It was dark now, and the fireflies were thick. They reminded her of the stars in the sky, how they twinkled.

"They're beautiful," she said. "The fireflies."

Chase took his eyes off her and looked out across the road. "They are. Did you know that in the south, there are places where entire mountain ranges light up with them? And they blink in unison. One mountain will blink, then the other will blink back."

"Really? That's cool."

"Scientists think they are communicating to each other."

"What are they saying?"

"Who knows? Maybe 'come to my side of the mountain and we'll party tonight.'"

Hannah laughed, then looked at her phone. "I should get going," she said. "Early day tomorrow."

"8 a.m.?"

"Nine," she said.

Chase laughed. "Jogging first?"

"Running."

Then she had a thought. "Why don't you come with me?"

"Me? Oh, I'm not much of a runner."

"I'll go easy on you, I promise. We'll do a light... *jog.*" She said the word teasingly.

She saw him hesitate, then nod. "Sure. Why not? I have nothing else to do while I wait for you to start working."

Hannah laughed. "Great. Be ready at 7:30. We'll head to the beach. That's my favorite place to run."

Then she walked down the stairs toward her Mustang, a smile on her lips and an unfamiliar flutter in her heart.

Chapter Twelve

Chase woke up early the next morning, thankful he had brought his running shoes. He wasn't really a runner, but he did put in a mile or two several mornings a week back home. It was a good way to stay in shape now that he no longer rode. He pulled on a pair of basketball shorts and a t-shirt and laced on his shoes.

Then he drove his SUV to Hannah's house, arriving ten minutes early so as to get the jump on her. She was waiting for him on her front porch.

He shook his head. He'd never get ahead of this woman.

Hannah was dressed in black spandex pants and a turquoise sports bra with a black tank over it. The outfit clung to the curves of her body. He tried not to notice.

"Good morning!" she said, climbing into the vehicle. She directed him into town. St. Ives sat on the shore of Lake Michigan, a little north of midway up the mitten. Several miles of uninhabited beach stretched up the state park, and that's where Hannah wanted to run.

"I'll pay," she said, leaning over him to hand a few dollars to the booth attendant. Her arm brushed his, and he could smell her shampoo. Something light and floral. The scent reminded him of the flowers that grew in the front flowerbed of his childhood home.

They ran for three miles. Chase kept up with her the first mile, then he started to lag behind. She wasn't kidding when she said she ran. She kept up a good clip the entire way. When he finally caught up to her, she was bent over, her hands on her knees, catching her breath.

"Not a runner, huh?" she said, squinting at him in the bright morning sunlight.

"You figured that out," he said, laughing and hugging his sides. "I'm definitely *not* a runner. I thought you said we were jogging!"

Hannah laughed, then looked at her watch. "Let's go," she said. "If you want me to be in the ring by 9 a.m."

They walked along the beach, catching their breath, and up the dune to where his SUV was parked. They got in, and he handed her a bottle of water.

"Is there a good place to eat in town?" he asked, unscrewing the cap on his bottle. The cool water tasted good going down.

"We don't have time to eat," Hannah said.

"You have to eat!"

She nodded toward the ignition. "Are we going or not?"

Chase shook his head and started the car. He drove up the divided highway that ran alongside the water and led back into the town of St. Ives. A touristy town, it was already bustling with people. Cute little shops lined both sides of Main Street. As he stopped at a light, ready to make the left turn to drive inland toward Fieldstone Farm, he saw a café on the corner.

"Best Clam Chowder in the Nation" read the sign in the window.

"I love clam chowder," he said. "There was a place near my old condo I used to go on Fridays, once a week, for the soup special. Gosh that was good."

"You must be hungry," Hannah said.

He was. His stomach was growling.

"It *is* pretty good," she said. "I meet Dad here a lot for lunch. When he's going to have to work late, or be out of town, he now insists we do lunch. He wants us to do one meal together every day."

"That's nice," Chase said.

Hannah shrugged.

Chase wondered what her relationship with her father was really like. Marcus seemed to realize the mistakes he had made earlier in life and to want to make up for them. He really seemed to love his daughter.

"Your dad cares a great deal about you," he said.

"I know," Hannah said quietly, looking out the passenger window.

"Are you having lunch with him today?"

"No. He's home for dinner tonight. I think he's lunching with *Marion*." She said the name with distaste.

"Marion?"

"His girlfriend."

So Marcus had a life outside of work and Hannah. The light changed to green, and Chase made the left turn onto the road inland.

"Let's eat lunch there," he said

"What? *Today?*"

"Why not? You're only ten minutes out of town. We'll go back, shower, work Grace, then take a lunch break."

Hannah looked over at him. She had her sunglasses on so he couldn't read her eyes.

"I guess," she said. "I'm pretty busy later though."

"Doing what?"

"Things."

"Hmm."

"What do you mean by hmm?"

"What other things?" He tried to imagine what else Hannah did in her spare time. "Do you like to read?"

"Yes. And I play some piano."

"You do? I do too!" For some reason he was very pleased by this. She liked music! "So where do you go when you hang out with your friends?"

Hannah turned back toward the window. "You ask a lot of questions," she said.

"I'm just trying to get to know you, since we'll be spending so much time together over the next ten weeks."

Hannah looked at him again. "I think we should stick to business," she said.

"But you invited me to run with you," Chase countered.

"Did you think this was a date?"

"What? No!" He felt his cheeks growing red. Never in his wildest dreams had he thought this was a date. "Don't flatter yourself."

"I'm not flattering myself! You'd be so lucky to have a date with me!" She huffed and crossed her arms. "I don't want to do lunch."

She was infuriating. He couldn't figure her out. He decided to end the conversation and leaned forward and turned on the radio. Bruce Springsteen's "Glory Days" blared loudly enough to drown out his thoughts, and he concentrated on getting them back home.

The lesson went well. Hannah was very focused when she was in the ring. Fortunately, Devon didn't come by. The other trainer was busy with students out in the front ring, jumping horses.

They kept things business-like, only talking about what related to dressage and to the horse. After two and a half hours of hard work, Hannah was sweaty again, Grace had a foam on her, and Chase was tired of standing. He was still starving. He thought about the clam chowder soup. He'd just drive himself there. It's be much more enjoyable without snarky Hannah anyway.

As they were leading Grace into the barn to wash her off, Devon showed up with a bay mare. He had just washed her off, and he put her in her stall before coming over to them.

"Hannah, I had a wonderful lunch yesterday with the Olympic committee members," he said. "I told them how magnificent you were."

To Chase, Devon always seemed like he was drooling. Not *actually* drooling, but emotionally.

He looked at Hannah with a longing that seemed inappropriate, almost as if he wished to own her.

"Thanks," Hannah said. Chase noticed that she avoided eye contact with Devon.

"How's your training going?" Devon asked, ignoring Chase.

Hannah turned on the water and started hosing Grace down.

"It's going great. Chase came up with a perfect music piece and has already choreographed it."

Devon finally looked at Chase and raised an eyebrow. "Already? That was fast. Just threw it together, huh?"

"Something like that," Chase said.

"Did you pray about it first?" There was a slight hint of mockery in Devon's voice.

"As a matter of fact, I did," Chase said. He kept his eyes on Devon's, silently challenging him to say more.

Devon considered him for a moment, then turned his attention back to Hannah. When he spoke, his voice was cheerful. "Yesterday you said another day for lunch," he said. "How about today? I found this new restaurant in town called Dooley's. They serve sandwiches on artisan breads."

Hannah turned and looked at Devon. "That's nice of you to ask, but I already have plans."

"You do?" Devon looked surprised. "With your dad?"

"With Chase," Hannah said.

Devon's eyes shot toward Chase, then back to Hannah. "Mind if I join you?"

"It's a working lunch," Hannah said. "We're going to go over the routine and make some changes." She glanced at Chase and smiled.

"I see," Devon said. "Well, maybe next time."

Hannah got the water scraper and ran it over Grace's coat, scraping the excess water off her horse. Devon turned to Chase. If eyes could shoot daggers, he was pummeling them at Chase.

"Have fun," he said to Hannah, his voice still cheerful. "I'll see you both around."

He turned on his heel and left. Hannah looked at Chase.

Chase frowned and crossed his arms. "You're using me again," he said.

"What? You invited *me* to lunch." Hannah dropped her eyes and picked at a bit of dirt on her shirt.

Chase had to admit that he was somewhat pleased that he had been chosen over Devon, no matter the reason. *Be careful, Chase, she's a viper.* His sister's words rang in his head. He pushed them aside. It was just lunch. Besides, he and Hannah needed to get some work done.

"Sure," he said. "I'll pick you up in an hour."

"How about I pick *you* up?" Hannah said. "We can take my convertible. It's a beautiful day out."

"Sure." A hot woman with a hot car. Not a bad way to spend his lunch hour. "Can I drive the Mustang?"

"Absolutely not," Hannah said. She smiled and led Grace to her stall. Chase followed.

"Well, then, I'll see you in an hour at the guesthouse," Chase said.

"It's a date," she said, latching Grace's stall door. Then her cheeks reddened. "I mean, not a *date*. A working date." She frowned. "You know what I mean."

Chase raised an eyebrow, enjoying her embarrassment. "Sure," he said. She turned and hurried off to the house to wash up.

Chase stood there for a moment and watched her. Then he put his hand on Grace's neck. "What do you think of your owner?" he said. "She's always scheming, isn't she?"

Grace perked her ears in Chase's direction, then nuzzled him. He rubbed the side of her face. "I sure do miss my own horse," he said. "But I've gotten used to it. Or as used to it as a man can get."

No longer having a horse to ride, especially Manny, felt like losing a limb.

"I've gotta go, Gracie," he said. Grace nuzzled his arm gently, as if comforting him. "I'm glad you like me, girl. I'm not sure your owner does. Or Devon. Or anybody, really, for that matter." He smiled. "But it's okay. I've gotten used to that too." He didn't care much anymore what people thought of him, that much was true. But he felt that he was starting to care a little bit about what Hannah thought of him. And that...well, that was dangerous territory.

Do the job, Chase, and keep it a job. That's all it is.

He gave Grace one last pat on the neck and headed back to the guesthouse to change clothes and get ready for Hannah to pick him up.

Chapter Thirteen

Louie's Sandwich Shop sat on a corner in St. Ives that looked across the street to Lake Michigan. They found a little table by the window.

Chase pulled out Hannah's chair for her.

"Thank you," she said.

She wasn't used to being treated so well. He had opened the restaurant door for her too. Most men didn't seem to think of chivalry these days. They were more concerned with getting something *after* the date, or, even more often in her case, with impressing her father. It seemed like everybody wanted something from Hannah. Nobody just wanted to be her friend because she was...just herself.

She wondered why. She had gone over that question so many times in her head. Why had her mother left her? She didn't remember being terrible as a child. She knew she was difficult now, but back then, she hadn't had the constant anger and defensiveness that flared up in her so often. As she grew older, she felt like she had to wrap herself in a bubble to stay safe.

"So this is the world's best clam chowder?" Chase said, looking at the menu.

"It is. And there is no clamming in St. Ives, so it's quite a miracle!" Hannah laughed. She loved the quirky little town that they had moved to when she was sixteen. The little tourist town had quickly felt like home. She loved being so close to Lake Michigan as well. Running on the lake shore had become one of her favorite things, next to riding Grace. It was a place she could be alone with her thoughts, and the sounds of the waves and the wind cleared her head.

Chase ordered a bowl of the soup and a BLT. Hannah ordered a cup of soup and a turkey club.

"Good choice. The BLT is one of my favorites," Hannah said. "I just had one the other day with Dad, so I'm turkey clubbing today." She laughed at her own joke.

"Better than the artisan bread Devon promised you?"

Hannah sighed. "I'm sorry. I just needed an excuse. Actually, I was looking forward to curling up on the chaise lounge in the screened-in porch with a pita and a book."

"Why don't you like him?"

"Why don't *you?*"

Chase smiled.

"So I guess we should get to work," Hannah said.

"No way," Chase said. "I need a break. You wore me out with the running and the horse training and the animosity."

"Animosity?"

"Yes. Between you and Devon. Between Devon and me. Between me and you." Chase smiled again, so she'd know he was teasing.

"I'm sorry," she said.

"Do you always apologize this much?"

"Actually, no. I never apologize."

"Why?"

"Because I'm never wrong."

She smiled and thanked the waiter, who had just brought the soup with little packages of crackers.

Chase laughed out loud. "Me either. How do you think *that's* going to play into this working relationship?"

"Well, the way I see it is, if we're both never wrong, then we must always be right. And if, by chance, we ever disagree, I'm *still* right."

"Ha! Wait a minute! How do you figure that?"

"Because I'm the girl," Hannah gave him the smile she used with her dad when she wanted something. "And because my father is paying you."

Chase laughed. She liked how his eyes sparkled. "Do you play that card often?" he asked.

"All the time."

She spooned up some of her soup and blew on it. Then she noticed that Chase had bowed his head to pray. She put the spoonful back in her bowl and bowed her head, keeping an eye on him. When he raised his head a moment later and picked up his crackers, she took another spoonful of soup.

"I'm sorry," Chase said. "Did you want me to pray out loud with you?"

"Um, no," Hannah said. She glanced around the restaurant to see if there was anyone in here she knew. Louie was up front taking orders. Her dad knew Louie because Marcus brought clients here often for lunch after a game of golf on the local course. He preferred it over the country club food.

"That would embarrass you," Chase said quietly.

"No," Hannah said quickly.

"Yes, it would," Chase said. "I understand. No worries." He smiled and took a bite of soup. "Oh my goodness! This *is* the best clam chowder I've ever tasted!"

"Told you so," Hannah said. She took another bite of the delicious soup. She liked how comfortable Chase seemed to be in his own shoes. She tried to remember what he was like when he was younger. There had been pictures of him with girls—lots of girls. She remembered that part because she had always been jealous. As a teenager, she's been too young for him, and she hadn't yet traveled in the upper-level dressage circles that he had. But now, she was twenty-four and he was thirty. They were both adults. And she was up on his level. Or at least, the level he used to be on.

She remembered the way Angela had treated him at the party.

"A penny for your thoughts," Chase said. "You're awfully quiet."

"I'm busy," Hannah said, holding up her spoon. She took another bite. The waiter brought their sandwiches.

Chase certainly *was* talented. He had come up with a workable routine for her in one day. *One day!* And she loved the music that he'd picked out for her and Grace. But she had no idea if he could stand up to the stress of the ring, of talking with the judges, or handling the other little things, like Grace's check-ins and everything else that went along with training a horse for an Olympic-level show. He'd certainly handled Devon well. So far, anyway. She hated the way Devon was condescending toward Chase. As if Devon was any better. He was just a young, upstart trainer who happened to be good at training jumpers.

And Devon was a jerk.

"So," Chase said. His mouth was full. "Sorry. Give me a minute." He held up a finger, chewed, and swallowed. "This sandwich is delicious too!"

"Louie's secret is lots of butter."

"And yet you like it. I thought you ate healthy."

"Where'd you get that idea?"

"The whole 'Your body is your temple' thing with Devon."

"Oh. Yeah, well, sometimes a girl's gotta live."

"So," Chase said again. "What do you think? After this morning's workout, are you comfortable with the routine?"

"I thought we weren't going to talk shop while we ate," she said.

"Fair enough."

Chase looked around the restaurant. "Tell me more about St. Ives."

"It's a tourist town, as you've guessed. We have a wonderful little shop that sells essential oils and candles, and I love the lavender. It's grown right here in St. Ives, at Hopeful Farm Bed and Breakfast. It's quaint. Anyway, we have the usual t-shirt shops, fancy restaurants, and beach hangouts."

"Why is it called St. Ives? Was it a Catholic settlement at one point?"

Hannah shook her head. "I'll show you after we eat," she said.

"Show me?"

"Yes. We have a statue of Mary Ives. The story behind it is quite romantic," Hannah said. "And sad. When we moved here when I was sixteen, I used to wonder if I'd ever find a love like Mary Ives had."

What had made her say that? Why was she suddenly all sentimental in front of Chase, who was little more than a stranger? She felt her cheeks redden again, and she looked down at her plate to hide the color. Devon and his friends would have teased her, but when Chase spoke, his voice was kind.

"And have you? I mean, you're only twenty-four, but do you think he's out there? This special man?"

Hannah looked up, into deep the brown eyes that she had memorized when she was younger. She didn't tell him *he* was the man she had dreamed about falling in love with. And now here he was, sitting across from her.

"No," she said quietly.

She thought she had found love once. For a brief two months. When her father had first hired Devon, the trainer came with all the trappings. Good looks, self-confidence, and a love of horses. For the first time ever, she'd felt herself drawn to someone in a romantic way.

They dated quietly, because neither of them were certain her father would approve. After the workday, they'd meet at a restaurant or at the beach. Devon was full of compliments and took her hand when they walked. She had felt the first fluttering of love.

Then, just two months in, she had learned something about him that changed how she felt.

"Devon seems to think he's your man," Chase said.

Hannah looked across at him to see if he was mocking her. His eyes were serious, questioning.

"He's not," she said. "We dated for about two months when my father first hired him. Then one day, I found out who he really was."

Chase raised his eyebrows.

"He saw a chance to be on the Olympic Nominating Committee," she said. "There was an opening, and they were looking for someone. He's so young, just thirty-four, so it was quite the thing that he made it. The woman who was leaving the opening...her term was up. She was in her forties and had a thing for him. He noticed her affections, and so he played into them. He brought her flowers, took her to dinner. He called her. I was with him one evening when she called, and he said all sorts of romantic things to her. He told me he was doing this for me. 'Once I'm on the committee, Hannah, you won't have to worry. You'll be a shoo-in.' That's what he told me. But I couldn't stand to see how he played her. I think she legitimately loved him. Or maybe she was just a cougar. But anyway, it was disgusting. When she left, she appointed him to fill her place."

"And that's how he got on," Chase said quietly. "Does anybody know?"

Hannah shook her head. "No. He advised me to keep it quiet. He didn't do anything illegal, but it wasn't nice. It was politics. When I broke up with him, he was all sweetness and apologizing, but he said it could ruin us both if someone found out about his affair with her. He didn't actually threaten me, but I think, if I brought it up, he'd make sure I didn't make the Olympic team. He has power. Maybe a lot more than we know about. Who knows who else he has been in bed with to get there?"

Chase was quiet. Hannah wondered if she had just said too much. What was it about this man that kept her talking?

Chase flagged down the waiter and got a refill on his iced tea before he spoke.

"Does he still see her?"

"No. Her husband got word that she had been cheating. He doesn't know it was with Devon, but it gave Devon the excuse he needed to call it off. He never cared about her."

"And now he wants you."

"He thinks he really loves me," Hannah said.

"Does he?"

"What do you mean by that?" Hannah asked, suddenly feeling defensive. Didn't Chase think she was attractive?

"Maybe it's your money," he said.

There was always that. Devon wouldn't be the first person after her trust fund.

"I've thought about that. But it doesn't matter, because he's not getting me." She put her spoon down firmly and picked up her sandwich.

"And yet you encourage him."

"I dance the dance," Hannah said. "Let's quit talking about Devon. It's ruining an otherwise great lunch."

"Sounds like a plan," Chase said. "Tell me what's good for dessert."

Chapter Fourteen

Chase and Hannah both ordered hot fudge sundaes after Hannah insisted they were the best thing on the menu. He watched her lick the chocolate off her spoon. She was smiling like a child.

"My father brings me here to celebrate after my big wins," she said. "This is always what we order."

"What are you celebrating today?"

Hannah thought for a moment. "That you and I haven't killed each other yet!"

Chase laughed. "True enough. Cheers!" He held up his spoon and they clicked them together.

"Tell me about Manny," she said.

Manny. Chase had had plenty of women in his life before he crashed to earth, but only one horse. Manny had been his best friend.

"Like I told you, I went to work for Hank Solomon when I was young. He started giving me riding lessons, and eventually I was helping with training. Then, when I was sixteen, this tall warmblood was brought into the farm. He was unruly, and no one could handle him."

Chase had been cleaning a stall out when Manny was brought into the arena. He remembered watching the horse from afar, while the trainer tried without success to put a saddle on him.

"I noticed that the horse was scared of having his left side touched. So I asked if I could try to ride him. Mr. Solomon said, 'Sure, why not?' I saddled the horse from his right and mounted from his right. Manny relaxed."

Chase closed his eyes for a moment, remembering his hand on the horse's warm neck, feeling the muscles under it loosen. Manny had even sighed, as if saying, "Finally, someone understands!"

"That seemed to solve the problem. Then we went for a ride out back in the acreage that Mr. Solomon owned so Manny could relax. By the time we returned, he was a completely different horse and let me do anything I wanted with him, even mount from his left side. But he wouldn't let anyone else handle him. After that, Mr. Solomon started calling me Alexander the Great, and Manny became my horse. I started training for high level dressage, because that was what Manny had originally been purchased for. And you know the rest of the story."

"Alexander the Great," Hannah said.

"Do you know the story?"

"Yes, of him and his black horse Bucephalus. But I want to hear you tell it!" Hannah's eyes were sparkling.

Chase grinned. He loved talking about horses, and she seemed to love it just as much.

"I *loved* that story as a kid," he said. He cleared his throat, laced his fingers together, and leaned forward for emphasis. "As you know, Bucephalus was a fiery black horse, just like Manny is. The story goes that

Alexander was sitting in the audience, watching as the horse was led into the arena to be presented to his dad, the king."

"Alexander was with his mom," Hannah said.

"Right. He was with Olympias, watching this magnificent horse who stood taller than any other Macedonian steed. The horse kept rearing up when anyone would come near him. The king said he was unmanageable and ordered him to be led away. As the attendants tried to lead the stallion away, Alexander stood and called out to them."

"He called them spineless," Hannah said, smiling. "I love that he had the guts to do that. He was just a kid."

"Sounds like something you'd do," Chase said, laughing.

"Hey! Anyway, go on..."

"So his dad, the king, reprimanded Alexander."

"Wait, you forgot the part about what exactly Alexander said," Hannah said.

"Who's telling this story?"

"In Plutarch's biography of Alexander, he wrote that the boy said." Hannah put on her best imitation voice. "'What an excellent horse do they lose for want of address and boldness to manage him.'"

Chase laughed. "Very good. And this made his dad, King Phillip, mad. His dad said something to the effect of 'Son, how dare you talk to your elders that way!'"

Hannah laughed. "Sounds like something my dad would say to me."

Chase tried to keep from agreeing. "But Alexander ignored the rebuke and offered to try his hand at handling the horse. He told his dad that if he couldn't manage Bucephalus, he'd pay for him."

"The horse wasn't named at that point. Alexander named him later."

"Shh. Spoilers," Chase said. "The king accepted Alexander's challenge. The crowd was laughing at him. But Alexander had noticed something the others hadn't. The horse was afraid of his shadow. Alexander walked forward and turned the horse to face the sun so Bucephalus couldn't see his shadow. He slowly approached him, took the reins in his hand, and mounted him.

As Alexander rode off, the laughter of the crowd turned to cheers. And when he returned on the horse a little while later, still on board, his father said—"

Hannah interrupted with her deep, storytelling voice: "O my son, look thee out a kingdom equal to and worthy of thyself, for Macedonia is too little for thee."

"Yep! Historians claim that that moment was the turning point of Alexander's life."

"Bucephalus was stolen once," Hannah said. "And Alexander promised to destroy the countryside and slay every inhabitant if his horse wasn't returned. Bucephalus was quickly returned with a plea for mercy."

"The two of them were inseparable," Chase finished. He stared at his iced tea and stirred it with his straw. "Until the horse died of old age."

Hannah sat back in her chair.

"What a nice story," she said.

"Except for the slaughter and war that comes after."

She laughed. "But to love a horse that much. I get that."

"Me too."

He watched Hannah across the table. She was gazing out the window, lost in thought. He followed her gaze. They had been lucky enough to get a table with a view. Louie's sat on the corner across the street from a parking lot for boats, and beyond that was Lake Michigan in all her splendor. He could see the waves crashing up against the black and white striped lighthouse.

"It's pretty out there," he said quietly.

"Yeah."

The soft light coming in through the windows softened Hannah's features, and for a moment, he saw a sad, lost little girl in the woman sitting there. He had a close-knit family and wondered what it would have been like to grow up without a mother. Or without a father. Marcus had admitted that he had never been there for Hannah. Chase knew her mother had left, but he didn't know the details. He wondered if Hannah ever saw her.

"Do you see your mom at all?" he asked

Hannah remained looking out across the vast Great Lake. "No," she said. "I haven't seen her since I was eight years old and she left me to wake up alone, wondering where she had gone. Dad, of course, was already at work that morning." There was a tinge of bitterness in her voice.

Wow. What parent could just go off and leave like that? Chase knew that if he ever had kids, he'd be there for them, always. Like his parents were for him.

He decided not to pursue it anymore.

"Are you ready to go?" he asked.

Hannah turned to him and smiled. "Yes." She reached for her purse.

"I've got the bill," he said.

"No, that's okay."

"Really. Let me treat."

Hannah nodded and put her purse aside. Chase flagged down the waiter and paid.

"So you were going to show me why this town is called St. Ives?" Chase asked.

"Yep," Hannah said.

When they got in the car, she turned toward the beach, in the opposite direction of her farm. The convertible top was down, and the wind blew their hair as she headed north on the divided highway, Lake Michigan at their left. Just up at the edge of town was a tall dune, the sand covered with rocks and grass. On top of it was a statue. Hannah parked the car in a little turnaround below the dune and got out.

"Come on," she said.

He followed her up the dune. When they got to the top, he could see that the statue was carved in the figure of a woman, her hands folded in prayer, her dress and shawl billowing out behind her as if in the wind from the lake. It was about the height of two men.

"This is Mary Ives," Hannah said. "Her story is almost as good as Bucephalus's."

"I can't wait to hear it."

"St. Ives used to be an unnamed fishing town. One day, Mary's husband and son went out and a terrible storm blew up unexpectedly. That happens around here. They never returned. She came up here every day to pray for their safe return, hoping that they weren't really dead. But there wasn't a trace of them to be found. Lake Michigan swallowed them up. After about a year, she gave up on seeing them alive and had a gravestone put in the cemetery with their names on it.

"But Mary continued coming up here to pray every day. She prayed for all the other fishermen who went out. She became a town icon, and people felt comforted by the fact that she was up here. In any weather too. She'd make the journey, it was said, anytime the fishermen went out. And if some of them didn't return, she'd make food for their families and take them care baskets. When she died of old age, the lines for her visitation wrapped around the church three times. They named the town after her.

"Is she really a saint?"

"Not officially. But to the people back then, she was."

He walked around to the front of the statue, where a bronze plate read:

St. Ives
Patron of sailors
Prayer warrior of the town

Chase looked at the statue, amazed at how soft the folds of Mary Ives's clothes looked in the stone. Her face was closed in the fierce concentration of prayer.

"I wonder how she felt when God didn't give her family back to her," Hannah said. "After all that pleading."

Chase looked over at her. The wind was whipping her hair loose from her ponytail. He couldn't see her eyes behind her sunglasses.

"Sometimes, we don't get what we ask for," he said. "God may have a better plan."

"A better plan than giving us our families back?"

Chase nodded.

"Explain."

He turned back to the statue and ran his hand over the stone. Mary Ives had remained faithful in prayer, petitioning for others even after she knew her own family wasn't going to return.

"Sometimes, the picture is bigger than us," he said. "I wonder how many families had their own faith strengthened as they watched Mary talk with God every day. She knew He was there, and she obviously trusted Him, or she would have quit talking to Him."

He glanced at Hannah through his own dark sunglasses. She was looking at the statue. "Hannah, do you believe in God at all?"

She snorted. "Of course I believe in God! I just don't think He's this approachable, cosmic being that my dad believes He is. Dad keeps talking about a personal relationship with Jesus. I don't think it works that way. I mean, how can it?"

"It's true. Jesus wants a personal relationship with us."

"With *us?*" Hannah said. "We're just these tiny beings, and most of us aren't even nice. I don't think for one minute that God wants to hang out with us."

"That's kind of what prayer is about," Chase said. "Hanging out with God."

"That's why I don't pray," Hannah said. "God would probably take one look at most of us and figure we're not worth it. Like Devon. You think God wants to talk to Devon?"

"Yes, I do," Chase said, although he hated to admit it. "It's a thing called grace."

"Hmph." Hannah crossed her arms. "Grace?"

"Your horse was named after a hymn. Do you know the story behind it?"

"I think we've had enough stories for one day," Hannah said. Her tone was tense. "Let's head back."

Without waiting for him to answer, she turned and walked back down the dune and got in her car. He followed, and as soon as he was buckled, she pulled out.

Don't try to talk about God, Marcus had said. *Show her Christ through you.* Chase had pushed her too hard.

They drove all the way back to the farm in silence.

Chapter Fifteen

Hannah rose early as usual and went for a run. Then she showed up promptly at 9 a.m. for her training with Chase.

She led Grace out to the arena where Chase was waiting for them.

"Hi," she said pleasantly.

She decided not to mention anything about yesterday. She had really enjoyed their lunch until he had brought up God. She had to remind herself not to trust anyone. She'd get hurt. Chase was like her father in the fact that he was dedicated to this "cause" of his. Look where it had gotten him—he had lost sponsorships and friends, and he had been publicly ridiculed because of his faith.

She had let herself get drawn into his stories about horses, and she had to admit that his good looks were a bit distracting as well. The moment she had first seen him, the old feelings had returned—her old crush on a stranger she had never met. Only now he wasn't a stranger. He was right here in front of her.

"Hannah?"

"What?" Chase was talking to her. She had been distracted, lost in her thoughts. Again.

"I asked if you wanted to do some warmups first."

"Sure."

She turned Grace into the arena and started a serpentine pattern back and forth across the space, stretching her horse's neck and other muscles. Then she entered her horse into a slow trot.

She was glad her nanny had tossed the scrapbook. She'd be mortified if Chase ever knew how much she had liked him. She *had* clipped photos and articles of *other* dressage riders too. And their horses. Mostly their horses. She had loved the sport from a very young age and had aspired to be like them. They were all her heroes. Chase was just a little above the rest.

Or had been.

"She looks good this morning," Chase said. "Let's work on the routine and polish it up some more."

The lesson went well. They kept to business. Chase didn't try to apologize for the uncomfortableness with which they had ended the afternoon. And he didn't pretend their small time of familiarity and fun had been anything more than a pleasant business luncheon. Not like Devon. Devon would have taken her interest as an open invitation to take her home with him.

Her stomach turned as she thought of Devon.

Hannah went home, showered, and sat down on her bed with Pussy Willow. Her wet hair was wrapped in a towel, and she felt a bit sleepy in the sun that was filtering through the sheer curtains onto her bed. The cat was stretched out in it.

She picked up her phone.

There was a text from Dierdre, the girl she sometimes rode with. Dierdre stabled her horse here at the farm and wondered if Hannah had a pair of reins she could borrow. She had left hers out in the arena and a mouse had apparently chewed on the leather.

Hannah texted back and told her yes.

She looked at her emails. A few informational ones about upcoming shows and registrations. She forwarded them to Chase.

That was it.

Hannah sighed and sat back against her pillows. She wouldn't really consider Deirdre a friend. She was more of a colleague. They rode together, and were friendly enough in the barn, but Dierdre never called her to go out or anything.

The only person who ever showed any interest in her was Devon.

She didn't really have any friends.

"Pussy Willow," she said, "you love me, right?"

In response, the cat came over and rubbed his head up against the back of her hand. "I love you too," she said, scratching him behind the ears. Then she moved to his lower back, just in front of his tail. He arched his back and purred in ecstasy.

Chase was nice. He was, in fact, the nicest person she had ever met. He didn't yell at her like her other trainers had. Yet he wasn't a yes-man, trying to say things just to keep her happy.

For some reason, Hannah suddenly felt like crying. She took a few deep breaths, wondering where all this emotion had suddenly come from. Focus was her strong point, but she had lost focus this morning in her wandering thoughts, and now she was losing focus again, ruminating over Chase.

She heard the front doorbell ring. Then Anastasia's footsteps as she went to answer it.

Pussy Willow perked up his ears. He was extremely shy. While he knew he was probably safe up here in her room, he wasn't taking any chances that a stray service repairman or visiting relative might find him.

"It's not for us," Hannah told him, scratching his ears again. "Really," she insisted. "I don't get company."

The cat didn't believe her, and listened, his purring having gone quiet. Hannah could hear muffled voices down below.

"Hannah! You have a visitor!"

Hannah looked at her cat. "Well, I guess I was wrong. Don't tell anybody," she said, kissing him on his head. As she got off the bed, he dove under the comforter, burrowing until he couldn't be seen.

"Silly cat," she said.

Hannah walked down the stairs, where Anastasia was standing, still speaking with a woman on the steps.

Anastasia turned to Hannah. "Miss Whitney, she says she's...she's..." Anastasia stuttered.

"Anastasia! Cat got your tongue?" Hannah said, stepping onto the marble floor in the entrance way. Her housekeeper seemed nervous. "It's okay. I've got it."

Anastasia looked pale as she stepped aside. What Hannah saw next made her stop in her tracks.

Standing at the doorway entrance, on the porch, was a tall woman in her forties, with shoulder length blonde hair. She looked the same as Hannah remembered, yet different, older. Her eyes were still that same brilliant blue, except now there were wrinkles around them. The shoulder-length hair was the same color as her own, only shorter than it used to be. The woman was dressed in a teal summer dress with tiny white flowers on it. She held a white clutch purse in her right hand and had on white, two-inch heels.

Hannah swallowed once. Twice. Out of the corner of her eye, she saw Anastasia.

"Miss Whitney, is it true? Is she who she says she is?" her housekeeper whispered.

Hannah nodded. "You can go now, Anastasia."

Anastasia disappeared.

"Hannah," the woman said.

"Mom?"

Hannah heard the word stick in her throat and come out hoarse. She was numb at first, then suddenly, a flood of emotions came at her. She was shocked, then torn between the desire to run and throw her arms around her mother, or to slap her. Instead, she kept standing about five feet away from the front door, her feet firmly planted in her home. *Her* home. This woman didn't belong here.

"Hannah," the woman said again. "Can I come in?"

Could she? Hannah had no idea. This wasn't Eva's home. Had never been Eva's home. Eva. When had she quit thinking of her as Mom and switched to Eva?

"Eva," Hannah said out loud. "Eva Whitney."

The woman nodded.

"Can I see some ID?"

It seemed fair. Hannah hadn't seen or heard from her mother in sixteen years. How was she supposed to know what she looked like?

The woman nodded and pulled her wallet out of her purse. She opened it and handed Hannah her driver's license. Hannah stepped close enough to take it from her and then retreated back to read it.

Eva Landings. Was she remarried? Or did she legally change it to hide? Either way, she had lost the Whitney last name. The birthdate matched. Hannah looked up.

"May I come in?"

Hannah nodded. "Come this way." She led her into the study. The morning light had moved out, leaving the room cooler but darker at this time of day. Hannah's stomach growled, and she realized she hadn't eaten lunch yet.

She motioned to one of the seats at the conference table. Eva sat. Hannah sat across from her.

"Does Dad know you're here?"

Eva shook her head. "No. I wanted to see you first."

"Why?"

Hannah wondered what the protocol was here. Should she offer her mom—this stranger—a beverage? Lunch? Should she show her out the door and tell her to never come back?

"Excuse me," Anastasia said. "I thought you might want some coffee."

Bless her. Anastasia brought in a tray with two cups of coffee, cream, and sugar. There were shortbread cookies as well.

"Thank you," Eva said. Anastasia nodded and left the room, closing the door silently behind her. Anastasia had only been with the Whitney's for a few years. Eva wouldn't know her.

"Nice," Eva said looking around. "I see you finally got the horse farm you always wanted."

Hannah couldn't wrap her head around any of this.

"What are you doing here?" she asked.

Eva tore open a packet of sugar and stirred it into her coffee. Her hands were shaking.

"I wanted to see you," Eva said.

"Why?"

Eva looked across the table.

"Because you're my daughter."

Hannah was suddenly angry. She stood. "Am I? Because mothers don't just walk off and leave their daughters!"

"Let me explain," Eva said.

"Explain? What on earth is there to explain?"

All the times that Hannah had dreamed of seeing her mother again, this wasn't how it had gone. Her mom had come back and they had flung themselves into each other's arms, crying, her mom apologizing and stroking Hannah's hair. There had been happy tears and a lot of embracing.

Instead, Hannah found herself wanting to throw this woman out. This woman with her neatly ironed clothes and bobbed hair wasn't the same, soft mother who Hannah remembered cuddling up to for story time. The clothes were cheap knockoffs, the shoes were not designer, and her face looked like it had seen too much sun. It was aged beyond her forty-eight years. This woman looked like she was trying too hard.

"Get out." Hannah said.

"It's not what you think," Eva said.

"What I think is that you abandoned us," Hannah said. "I got up that morning and sat on the couch an entire day, waiting for you to come and take me to school. An entire day! I sat on the couch where I could see out the front window, so I wouldn't miss you pulling into the driveway. I figured you had just gone somewhere in an emergency and forgotten to leave me a note."

"I left your father a note."

"When was dad ever home to read a note?" Hannah was shouting. She could hear herself, but she couldn't stop. "I never thought that you'd leave *me*, Mom! What did I do to deserve that? Was I not enough for you? Was I too much? I tried to be the best little girl I could be! What did I do wrong?"

Hannah was crying now. That's something else that Hannah Whitney never did—cry in front of people. Never show fear. Never, ever, let them see you cry. She suddenly hated herself.

"Get out!" she screamed, pointing her finger at the door of the study. "Get out now!"

Eva stood. "I didn't mean to leave you. It just happened. You just need to listen."

Hannah grabbed a box of tissue and threw it at her mom. She actually threw it. Suddenly, she didn't know who she was anymore, and it scared her.

"Get out!"

Eva stepped back, ducking from the tissue box, caught her heel on the carpet, and almost fell over backwards. She caught herself.

"I'm so sorry," she said. "I just came to apologize. I'm so, so sorry." Eva was crying now. She took the time to open her purse as she was leaving and pull out a business card.

"Here," she said, reaching toward Hannah.

"Get out," Hannah said. Her voice was quieter now, and she put an edge into her words. "*Now.*"

Eva laid the business card on the table, turned, and walked quickly out of the study. Hannah watched her go across the marble foyer and heard the front door close behind her.

She ran to the door and watched through a small side window as her mother climbed into an economy-sized sedan and drove away.

Then Hannah went back to the study, closed the door, and sat down at the conference table. She hung on to the sides of the table, willing her heart rate to slow back to normal. She took a few deep breaths, practicing what she had learned in competition, until the world quit tipping, and she felt somewhat normal again.

Then she picked up the business card and read it.

Eva Landings
Interior Designer

It had a phone number and address. Her mom was nearby. She was in Grand Rapids, just a stone's throw from St. Ives.

Hannah crumpled the card up and threw it on the ground.

"I hate her," she said. Then, knowing that wasn't true, she put her head in her hands, and cried.

Chapter Sixteen

"Hannah, you need to focus," Chase said.

They were together for their evening riding lesson. She was supposed to be working on her pirouettes, but she kept coming up short, and Grace was getting frustrated. He could see the horse's ears swiveling back and forth as she tried to discern her rider's cues.

"I'm sorry," she said.

Hannah hadn't been on her game today. First, this morning, she had seemed out of it. And now she was *really* not focused, and her eyes had a slightly puffy, red look, as if she had been crying. Unfocused and crying. He couldn't imagine Hannah Whitney doing either.

"Is there something wrong?"

Hannah shook her head. "I'll do better."

She tried to execute the pattern, then messed up halfway through the pirouette. Again.

"Bring Grace into the middle."

"I'm fine. Let me try again."

"Hannah. Bring your horse here." He made his voice gentle but firm, like he would do with Manny when he wanted the horse to know that he wasn't going to punish him, but that it was in his best interest to listen.

Surprisingly, Hannah rode into the middle of the ring and stopped in front of Chase.

"I'm sorry."

He wondered what was up. Was it because of their luncheon yesterday? She had been acting weird since then.

"About lunch yesterday," Chase said. "I'm sorry I brought God up. Actually, I didn't bring God up. You did. But anyway, I'm sorry. I wanted—"

"What? No. That's not it. It's..." Hannah shook her head. "I'm fine."

"You're not fine at all."

"I am. How do you know? You don't know me."

"I don't, but I know what it's like to lose focus. Or have you forgotten the pattern?"

They looked at each other for a beat.

"You're upsetting your horse," Chase said.

Hannah put a hand on Grace's neck and petted her. The mare bent her neck around so she could nuzzle Hannah's boot.

"Why don't you go on the rail and let her do a relaxed walk. Give her her head."

Hannah nodded and returned to the rail in a counter-clockwise direction. She rocked slightly in the saddle, using her weight to elongate Grace's stride into an extended walk. She loosened her reins, and the mare dropped her head, stretching her neck out and relaxing her muscles.

"Take a few deep breaths," Chase said.

He watched as Hannah inhaled and exhaled a few times. She was going through the motions, but her shoulders were still up near her ears. There was tension radiating through her whole body.

"Was it Devon?" Chase asked.

"Devon?" Hannah said. "No...I told you, it's nothing. Geez. Can't I have one off day?"

"You told me you don't have off days."

He watched the two of them walk some more. He decided to go take a seat in the judge's booth. They walked for about five minutes before she spoke again.

"Is this all we're going to do? How is this going to get me into the Olympics?"

"You're not going anywhere if you don't learn to focus. Whatever happens outside of the ring, you have to leave it outside of the ring. When you're in the ring, nothing else exists except for you and the horse. Nothing."

"How do you know? You're obviously not good at focus."

Chase smiled. "You're right. I'm not. I blew an entire career because I couldn't focus. Do you have any idea how much I regret that?"

"Do you have any idea how much I don't care?"

Chase took in a slow, deep breath, pushing down his rising frustration. He couldn't figure her out. Yesterday, he had seen a different side to her, but now she was all defensive and mean again.

"I don't care that you don't care," he said, realizing how immature that sounded. "I'm just here to train you and your horse. Are you going to let me do that?"

His sister said he had a stubborn side and needed to think before he spoke. He didn't think that rule applied with Hannah.

Hannah jerked her head in his direction. "You don't care? Fine. Then you're fired."

"You can't fire me."

"Just watch me."

She was angry about something and looking to pick a fight. He wasn't helping by letting her bait him.

Please, God, he prayed. *Help me be nice.*

"Let's have Grace do a counter-canter so she can end on a good note, and we'll call it a day."

"We can't call it a day. I have trials in less than ten weeks!"

Hannah picked up her reins. "Turn on the music. I want to do the routine."

Chase looked at the horse. Grace seemed relaxed, despite her owner's tension. She seemed ready. He leaned over and turned on the boombox. He was still using it, despite Hannah's urging for him to put the music over their electronic system. He knew he was doing it out of stubbornness, just to annoy her. But he needed to feel that he was in control of *something.*

As the first chords echoed across the ring, Hannah turned her horse into the middle and got ready to begin.

They rode, and they rode hard. He stopped her a few times to correct something, and she did as he said. She suddenly seemed to be trying harder than she ever had. An hour went by. Then two. Grace had a white lather on her. Loose strands from Hannah's ponytail were plastered against her neck when they finished the routine for yet another time.

"That's good," Chase said. "Enough for the day. Cool your horse off."

Hannah patted Grace on the neck and nodded. "Good girl," she said. Her voice was softer, and her shoulders had relaxed a little bit. But he could still see in her eyes that she was troubled.

"If you want to talk about it—" he started.

"I don't."

"Was it something I said or did?" He tried to soften his tone. "If so, I'm sorry. You have enough stress without me causing more." He expected an angry retort. But instead, she looked at him, and for a moment, he saw the woman he had seen at lunch yesterday. The softer Hannah.

"No," she said. She seemed like she wanted to say more. "There's just...something...that came up. I'm just having a bad day."

"Hannah, I'm your trainer. I need to know, or I can't help you."

She shook her head. "I'm fine," she said. She was lying. "I'm sorry I was such a jerk today. This is why I'm alone." She gave a half-hearted laugh. Hannah Whitey playing the victim? A lot of firsts today.

He wanted to ask *who* had hurt her. There were so many people to choose from. But she was gone, back inside the barn to untack Grace and to walk her until she was cool. Devon wasn't around, which Chase figured was probably a good thing for Devon. Hannah seemed like she was in a mood to kill.

He decided to leave her alone and go back to the guesthouse. He had work to do anyway and wanted to get a head start on plans for their lesson tomorrow morning.

147

Chase did about an hour's more work, then went into town and did some grocery shopping. He loved St. Ives. The streets were quaint, busy with tourists wearing souvenir St. Ives t-shirts and hats. Most were dressed casually in flip-flops, sandals, and tank tops, their shoulders reddened from too much time on the beach. Some of them carried ice cream cones or bags of salt-water taffy. It was a typical beach-side tourist town, reminiscent of some of the ones he had seen on Illinois' coast near his home.

He stopped in a little shop called Camilla's Soaps and Candles and bought a lavender-scented candle for his sister. The label said that the lavender oil was from fields right here in St. Ives, at Hopeful Farm. He remembered Hannah saying how much she loved the smell. In the center of town, near the gazebo, was a farmer's market, and he purchased sweet corn, tomatoes, and cucumbers.

When he got home, he made himself an Italian salad, cutting up the garden cucumbers and tomatoes, adding onion, and mixing it in canola oil, vinegar, salt, and pepper. He put it in the fridge to chill while he shucked the corn and fired up the electric grill on the back porch for the steak he had bought. He loved this town and this house. He could live here forever.

After dinner, he was sitting on the front porch swing, thinking about his horse and missing him, when Marcus drove up in his sporty blue Corvette. He got out. He was dressed down, wearing khakis and a polo instead of his usual business suit.

He walked up to the porch and sat down on the plastic chair across from the swing where Chase was sitting.

"Hey, son," he said.

"Hey," Chase said.

"Hannah seemed upset during dinner tonight. She was toying with her food and very quiet. That's not like her. She almost always has something to say. She insisted she was fine, but she's not. I wondered if you knew what the problem was."

Chase shook his head. "She was having trouble focusing today at the lesson as well."

"That's not like her."

"I didn't think so."

The two men sat in silence. Chase thought of Devon and his predatory attitude. He wondered if he should say anything. Maybe he should also tell Marcus about their discussion at lunch yesterday and how Hannah had become angry when he mentioned God. But he didn't feel right discussing what she had shared with him in confidence with her father.

He decided to go with Devon.

"How long has Devon worked here?" he asked.

Marcus thought for a moment. "Two years. I hired him when the last trainer moved on. Hannah has always had her own trainer, and then we keep a second trainer around for the jumpers and a few dressage folks."

"Where did you find him?"

"He came highly recommended. He's a young guy, but he's done quite a bit of work in the sport, and he's also pretty high up in the social circles. It's good to know someone like that." Marcus glanced at Chase and smiled. "Politics. You know."

Chase knew all too well the politics in the higher paying sports world.

"So you like him?"

Marcus turned to Chase again. This time he looked concerned.

"Shouldn't I? Has he been mistreating the horses?"

"No, nothing like that," Chase said. "I was just asking."

"He seems okay. He's arrogant, but a lot of our athletes are. They're spoiled. Raised with inherited money. Devon is one of the few who has worked his way to the top. He doesn't come from money. I think Hannah had a little crush on him at first, but that seems to have gone by the wayside, thank goodness." Marcus's phone beeped. He took it out, glanced at it, put it back in his pocket. "Is he bothering you?"

Chase wasn't sure how to answer that. If he said yes, he'd sound petty. If he said no, it was a flat out lie.

"He's okay," Chase said. Now, mentioning Devon's predatory demeanor suddenly didn't feel right. Maybe Chase was just being too sensitive. Hannah seemed to be handling Devon just fine. So what if Devon disliked Chase? Wasn't he used to people ridiculing him?

"How is Hannah treating you?"

It was the second time in two days Marcus had asked.

"You seem awfully concerned about that," Chase said. He met the other man's eyes. "Is there something I need to know?"

"Nothing you probably haven't already found out," Marcus said. "I hate to speak ill of my own daughter, but she can be a handful. She knows what she wants, how she wants it, and she intends to do it her way or else."

"Even though I'm the trainer."

"Yes."

"I've noticed a little bit of that," Chase said. He couldn't help the smile that came to his lips. Marcus laughed heartily.

"I like you, Chase. You're a good, honest man. Just keep your head up. This is a tough business. Let Devon do his thing. You focus on Hannah, and all will be well. I have a good feeling about you."

Marcus stood, brushed his khakis off, and pulled the keys out of his pocket. "I'm sorry to have bothered you. If you find out what's up with Hannah, let me know."

"Sir, that kind of feels like spying on her," Chase said.

Marcus looked at him thoughtfully. "It does. Well, if there's anything drastic, then let me know. Otherwise, I'll trust you with my daughter." He paused, jangling his keys. "She's all I have, you know. I love her dearly."

"I know," Chase said. "I'll let you know if I find out anything concerning. She told me she was allowed to have a bad day. I think she's right."

Marcus nodded. "I tend to make mountains out of mole hills when it comes to Hannah," he said. "I can run multi-million dollar companies and make decisions that affect the lives of thousands of my employees every day, but when it comes to my daughter..." he shook his head. "I just want her to be happy."

Chase watched him as he went down the steps to his car. Marcus got in, turned around, and headed back to the house. As the headlights disappeared beyond the trees, Chase wondered, once again, what he had gotten himself into. Hannah Whitney very well might be the way for him to get back into the sport. Or she might be the end of him.

Chapter Seventeen

Hannah's dad walked in the house around 9 p.m. Hannah watched as he came into the study where she was reading, put his keys in the bowl on his desk, and loosened his belt. He sat down in his swivel chair behind the big cherry desk and sighed.

"You doing better?" he asked.

Hannah was antsy and upset. She glared at him, even though she knew it wasn't his fault. Or was it? Was he the reason her mom had left them?

"Were you with Marion?"

"Marion? No, I went to check in with Chase."

"Were you talking about me?"

Marcus watched his daughter for a moment. He was always slow to respond. As long as she could remember, he would weigh his words before he spoke. He did that more now, seemed more thoughtful, since he had found Jesus.

"Yes," he said. "I asked how you were doing."

"What did he say?"

She pretended like she didn't care, but the truth was, she did. She cared a lot about what Chase Livingston thought of her.

Pussy Willow wandered into the room and rubbed up against her leg. She bent down, picked her cat up, and put him in her lap.

"He said you're doing fine," Marcus said.

She scratched Pussy Willow behind the ears. "Good Puss," she said. He purred in response.

"Are you?" her dad asked.

She looked up at her dad. "Yes! Why wouldn't I be?"

"You seemed preoccupied at dinner tonight. Even a little stressed."

"I'm always stressed," Hannah said.

"I know."

"When are you seeing Marion again?"

Marcus swiveled around in his chair, so he was looking out the big glass windows at the dark sky. The only light in the room was the desk lamp Hannah was using to read with, so the stars were visible. "Tomorrow for lunch. We're trying to have lunch every day. I'd really like to invite her over for dinner more often."

"Go ahead. It's your house too. I can eat alone in the kitchen," Hannah said.

"Why do you dislike her so much?" Marcus said, turning his chair around to look at her again. His voice had gone tense. He seemed a little frustrated.

Good, Hannah thought.

"She's not my mom," Hannah said.

"She's not trying to be," Marcus said. "She just wants to be your friend. Geez, Hannah, we have this conversation almost every day."

"I don't want her in your life."

"Don't you think it's time I get to have some fun? I raised you alone. I've worked my fingers to the bone for decades to give us all of this." He made a sweeping gesture with his arms. "Now, I just want someone to hang out with, maybe go to a movie with, have lunch with, laugh with. Marion is kind, and she and I share a lot of the same interests. I really like her."

Her dad had met Marion a year and a half ago at a pharmaceutical convention. He was speaking about his latest drug, and she was the public relations person assigned to run the convention. She lived only about thirty minutes from St. Ives, and he had asked her out the following weekend. She had never married and had no children of her own. She said it was because she got too consumed with her job and never took the time, a move which now she apparently regretted.

"I guess," Hannah said.

"Maybe you should try dating." Her dad never asked about her love life, for which she was grateful. She didn't have one. Oh, she had plenty of *opportunities*. Men were always asking her out. She was pretty, she had money, and she oozed confidence. But they always seemed boring, or petty, or just wanted to get her in the sack. So she hadn't dated in a while. Not since Devon.

She thought briefly of Chase, and how he talked so fondly of his horse. And how he didn't use the crude jokes and teasing voice that the other men she had dated used. He held himself with a quiet confidence despite what he had been through. Or maybe *because* of it. Chase knew who he was, and he didn't seem to care of she liked him or not. It was a little intoxicating. Most men fawned over her and did anything to please her, so desperate were they to be with her.

And her money.

She sighed a little too loudly.

"Well, I don't like her." Why was she picking on Marion? The truth was, Marion had always been sweet and nice to her. She didn't deserve the way Hannah treated her. Every time she invited Hannah out with them, Hannah refused, unless it was a holiday. A few times she had let Marion join them for dinner here at the house. Twice, maybe.

But why was she so angry with Marion *tonight* in particular?

She thought about Eva's visit, and knew that that was the reason. Here was Marion, bending over backwards to show Hannah some love, when her own mother had never tried that. Until now.

She looked at her dad again, sitting in his big desk chair. He looked tired. He did deserve some happiness. She decided not to tell him about Eva, since she had sent her away.

She didn't want to see her mother again. Bringing her into their life would only confuse things. She had the trials to think about. She had a new trainer. A new routine to learn. She didn't need Eva to come in and mess things up.

"Yes," she said. "You do deserve to be happy."

For the third time in two days, Hannah thought she might cry. She bit her lip. What was *wrong* with her? She kept seeing her mom opening the sugar packet with trembling hands, her new clothes bought off the discount rack. Her inexpensive car parked out front. Her mom had given up all of this for what? A life without money? Without power? Without *them?* Was it worth it? She wanted to shout, to say, "Look what you missed out on, Mom! Look what we have and you don't!"

"Hannah?"

Her dad's voice broke through her thoughts.

"Hmm?"

"You know I love you, right? I'm sorry for the way things used to be. I'm trying to make up for that."

And here was the one person who truly loved her. She knew that now. "I know, Dad. You've told me. I know you love me." Hannah swiveled in her chair, disturbing Puss. She met her dad's eyes. "I love you too."

Marcus smiled the smile that lit up his face.

"I need to get some rest," Hannah said. "I have an early day tomorrow." She rose, setting Pussy Willow gently on the floor. She went over and kissed her dad on the cheek. "Good night, Daddy. I love you."

Marcus, in an unfamiliar gesture, stood and wrapped his arms around her. She could smell his aftershave, faded at the end of the day. He held her there for a moment, awkwardly, then he let her go.

She stood still, uncertain how to respond. Then she put her hand on his shoulder and gave it a squeeze.

She turned and went upstairs to bed.

Hannah couldn't sleep. She kept tossing and turning, thinking about her mom. The business card remained crumpled, now laying on her nightstand. She opened the drawer and stuffed it in, shutting the drawer firmly, as if that would erase the reminder of her mom's visit.

Finally, somewhere around 2 a.m., she fell asleep. When her alarm went off at six, she was exhausted. She sat up and looked across the room at the words opposite her bed. She had stenciled them on when she was sixteen and knew she wanted to be an Olympic champion.

Don't wish for success.
Make it happen.

So that's what she would do. Sleep was for the weak. She got up, drank some water, brushed her teeth, and dressed for running.

By the time she got to the riding ring with Grace, she was more awake.

Chase was there with his yellow notebook and that stupid boombox.

"I made a few tweaks yesterday," he said, with no formal good morning or hello. He was all business. For some reason, that annoyed her.

She watched silently as he sketched a few things out for her.

"Okay," she said. "I think I've got it."

He asked her to warm up. She felt the comforting muscles of her horse move under her. This was where she knew she was in charge. Here, on top of Grace, controlling a twelve-hundred-pound animal with a light touch, was where she was meant to be. And Grace loved her. Unconditionally.

How many times had she run to Grace's stall and hugged her when she was hurting? She told Grace all her secrets. She often spent lunchtime with her, down by the pond under the willow tree. She spent more time with her horse than with people.

They worked together for an hour, and Hannah felt her muscles growing fatigued. She'd have to nap this afternoon.

No, sleep was for losers.

A vision of her mom floated in front of her eyes. She closed them briefly.

What was her mom doing coming back into her life *now*, after all these years? Was she after Hannah's money? What else could it be? There was certainly no other reason. She didn't love Hannah. She had proven that the day she walked out the door.

Suddenly, Chase turned the music off. "Hannah, ride into the center of the ring, please," he said.

Hannah slowed Grace from the trot they were in and turned her. She rode up to where Chase was standing and stopped.

"Where is your head?"

"I'm doing what I'm supposed to do," Hannah said. "I don't know what you mean."

"Yes, you're going through the motions of what you're supposed to do, but your head isn't in it. You're riding from muscle memory."

"How can I do that when I'm riding a pattern?"

"I don't know, but you're doing it. Your presence looks weak; your display is half-hearted. You are running out of time. You need to focus."

His words were soft. Hans would have been shouting at her by now. He probably would have been waving his riding crop around in the air.

"So?"

"*So?*" Chase echoed. He let out a breath of air. "So? Do you want to make the team or not?"

Hannah thought of all the crap she had put up with from Devon. And Hans. And everybody, just so she would be on the Olympic team. It was her goal. Her *only* goal. Nothing else mattered. Nothing.

"Of course I do!" she said. Her anger flared. "Why on earth wouldn't I?"

"Then you need to focus!" Chase said. "By now, most of the riders already have their pattern and have been practicing for months. Not you. If you don't focus, you'll never get this."

"What do *you* know about focus?" Hannah said. Did he have any idea what she was going through? How was she supposed to focus *now?* She felt a new surge of anger toward Eva, almost hating her. She had waited so long for her to return, and Eva picked *now?* Hannah felt the heat rising in her face. She took a deep breath to calm herself.

"I know *a lot* about focus," Chase said. His voice was even. "I told you. Losing it cost me everything."

"You never told me why," Hannah said. "You never told me why you lost focus that first time."

She met his eyes, challenging him. She could see him fighting back the anger, but she was in the mood for a brawl. "If you want me to trust you, then I need to *know* you."

There was a moment of silence as Chase considered. Grace snorted and pawed the ground, eager to continue. Hannah put a soothing hand on her neck.

"Okay," Chase said. "But this goes no further than here. Understand?"

He waited until she nodded. He sighed again. There was a lot of deep breathing going on. He walked over to the side of the horse and gazed up at Hannah.

"I was having an affair with Marina Zlovsky," he said quietly.

Hannah felt her eyes go wide. "Marina Zlovsky?"

"Yes. The three-day event gold medalist. She hated her husband, who happened to be the owner of her horse. They had met and married young. He kept her supplied with horses, but not with love. We were teammates the first time I went to the Olympics, and teammates again the second time. We started seeing each other about a year before my last Olympics. We kept it quiet because she was married. So we stole away to be alone together when we could.

"I loved her. Deeply. I had a ring and had planned on asking her to leave her husband and to marry me. I didn't feel bad about it because he was mean to her. But first, I was going to buy her horse from him. Before he found out about the affair. I had it all planned out in my head."

Hannah realized she was staring at him. She had never dreamed . . .

"I know. It was horrible," he said. "*I* was horrible. But there it was. I really loved her."

"So you were distressed over a woman," Hannah said. "You were nervous about asking her to marry you. About destroying her marriage to be with you?"

The anger that had been inside her for the past twenty-four hours surged up in her head. She felt the heat flush her cheeks and swell her chest, felt her heart pounding. Marina had a young kid at the time, she remembered. Would she have left her behind to be with Chase? Would he have asked that?

"You were terrible," Hannah said.

Chase nodded.

"Well, then," Hannah pulled Grace aside. "I don't want to hear any more," she said.

"But there's more to the story," Chase said. "I don't want to leave it with you thinking I'm this marriage wrecker who—"

"I said *enough*," Hannah said. "I want to get back to work. No. Never mind." She quickly dismounted. "I'm finished today." She handed Grace's reins to Chase. "You can cool her off."

"Hey," Chase said. "We're not finished! Look, I'm sorry. I'm not a jerk *now*. Not like I used to be. Let me finish the story so we can talk about focus."

"I don't even think you know what you're doing," Hannah said.

Chase raised an eyebrow. "You don't think I know what I'm doing?"

"No. How can I learn from you? Especially about focus?"

"Hannah, I screwed up a lot, and I've paid the price. Let me teach you what I've learned."

Hannah spun on him. "What you've learned? It seems to me as if you've gone backwards. You were an Olympic winner! And now you're..." She stopped.

"I'm what?" Chase said. His voice was quiet, even.

She had gone too far. "Never mind. Let's get back to work." She suddenly felt fear in her stomach. A fear that he, too, would quit. She grabbed her stirrup and tried to mount, but Grace was too tall. "Here. Give me a leg up." She wanted to take it all back. All of it. She wanted to rewind everything and go back to yesterday's lunch when life wasn't so complicated.

"No. Finish your sentence. I'm what?"

Hannah looked at him. "You're..."

"Go ahead and say it, everybody else does."

She was quiet.

"You think I have a big 'L' on my forehead." He said it as a statement, not a question.

"Well," she said. There was no turning back now. Her temper rose again. She could feel it, feel him getting ready to leave her. "Let's face it. You *quit.* You were out there winning, and then one day, you just quit. You gave up. Losers quit when they fail. Winners fail until they succeed. I don't want to be a loser."

They stared at each other, and she saw hurt in his eyes, quickly replaced by anger. He tossed Grace's reins at her, slammed his notebook closed, and walked out of the arena. She stood in the silence he left behind and felt empty.

Chapter Eighteen

Chase was so mad he wanted to shout, to pound something. His heart hammered in his chest as he stomped back to the guesthouse, went inside, and slammed the door. He reached for his suitcase and threw it on the bed, stuffing his clothes into it. His sister was right. This was too much. Hannah was a spoiled brat—a *mean* spoiled brat—and no amount of money was worth this trouble. He slammed the suitcase closed and opened the other one.

As he tossed in his shoes, the two ties he had brought, and his swim trunks, he thought about his sister back home, working at the diner, coming home to Tyler at night.

Well, he could get *another* job to help her pay off her debts. He might be able to teach piano. Or maybe he'd start his own business online. He'd work in a factory if he had to.

Anything to get away from Hannah Whitney, Devon, and this insane cast of spoiled characters.

Then he thought of Marcus Whitney, and his kind face and worried eyes.

"My daughter is lost," he had said that first day.

Chase sat on his bed and put his head in his hands. If he left now, he'd never have another chance again to get back into the world he loved. He loved horses like he loved breathing. Their absence had left a huge hole in his heart that nothing else on this earth could fill. Nothing.

He thought again of Manny. There would never be another horse like Manny. But there *were* other horses. And he could train them, train others, maybe even show again someday if he could just get Hannah to the Olympics.

And he had to face it. The money here was good. For what Marcus Whitney was paying him for these ten weeks, he'd have to work over a year at most other jobs.

He sighed heavily and kept his head in his hands. *What do you want from me, God?*

Chase always spoke to God like he was another person in the room. He believed that that was what God wanted from us all, a personal relationship. Chase often told, asked, questioned, and sometimes just chatted with God about a lot of things. He didn't have the emotional makeup to sit quietly in a meditative state and pray, so he had taken up the habit of conversation with God.

It didn't matter if he voiced his fears or confusion, because God already knew what he was thinking. There was no sense in hiding any of it.

She's driving me nuts, Chase prayed. *I'm not even sure I like her. And I definitely don't like Devon. Marcus is okay. But God, did I understand You wrong? Should I really be here? What am I doing?*

The room remained quiet. Chase could faintly hear the birds chirping outside the window.

I need a sign, he said.

He had only been here a few days, and he and Hannah had fought several times, he and Devon had an instant shared dislike of each other, and he had been ridiculed at a party. Also, he could see the looks on the stable hands' faces in Hannah's own barn, even though none of them said anything to him personally.

What good was he to Hannah anyway? He wasn't even sure he could *get* her to the Olympics. What if his very presence alone was hurting her chances? Nobody wanted to be seen with the has-been wonder kid zealot.

God, give me a sign, he prayed.

The room remained silent. After a few minutes, he lifted his head and looked at his suitcase. Did he really want to leave after less than a week? What if Hannah was right? What if he really *was* a quitter?

He stood and went to the window that overlooked his little backyard. A squirrel was eating berries off a tree, balancing precariously on an extended branch. The squirrels trusted that they wouldn't fall. After all, climbing is what they were created for. Did a squirrel ever think twice about climbing a tree?

Riding was what Chase was made for. He knew that in his bones. Riding and training.

"But there are other ways to be around horses," he said quietly, to no one.

The squirrel dropped a berry from the twenty-foot tree and looked down at it, then quickly moved on to the next berry, giving that one up for lost.

Maybe Chase needed to move on. Maybe horses were a thing of his past.

He felt confused. He looked at his suitcase again. A new surge of anger went through him.

No. He wasn't going to let anyone else take advantage of him. He had had enough of ridicule, bullying, and bad media coverage. He had gone into hiding for a reason. He never should have said yes to Marcus Whitney when he'd called. He'd go back to his previous job as an insurance agent, if he could get it back, and he'd work hard like most Americans did to get his paycheck. He wasn't going to let some hot-headed, arrogant woman destroy his life. He had already done that once. Never again.

He threw his toothbrush and toothpaste into his suitcase, carefully packed his laptop and iPad, and closed the lid.

He'd leave first thing in the morning. No, he'd leave *now*.

He grabbed both suitcases, one in each hand, and headed toward the front door. Just then, the doorbell rang. He stopped in his tracks, setting the suitcases down.

He could see a silhouette in the bubbled glass that ran alongside the door frame. It looked like Hannah. After a moment, the doorbell rang again.

He huffed and walked over, throwing the door open. "What do you want?" he said, hearing the anger in his voice.

"Can I come in?" She was still in her riding clothes, dirt staining her shirt. She looked disheveled, her hair coming out of its ponytail. Her eyes were red.

Chase hesitated, then stood aside so she could come in. He shut the door behind her. He saw her eyes roam past him to the two suitcases.

"Are you leaving me?" she said.

The way she phrased it stopped the sharp retort he had ready. She hadn't said "are you leaving?" She'd said "are *you* leaving *me?*" There was something in her tone. Fear?

"Yes," he said. "Hannah, you and your horse are both talented, but I don't need this. You argue, and you do everything your way, as if my training techniques are just a suggestion. Devon is a jerk, and the few friends of yours I have met, hate me. You yourself are embarrassed by me. I figure it's best for us if I just leave."

Her eyes were wide. "You can't," she said. For the first time in the short week he had known her, he saw Hannah Whitney look frightened.

"I *can*," he said. To emphasize his point, he moved the suitcases closer to the door, setting them down with a thump. "I need for you to leave now. I'll call your dad and tell him he only owes me for the week."

Chase opened the door and motioned for Hannah to leave.

"I came to apologize," she said. She blurted the words out quickly, as if she wanted to say them before he walked out. "I know I'm not easy to work with. And I'm sorry for what I said. I didn't mean those things. Really, I didn't."

"Hannah," Chase said. He sighed and ran his hand through his hair. "I know you have issues. I've seen quite a few of them surface in the short time I was here. And I can't imagine what it must be like to have your mom walk out on you. But you're too driven. It's hurting you, and you're taking it out on others. Whatever you're running from—or *to*—I'm not going there with you."

"I'm sorry," she said, coming closer to him. "*Please*, let's talk. I'll tell you what was bothering me today." Suddenly, her eyes filled with tears. He saw her swallow, pushing the emotion back, but it was too strong for her. She turned toward the kitchen, away from him, so he couldn't see her face. "I know I'm hard to work with. I don't know why. I don't know what's wrong with me. I feel...lost."

This is why you're here. The voice was in his head. A simple peace came over him then, the anger left, and he was suddenly filled with compassion. He quietly shut the door.

"Let's go sit down," he said, and led her into the little living room. He took a seat on the couch and motioned for her to sit in the wingback chair opposite him. He handed her a box of tissues.

"My mom came to see me yesterday," she said.

"Your mom?" Chase said.

"Yes. I haven't seen her since I was eight. And she just showed up at my front door. No warning. Nothing."

Hannah took a tissue and wiped her eyes.

"What did your dad say?"

"I didn't tell him."

She hadn't told him? "Why not?"

She shrugged. "I want to pretend it didn't happen." She said it quietly. She suddenly seemed so young, so vulnerable. All her anger was gone, and in its place was a scared little girl.

"But I thought you'd want to see your mom," Chase said, imagining if his own mom had shown up at his door.

"I thought so too. I always imagined that moment. My dream come true. What I had always wanted. But you know, she *did* leave me. And mostly all I felt was anger. And sadness."

Chase was quiet, letting her talk.

"I don't trust people," Hannah said. "I learned not to. You see what it's like in this world. It's competitive, everyone goes for the jugular." She gave a little laugh and blew her nose.

She met his eyes. "I need you to help me, Chase. Please. I'm so sorry. I don't think you're a loser. Actually, I think you might be the most real, genuine person I've ever met. You're kind to me, and I believe you actually care if I win or lose."

Chase nodded. "I do. I'm not just in this for the money."

"I know that. I do. I will try harder. I'll do better. I'll quit arguing. If you want me to start at 8 a.m., I'll find another time to run."

He watched her for a moment, considering.

"Oh, Hannah," he said, finally. He learned back against the couch. "You need to tell your dad about your mom visiting."

"I know."

"And you'll listen to me and let me do my job, which is to train you? You won't argue?"

"I'll try not to." She smiled a little bit, through her tears.

"Okay then," he said. "I'll stick around a little while longer. We'll try this again."

She lifted her chin and squared her shoulders. "Okay, then! Thank you!" she stood, and he stood as well. She walked over to him and embraced him in a hug. He was startled at first, but she held him for a moment, then pushed back. She was smiling. "You're the best," she said. Her eyes had their sparkle back in them. He could swear she was blushing.

He smiled and led her to the door, let her out, and watched her drive away. The scent of her shampoo lingered, mixed with leather and a slight tinge of sweat. He remembered how her body had felt next to his. Yes, he was her trainer, and she was his student. But they were also only a few years apart in age. He was a man. And she was quite a woman.

He closed the door and went back inside the house to clear his head and unpack his suitcase. He pushed his interest in Hannah back down, and instead, focused on what he would need to do tomorrow in order to move her lessons forward. They had lost a lot of time today, and time was running out. The trials would be here before they knew it.

Chapter Nineteen

Hannah drove back to her house and sat in her Mustang for a moment. She hadn't meant to hug him, but she had been so grateful. His body against hers had felt wonderful, and her stomach had started to tingle as the hug had turned into something...more. She hadn't wanted to let go. His scent, something masculine and organic, still clung to her hair, and she remembered the feel of his muscular back against her hands.

She shook her head to clear it. This was her *trainer.* He was here to work. She had no right to expect anything else, and emotions would only ruin her chances of winning.

Focus. It was all about focus.

She went in the front door of her house and heard her dad coming down the stairs.

Tell your dad about your mom's visit. It was Chase's voice in her head. She would. She had told him she would. Just not tonight.

Her dad stopped in the foyer, looking at her, a folded newspaper in his hands. "Have you been crying?"

She brushed her eyes with the back of her hand.

"No. I mean yes. But I'm okay."

Marcus stood there for a moment, considering. "Is this about Chase? Did he upset you?"

Hannah shook her head. "No, Daddy. Everything is fine. I got upset and said some things to him. I... yelled at him."

She saw the look of disappointment in her dad's eyes. "No, it's okay," she said quickly. "I went to apologize. I promised to work hard and not to cause any more trouble."

"Hannah, he's all you have left," her dad said. "You realize that, don't you?"

She did. She had called trainers herself. Chase was it.

"I do," she said. "He's just so infuriating, sometimes. And I'm not a very patient person."

Her dad raised both his eyebrows at this. "No, you are not," he agreed. He came forward and wrapped her in a hug. This time, she let herself melt into it. It felt good to be held by this man who loved her so much. She should tell him. She should tell him right now about Eva.

"If you're okay, I have a phone call to make," Marcus said, pulling away. He squinted at her over the top of his reading glasses.

"I'm okay," she said. The conversation about Eva could wait. He sounded busy. If she told him, there would be a long discussion and questions she couldn't answer. Also, a part of her wanted to keep her dad to herself. She didn't want to share him with Eva, and she knew that her mom's return, for whatever reason and for however long, would take up a huge chunk of emotional space. This past year, she had felt like she was finally getting her dad in her life. She didn't really want to bring Eva into the picture now.

He walked into the study, then stopped and turned. "I'll be late for dinner tonight," he said.

Hannah looked at the grandfather clock against the wall. It was already 7 p.m. "I'm really tired. Is it okay if I just grab something quick and then go to bed? I'd like to be in bed by nine. Chase is working me to death." She laughed to lighten the mood.

"Sure, honey," he said. He glanced at his watch. "I'm going to go make this call. Good night. I love you."

"I love you too, Dad," Hannah said. She watched him go into the study and close the French doors. Then she turned and walked slowly upstairs. She was exhausted.

Over the next two weeks, Hannah worked hard at memorizing their pattern. She didn't yell at Chase (much), and she tried to listen to his advice. In return, or maybe just because he got tired of carrying the boombox, he started playing her song over the speaker system.

She and Chase agreed not to ask each other personal questions, but to focus on work. Devon was away at a horse show with some of his students, so neither she nor Chase had to deal with him. The barn was quieter with his six students gone, and Hannah used the time to really focus. By the end of the week, now fourteen days in with Chase, she was feeling good about life.

"Has your mom tried to contact you again?" Chase asked one day, as Hannah was warming up Grace.

"We agreed not to talk about personal things," Hannah said lightly. It was easier that way.

"I know. Just wondering."

"No, she hasn't."

"Have you told your dad yet?"

"No, I'm just waiting for the right time." Which was true. Or maybe the right time would be never.

They ate at Louie's a few times, and he told her a little bit about his sister, but mostly they talked about horses. Their agreement to stay away from personal conversation seemed to be greatly helping their relationship.

But every time she was near him, her heart wanted more. More time with him. More conversation. She wanted to learn more about what made this handsome man tick.

Focus, Hannah, she kept telling herself. But the truth was, she was all too aware of how she felt. Now she had to make the Olympics for sure. Because if she didn't, she'd have no reason to keep him on as a trainer. And then he'd leave her, like the others had.

Their evening riding session came to an end. They had been through the entire routine twice. Hannah had it memorized, and she and Grace had performed without error. They just had to work on fine-tuning their elements.

She was thrilled. She brought Grace into the center of the ring.

"That was incredible!" Chase said. They fist-bumped. "I'm so excited! Wow!"

Hannah laughed. "Me too." She pulled her thin, leather riding gloves off. "Whew. I'm really beat today."

"It's the heat," Chase said. He took his Cubs cap off, rubbing the sweat from his forehead. "And that maniac run this morning."

Hannah laughed. "You just can't keep up," she said, teasing him.

"Who can? I doubt *Grace* could've kept up with you today." He had been running with her a few days a week. They went early, 8 a.m., before her morning lesson. It made her happy that he was making concessions for her. She was trying very hard to behave herself.

"It was the dunes," she said. "That's why I usually run around here. The dunes are a killer."

"I thought I was going to die," Chase said. "And there you were, booking up the dune like a gazelle. It made me feel less manly."

"Less manly?"

"Yeah. Like that awkward moment when you're wearing Nikes, and you can't do it."

Hannah laughed out loud.

"Sounds like your lesson is going well." The voice came from behind them. They both turned, startled, to see Devon. He was back.

"Yeah," Hannah said, wiping a tear away from her eye from the laughter. "Chase just told me a joke. That's all." She stifled another giggle. So now she was *giggling?* She was so happy right now that even the sight of Devon wasn't bothering her. "My routine is going really well. I'm excited about it!"

"I see," Devon said. He watched them for a moment.

"How did the horse show go?" Hannah asked.

"We placed in the top three in all of our classes," he said. "Tiffany did excellent. All that hard work paid off. Looks like she might be a Nationals winner for sure."

"I'm happy for her!" Hannah said, and meant it.

Chase put his hand on Grace's neck and rubbed the horse affectionately. "You ready to call it a day?" he asked Hannah quietly.

"Yes," she said. She handed him her gloves and crop and dismounted.

"Are we running again tomorrow?" she asked Chase. She hoped he'd say yes. She'd have to go easier on him if he agreed.

"If you promise not to kill me."

"I promise. Let's just stay around here. No dunes. Just paved roads."

"Sounds good."

"Thank you," she said, trying to hide the smile that crossed her face.

"For what? For letting you humiliate me another day?"

"For the routine. It...I just feel really good about it." Before she realized what she was doing, she gave Chase a brief hug. Then she laughed and took her gloves and crop from him. She felt lighter than air. "See you in the morning then."

Chase nodded. She turned Grace and walked out of the arena. Devon followed her.

"So you're happy with him?" Devon said when they were out of Chase's earshot.

"Yes. He's working out. Wait until you see my routine." She tied her horse up at the wash stall and took her saddle off. She handed it to Devon.

"Don't let him mess with your head," Devon said.

"Chase? He's not. We're just working."

"He looks like he wants more than work."

Does he? Hannah wondered. Chase had been friendly toward her but had never once suggested there was anything more between them. As much as she would like for there to be, she'd never initiate it herself. Not now, especially. Maybe not ever. It was enough just to be working with him.

"He'll embarrass you," Devon said. "Is that who you really want to be seen with at the trials? His name will go on all the paperwork as your trainer. The judges will see. I'm sure the media will be there."

"So?" Hannah concentrated on washing her horse off. Devon was really starting to put a damper on her mood. She wished he was still away at the horse show.

"So? It'll hurt your reputation," Devon said. "Nobody likes him, Hannah. He's an embarrassment to the sport. I'd hate to see you not get chosen based on that."

She couldn't tell if it was a veiled threat or not. She turned the water off and walked around her horse where she could see his eyes. She started to scrape the water off Grace's coat.

"Do you really think having him as my trainer will hurt me?"

Devon shrugged. "I'm just telling you what I've heard. There has been talk."

"Who else would train me?"

Devon shrugged again. "You have the routine choreographed now. You don't need him. I can find you someone."

"No one else is available," Hannah said.

"What about me?"

There was a long silence. Finally, Hannah said, "It wouldn't be appropriate since you're on the Olympic nominating committee."

"There are no rules against it."

"It just doesn't feel right." *Think, Hannah. Think.* "If I get picked, people would think it was because you were my trainer. I want to get in under my own talent."

"Hmm. I guess that makes sense."

She finished with the water scraper and toweled Grace's head off. Then she untied her. "Can you be a doll and put my saddle away for me? Please? I'm exhausted. I want to put Grace in her stall and go get some dinner. I'm turning in early tonight."

"Sure," Devon said.

"Thanks, Devon. You're awesome." For added emphasis, Hannah stood on tiptoe and kissed him on the cheek. As she walked away, she could feel Devon's eyes on her back. Her good mood had disappeared, and she felt the old tension and worry creeping back into her shoulders. She should never have hugged Chase, especially in front of Devon. She had just been so happy!

But Devon was watching them. She'd have to be careful now that he was back.

Chapter Twenty

The next evening, Marcus Whitney invited Chase to the house for a talk. He had sounded firm on the phone. "Come at 7 p.m.," he said. "There's something we need to discuss."

Chase was a little nervous. He knew that Hannah was out buying new riding clothes, so he'd be alone with her dad. What could Marcus possibly want to discuss?

Anastasia let Chase in and led him to the study. Marcus was sitting behind his huge cherry wood desk. He stood and motioned for Chase to have a seat at the conference table. Chase pulled out a chair and sat.

Marcus got up and closed the doors to the study. It was getting dark outside, and the study was dimly lit by recessed lighting. Chase could see shelves of leather-bound books lining the north wall behind the conference table. The room was beautiful.

But judging by Marcus's solemn demeanor and the closed door, he wasn't here for pleasantries.

"Sir, is everything okay?" he said after a few moments when Marcus still hadn't spoken. Marcus was running his fingers along the spines of his books.

"I'm trying to figure out how to say what I want to say," Marcus said. "I'm usually not a man to mince words."

"I guess the best way is to just say it," Chase said. *What could this be about?*

Marcus turned so his eyes were on Chase. He was still wearing his light gray business suit from work. He had a white shirt on underneath, boasting a light gray pinstripe. The burgundy tie looked like pure silk. He was an imposing sight.

"I didn't hire you to date my daughter," he said.

"What?"

"Or hit on her. Or flirt with her. Or whatever it is you're doing." There was anger in his eyes.

"Um, sir, I'm not—"

"Listen to me, Mr. Livingston," he said.

So now it was *Mr. Livingston?* What had happened to Chase? Or son?

"She's vulnerable. Hannah may seem like a sharp woman, but she's vulnerable when it comes to men. She really wants to be loved. She missed that when she was growing up. That's what I've learned in the many years of therapy I've had. She is looking for love. You're not the man to give it to her."

Chase raised his eyebrows. Where on earth did he get an idea like this? "But I'm not—"

"I haven't given you permission to speak," Marcus said, cutting him off.

Chase dropped his eyes. "Yes, sir." 'Sir' seemed to be the most appropriate title at the moment.

"Are you trying to date my daughter?"

Chase looked up at him. Was he supposed to answer? Was it okay to talk now? He waited, and Marcus raised his eyebrows.

"No. Absolutely not," Chase said, his mind spinning, trying to think if he had in any way encouraged this. "Why? Has Hannah said something?"

"No. This has been brought to my attention by others."

"Devon." Now it made sense. Chase remembered the spontaneous hug Hannah had given him last night and the look in Devon's eyes.

Marcus neither acknowledged or denied the fact. "But I don't need anyone to tell me these things," he said. "I know my daughter. She has been walking around here like she's floating on air. She's happy. She's distracted. She's preoccupied. Because of you."

He frowned at Chase. He seemed more concerned than angry. But still.

"Sir, I think she's just excited about her routine," Chase said truthfully. "You should come and watch it! She finally has it memorized, and her ride yesterday— and today!—was just spectacular! If she's walking on air, it's because she *is*. That's literally how she and Grace look when they perform."

Chase realized, as he talked, how excited he was for Hannah and her horse. He felt proud at having helped them get this far so quickly.

"Son, I know what falling in love looks like." His voice was softer.

Chase was honestly taken aback.

"You think she's *in love* with me?"

"Don't you?"

Chase thought about it. Hannah had been happier this past week or so. She seemed to want him to spend time with her. She had invited him jogging. They had had lunch a few times. She was eager for her lessons to start. She had even suggested they work extra hours some days. He figured it was all part of her driven personality.

And the fact that he seemed to be her only friend.

"Um, I really can't say."

"For now, forever, you need to put that thought out of your head."

"Sir, the thought was never really there," Chase said. Although if he were honest . . .

"This is a business arrangement. That's all it is."

"I realize that."

"Devon—yes, it was Devon who brought this to my attention—has suggested that I fire you."

Of course he would. Chase felt his anger rising. What right did he have? Devon acted as if he owned the place. But *fire* him? What if Marcus did?

"I thought you couldn't find anyone else to train Hannah," Chase said.

Marcus shrugged. "We have the choreographed routine now. That's what we really needed. Devon has even suggested the names of some trainers."

"Who? Himself?"

The corners of Marcus's lips twitched.

Chase stood. "Sir, Devon hates me, and he's just looking out for himself. This is unfair, and if I could just tell you—"

"Relax, Chase. Sit down." The words were firm. Chase sat.

"I'm no fool," Marcus said. "I know when I'm being played. Devon is walking a fine line here."

Chase took a deep breath to steady himself. He realized his hands were shaking. "So you're not going to fire me?"

"No. I'm not going to fire you. But you'd be wise not to take advantage of how Hannah feels about you. It would be easy to do, considering your background."

"My background?"

"She idolizes you."

"She's embarrassed by me!"

Marcus walked over to the bookcase and opened a drawer. He pulled out a brown, leather-bound book. It was about twelve inches by twelve inches in size and had yellowed newspaper clippings sticking out from the pages. He set it down on the conference table in front of Chase with a thump.

"Open it."

Chase opened the first page. Someone had drawn a banner across the top in green marker. It read, *My Olympic Heroes.* There was a cutout of the five Olympic rings glued under it. He turned the page. There were a few pictures of show horses, cut out of magazines. He recognized them.

"Keep going," Marcus said.

Chase turned another page. There he was, staring out from a magazine page, clipped and glued in. He had on his riding hat and was holding a ribbon. It was a show he had been in before he won the gold, when he was just making a name for himself. He turned more pages. There was his face, again and again. She must have found every article written about him. There were other pages, dedicated to different riders, and some to horses too, but mostly, the pages were filled with him.

She had collected his sponsorship ads too. Him holding a Cordova saddle and Cordova bridles. Horse feed. Fly spray. A riding jacket. His face stared out at him from the pages.

"Hannah started this when she was twelve," Marcus said. "And you were...?"

Chase turned the page to see himself holding the gold medal, sitting on Manny, and smiling for the camera. That one was taken when he was offered the toothpaste ad.

"I was eighteen," he said.

Marcus didn't say anything.

Chase flipped through the rest quickly. His second Olympics. She had articles about the trials, about the games themselves. There was a photo of him getting thrown off his horse. Then . . .

He turned the page. There were about a dozen pages left in the book. They were all empty.

"What's everybody doing?"

Both men jumped and turned toward the study door. Hannah was standing there, shopping bags in her hands.

"What's up?" she said again. "What are you looking at? Can I see?"

Her eyes traveled down to the book, and she turned pale.

Chapter Twenty-One

Hannah knew what it was the moment she saw it. She met Chase's eyes, then looked at her father.

"How *could* you?" Her voice was a whisper.

"Chase was just leaving," her dad said. Chase closed the scrapbook and quickly stood. He left the room, not meeting Hannah's eyes, brushing by her on the way out. She heard the front door close.

"How could you?" she repeated to her father. "Where did you even find this?"

"Your old nanny gave it to me several years ago," he said. "You threw it out."

"I threw it out for a reason!"

Hannah felt her face turn red. She had never been so embarrassed in her life. "Dad, I don't even know what to say. I can't imagine why you would think it's a good idea to show him this...this...spectacle. I was just a *kid!*"

She saw the look of shame in her dad's eyes. He had screwed up, and he knew it. She marched over to him, grabbed the scrapbook, and hauled it and her shopping bags up the stairs to her bedroom.

"Hannah, come back," he called after her. "Let's talk. I'm sorry."

She ignored him and slammed her door, startling Pussy Willow, who had been asleep on her bed. She threw her bags on the floor and sat on the edge of her bed.

"Oooh!" she growled, and pounded her pillow for good measure.

Her phone beeped. Was it Chase? She took the phone out of her purse and looked at it. It was just a reminder from her running app.

"Oh my *gosh!*" she said to her cat. "I can't believe this is happening. He *showed* Chase, Puss!" She pulled the scrapbook out of one of her bags and set it on the bed beside her. She opened it, leafing through. It was worse than she remembered. Chase was on nearly every page. She looked like a stalker. She looked immature. She looked...crazy.

"Oh my gosh," she said again.

She went into the bathroom and took a long, hot shower, trying to wash away the stress. Then she put on her most comfortable pajamas and climbed into bed. There was a knock on her door.

"Go away," she said.

"Hannah, your dad wants you to eat something." It was Anastasia.

"I'm not hungry."

"Maybe I could just put it on your dresser for later?"

"No, Anastasia, thank you. Please take it away."

"Okay, Miss."

Hannah listened as the housekeeper's footsteps went back down the stairs. It wasn't even nine o'clock, but she turned off her light and crawled into bed.

There was nothing else she could do. Maybe she'd never come out of hiding again. Ever.

The next morning, she didn't go for her run and stayed in bed until she was sure her father had gone to work. She put off leaving the house as long as she could. She didn't want to see Chase.

"Puss," she said to her cat. "I can't go out. Ever."

Puss nudged her hand with his head. She petted him.

There was a little framed picture on her nightstand of her winning her first horse show ribbon. She had ridden a pony her father had leased when she was ten. Her dad was standing beside her, smiling. It was one of the rare times he had showed up. She had framed it because it was her first success and the beginning of her Olympic dreams. Underneath, on the bottom of the frame, she had written:

"Once upon a time you were a little girl with big dreams that you promised you'd make real someday. Don't disappoint yourself."

Pussy Willow nudged her, and she absently petted his head. "You're right, kitty. I'm the only thing getting in my way."

This was *it*. She was living her dream. She had a killer routine, a fantastic horse, and a trainer willing to take her all the way.

She'd put her chin up like she always did and carry on. What else was there to do? It's not like she hadn't been embarrassed before.

She took a deep breath to steady herself, and then got dressed to go to the barn.

Chase was waiting for her in the ring when she arrived. Devon was teaching a student, and everybody else was at work. The arena was quiet. They were alone.

"Hey," Chase said.

"Hey," Hannah said. She walked Grace over to Chase as was their custom now. He always gave her a leg up onto her horse.

But this morning, instead of offering her a hand, he said, "I want to talk about it."

"Well, I don't," Hannah said.

"Why didn't you tell me?"

"I threw it away years ago! I was just a kid. I wanted to be like you when I grew up, okay? That was it."

"And then I disappointed you."

She finally met his eyes. They were kind, questioning.

"Yes," she said quietly.

"So this is personal for you."

She swallowed and nodded.

"I'm sorry."

Hannah raised her eyebrows. "Sorry? What for?"

"For making you think...that I was better than I was. Hannah, I'm just a man. Imperfect. I'm nothing to pursue, either in or out of the show ring."

What was he talking about? Hannah studied him for a moment, but he didn't say anything else.

"I'm really embarrassed," she said, and laughed a little bit. She looked away from him and felt her cheeks turning red. "I thought that scrapbook was gone. I had no idea Dad still had it. You must think I'm some obsessed fan. That I'm crazy."

Chase smiled then. Not a laugh, like he was making fun of her, but a truly friendly smile of agreement. "I know all about being embarrassed," he said. "You'll live."

"Hmph," Hannah said. "I don't think you realize quite how embarrassed I am."

"I can top you. I fell off my horse in the middle of my Olympic performance."

"I filled a scrapbook full of pictures of my trainer."

"I lost the gold medal for my entire team," Chase said.

"I've lost at least four trainers due to my bratty attitude."

"Hmm. That's tough to beat," Chase said, rubbing his chin thoughtfully. "I lost all of my sponsorships, my house, and my horse."

"I don't have any friends, my mother left me, and my dad is going through a mid-life crisis."

"I was working as an insurance salesman before your dad hired me."

Hannah raised her eyebrows. "Wow. Well..." She thought. "I didn't tell you about the posters of you I had plastered on my walls when I was a teenager. Now who's embarrassed?"

"Yeah, well, I went on national television and told people I saw an angel."

Hannah snorted. She actually snorted. "Okay. I can't top that. You win," she said. She started laughing, and Chase joined her.

"So we've established that we're both crazy, and we're both a mess," Chase said. "Is that right?"

Hannah nodded. She was laughing so hard she had to wipe the tears from her eyes. She felt a great sense of relief.

"Okay, then. Let's get to work." Chase moved to Grace's side and offered his cupped hands. Hannah stepped into them and mounted her horse.

She rode well. The routine was going smoothly, and Grace loved working. When Hannah finally pulled her up to quit, the horse shook her head, wanting to do more. But Grace had a white lather on her, and Hannah was sweating. "We need a break, girl," Hannah said. "We'll come back to it later today."

Chase was giving them other exercises in the afternoons—bending, stretching, and building their strength and endurance. He had them on a nice, predictable schedule, and Hannah liked it. She always knew what to expect.

She hopped down off Grace. "I'm so happy with how she's doing!" Hannah said. "Thank you! And thank you for understanding about...you know." She couldn't hide the smile that spread across her face.

"No worries," Chase said.

Hannah stepped forward to give him a hug, but he pulled away.

"Not a good idea," he said.

"What?"

Hannah had always been expressive. She tended to throw herself at people when she was excited. She had hugged Hans many times, much to his cold, German distaste. She hugged Anastasia when the housekeeper baked Hannah's favorite chocolate cake, or decorated for Hannah's birthday parties, or remembered not to dry her favorite pair of jeans in the dryer. Likewise, she was just as emotional when she was upset. She had been known to throw glasses of water at people.

"It's not a good idea for us to hug," Chase said.

Hannah felt herself tightening up with fear. Had she gone too far? Had she insulted him? Was she pushing him away?

"Why?"

"Your dad thinks we have something going on."

"*Us?*" Hannah said. "That's crazy. Why would he think that?"

"That's what I wondered," Chase said. "I told him that I'm your trainer, and you were simply excited about how good you're doing."

"Exactly. That's exactly all it is," Hannah said. But inside she was starting to hurt a little. It felt like she had been poked in the gut.

"Exactly," Chase echoed.

"Where would he get an idea like that?" Then she remembered. She had hugged Chase yesterday in front of Devon. "Augh!" she growled. "Devon!"

"Don't say anything to him," Chase said. "I've already talked to your dad. It's all good."

"That's why Dad showed you my scrapbook," Hannah said. It was all starting to make sense now.

"He told you not to take advantage of me, didn't he? Not to play on my feelings?"

Chase nodded. "He thinks you still have a thing for me."

"Ha!" Hannah said. "I *had* a thing for you. Maybe a small crush. Geez, I was just a kid then."

"I know."

"Okay. I won't mention it." Hannah sighed, long and heavy. Then she peeled her riding gloves off and walked Grace out of the arena so Chase couldn't see her face. A little part of her was wishing he did have a thing for *her*, that he felt the same way about her that she was starting to feel about him. The old crush was still there, only it was a big girl crush now.

Focus, Hannah, she told herself, and it was Chase's voice she heard in her head this time. Not her own. *You only have a few more weeks. Focus.*

She lifted her chin and went into the barn to wash her horse off.

Chapter Twenty-Two

Chase stayed in the arena and busied himself with the speakers. He didn't want to follow Hannah into the barn. He hadn't been able to stop thinking about her since his talk with her dad last night and seeing the scrapbook. At first, he was mortified that she had followed his career so closely and not told him when they had first met. Judging by the number of pictures of him and Manny, she had read every article ever published about them. He had even seen a few hearts drawn on some of the scrapbook pages around his pictures. No wonder she was embarrassed.

Then there had been Marcus's firm warning not to play into his daughter's crush from so many years ago.

The whole thing would have been funny if Chase hadn't had any feelings for Hannah. She was a grown woman, twenty-four years old, and very attractive. What's more, he was drawn to her strong personality and persistence. He had never met anyone who worked so hard and complained so little. At the end of their days, Hannah must have been exhausted. Yet she still found time to lift weights and run, memorize her pattern, and take care of her horse. She had never once complained about any of those things.

Did he love Hannah? Was she falling in love with him? He thought about Marcus's words. Chase knew a relationship would be detrimental right now. She had to focus on winning. If she got distracted by love... well, look what had happened to him.

Chase realized he still had Hannah's riding crop and needed to return it to the barn. He waited until he saw her leave and walk up to the house before he went inside. He found her spot in the tack room and hung the crop on a little peg beside Grace's bridle. He was turning to leave when he heard voices. Two men were talking and laughing.

"She sure is!" It was Devon's voice. "But if you think she's athletic on a horse, you should see her in bed!"

There was more laughter, then the other voice said, "You're playing with fire if you mess with the boss's daughter."

"Oh, she likes me," Devon said. "No worries there. I have her wrapped around my little finger. I figure we'll marry."

"That'll set you up real nice," said the other voice, which Chase identified as Devon's assistant trainer. "You'll be in tight with Daddy Moneybucks."

"That's the plan," Devon said. "That and having Hannah on my arm. She's gorgeous."

"And apparently good in bed."

"Because of me. Horses aren't the only thing I train."

More laughter. Chase felt anger rising in him. How dare they talk about her that way! The voices were moving toward him now.

Chase stepped out of the tack room, so he was standing in front of them. They stopped.

"You shouldn't talk about Hannah that way," he said.

Devon grinned, showing his wolfish teeth. "Oh look, it's Wuss Livingston. What are you going to do about it? Call down a few angels to fight for you?"

Both men laughed. Chase felt the blood rushing to his head, his heart hammering.

"She'll never be with you," Chase said, vaguely remembering in the back of his mind that Hannah had told him to be nice to Devon. "She's better than that."

"She will," Devon said. "I was her first. I know how she likes it."

Chase grabbed Devon by the front of his shirt and slammed him up against the wall. He heard the air whoosh out of Devon.

"If you so much as lay a finger on her..." Chase said through gritted teeth.

"You'll what?" Devon said, gasping. He was really in no position to argue. Chase was far stronger than he was. The man had guts; Chase had to give him that.

"I'll send you to Hell," Chase said. He glared at Devon for a moment, his eyes burning into the man. Then, roughly, he let him go. Devon brushed his shirt off.

"You ever touch me again, Wuss, and I'll have you fired," Devon said. "Your days here are numbered. You just remember that."

Chase forced himself to breathe evenly and relax. This man wasn't worth it. He deserved a good pounding, but he knew that's not what God would want. Plus, Chase didn't want to cause trouble. Not now. Hannah didn't need the stress. And right now, Devon had the power to place her on the Olympic team if she scored well. Or keep her off.

It took all his strength to leave, but Chase turned and walked out of the barn. He didn't look back. The walk back to the guesthouse was long, and by the time he got there, he had calmed down a little bit. He poured himself a glass of iced tea and sat down on the sofa in his living room. After a few moments, he opened up his iPad and got to work. Hannah needed to strengthen the middle of her routine, around the third minute. He'd work on that.

Right now, the only way he could help her was to give her the best work he could offer. Then, she could win her way out of Devon's clutches. If she scored high enough in her routine, there would be no way he could deny her entry onto the Olympic team.

The next week went smoothly. With the end of summer, the fall horse shows were in full swing, with riders contesting for those last points that would either give them year-end awards or make them wait until next spring to try again. Devon and his students were off to another show.

Chase and Hannah worked hard all week. He had strengthened her routine, and Grace had handled it well. They both looked spectacular.

One evening, after a long, hard day, they were sitting on the fence drinking bottles of chilled water. Hannah had just put Grace away for the night, and the barn help had gone home. The sun was setting. Both of them needed to go back to their houses and shower, and Chase was thinking longingly of his bed. They had started the day off with a three-mile run, worked Grace for a total of four hours, and lifted weights. He was exhausted.

"I love it when Devon's gone," Hannah said out of nowhere.

That brought up the lingering feelings Chase still had about his run-in with Devon last week. He hated the way Devon treated Hannah, and especially how he talked about her.

"You were right about us not hugging," she said. "He would hate it."

"Why do you let him treat you that way?" Chase said.

Hannah shrugged. "There's a certain amount of his crap I have to put up with, because he's on the Olympic nominating committee. I told you this already."

"But there's a limit."

"What can I do about it? He's just obnoxious. I tolerate him. That's all. It's not so bad."

"He talks about you behind your back," Chase said. What was he doing? Hadn't he decided already that Hannah didn't need any more stress?

"What?" She looked at Chase. "What does he say about me?"

"I heard him telling his assistant trainer how good you are in bed."

Hannah looked forward, and he saw her jaw set in a hard line.

"Sounds like that two months you guys dated meant a lot to him," Chase said. He was surprised how much that thought bothered him, even though he knew Devon's feelings for Hannah bordered closer to ownership than love. "He thinks you'll start seeing him again soon."

"I never slept with him," Hannah said. "I wouldn't. Ever. Not with that snake."

Chase was quiet.

Hannah turned to him. "You thought I did? You *believed* him?"

"Hannah, you're a grown woman. I don't know. You do what you do."

"I can't believe you believed him." She looked down at the ground and fiddled with her boot.

"If it helps any, I almost beat him up."

Hannah looked over at Chase. "You did?"

"I threw him up against the wall. I would have liked to have done more, but I kept hearing your voice in the back of my head, warning me to be nice so he'd pick you for the team."

Hannah smiled and took a drink from her water bottle. "Thank you. I'd have liked to have seen that. Why didn't you tell me?"

Chase looked out across the arena, past the barns. The sun was setting. He wished he was at the beach on Lake Michigan right now, watching the sun sink into the water. But he was happy here, too, he realized. Beside Hannah.

"I didn't want to stress you out," he said.

"And yet you're telling me now."

"I think you need to know. You need to be careful."

Hannah took another drink of her water.

"I don't know why he's so upset with me," Chase said. "He truly hates me."

"He's jealous," Hannah said.

"But you and I are not an item. And you've had a lot of other boyfriends, right? I mean, what about them? Why is he singling *me* out?"

Hannah was silent.

"You *have* had other boyfriends? He mentioned he was your first."

"Wow. He said a lot," Hannah said.

She was silent for a moment. *Hadn't* she had other boyfriends? He couldn't imagine that a woman as beautiful as she was hadn't dated all through high school, at least. Her sport didn't leave much room for a relationship now, but there had to be a time when she was a teenager, right?

"No. I don't date," Hannah said. "I've gone out a few times. But there just hasn't been anyone who's caught my interest."

Chase thought about the scrapbook, and the pictures she had of him.

Hannah's water bottle was empty, and she crushed it with her hand. "I can't believe he said those things. I can't believe it!"

She dropped it on the ground, hopped off the fence, and stomped on it. "I'm pretending this is his face," she said.

Chase laughed. He did the same and jumped off the fence, crushing his bottle under his heel.

When they were done, Hannah looked up at him, her anger spent. "I never slept with him. I never slept with..." her voice trailed off. "I've never."

Chase was speechless. She was a virgin? This take-charge woman who could have any man she wanted... he hadn't expected that. Not at all.

"What?" Hannah said. She leaned back against the fence, looking off at the sunset. "You're surprised?"

"No," Chase lied. "I mean, yes. I don't know."

"Are *you?*"

"Me? Am I a virgin?" He laughed. He felt his cheeks growing red.

Hannah glanced at him, then back at the sunset. "I've embarrassed you," she grinned.

"I'm used to it," he said, trying to lighten the mood. "You certainly do say what's on your mind, though."

"Well, *are* you? I told. Now it's your turn to tell."

"What are we, in middle school?"

"Gosh, I hope not. Not if we're having this conversation!"

Chase laughed again. Then he sighed. "No. Marina. Remember?"

"Ahh, the woman who broke your heart."

"Yes."

"Was she the only one?"

"Yes."

"Hmm." Hannah thought for a moment. "That was back when you were twenty-two. And you're thirty now?"

"It has been a long, lonely time," Chase said.

They both laughed. Then Hannah looked over at him, her eyes serious. "Why?"

"Why? You're asking the has-been wonder kid who talks to angels why nobody wants to be with him?"

But Hannah didn't laugh.

"I'm waiting," Chase said seriously.

"Oh," Hannah said. "Because of the Jesus thing."

"That. And because I want it to be the right woman. The only woman. If I ever give my heart away again, I want it to be forever."

Hannah turned to look at him. "I thought guys didn't care about that sort of thing."

"I do."

He saw her eyes narrow slightly, then soften. She moved a little closer to him and tilted her head up to look into his eyes. He could smell the light scent of her shampoo, mixed with the warmth of her body. Her lips looked soft, slightly parted as she looked up at him. He wanted to pull her into his arms and kiss her.

"Chase..."

"Hannah," he said, stepping back and looking at his phone. "It's late. We should go home."

She dropped her eyes and turned away from him. He had hurt her.

"You're right," she said lightly. He noticed the slight lift of her chin. She did that when she was trying to be strong. "I have a lot to focus on, and a long day tomorrow." She stretched. "And I'm exhausted!"

She bent down and picked up both of their crushed water bottles.

"I'll see you tomorrow," Chase said.

Their eyes met again and held for a moment, then Hannah nodded. "Yes. I'll see you tomorrow."

She walked away, and he stood there for a moment, watching her go and regretting that the world, and their roles, weren't just a little bit different.

Chapter Twenty-Three

A few days later, Hannah wrapped up her session and returned to her bedroom to find a letter sitting on the dresser among the other mail that Anastasia had brought in. It didn't have a return address. She carefully opened it and unfolded the letter inside. It was handwritten on a page of lined stationary that had bluebirds on it.

She quickly looked for the signature line. It was signed *Mom.*

Her heart started to hammer in her chest, and she folded the letter up and put it back in the envelope. Then she paced back and forth in her room.

What did her mom *want?* Hannah decided she wouldn't read the letter. She wouldn't give her mom the time of day. Not after all these years. Not now.

But curiosity always got the best of Hannah. After no more than two minutes of pacing, she returned to the dresser, ripped the letter out of the envelope, and began to read.

Dear Hannah,
  I am so sorry I upset you the other day.

The other *day?* What about upsetting her fifteen years ago?

I would greatly like for us to meet again. There is so much I want to tell you. But most importantly, I have something I want to give to you. It's from your grandmother. I don't have your phone number. Please text or call and let me know when and where you are available.

Love,
Mom

There was a phone number at the bottom.

Hannah was angry. Eva had signed the letter *Mom.* How *dare* she? Well, Hannah wouldn't reply. That would show her. The whole gift thing was a bribe, just something to get her to agree to meet her.

From her *grandmother?*

She vaguely remembered the older woman, who had seemed frail the few times Hannah had seen her. She had died when Hannah was only five. Her grandfather—her mother's father—had died when Hannah's mom was just a child. Her other grandparents had also passed on early. Hannah had never really had grandparents.

What gift could her grandmother have that Hannah wanted? Nothing that she could think of. Nothing that she'd *want*, certainly. She barely knew the woman.

Still, she wondered what it was.

Hannah sighed loudly. She paced a few more times.

"Dang it!" she said, knowing that she would meet her mom. If curiosity killed the cat, and Hannah was a cat, she'd have gone through all nine lives by now.

She sat down on her bed and texted the number.

Tomorrow at noon. Louie's.

She sent a link with the address. Then she waited. Almost immediately, she got a reply.

Thank you, Hannah! See you then!

Hannah sent a "thumbs up" emoji and tossed her phone on her bed.

"I must be crazy," she said to Pussy Willow. He meowed, as if agreeing with her. Then Hannah went to get ready for bed. She'd need to be well rested for tomorrow.

Hannah arrived at Louie's twenty minutes early. Her dad had taught her that to have the advantage in a meeting, you needed to get there first and pick your seat. She chose a small table near the back. It didn't offer a good view of Lake Michigan, but it would give them privacy. She had her back to the wall, so she could see her mom come in through the door. Her mom would be sitting with her back to the door, then, forcing her to focus on Hannah.

Eva came exactly on time. She was dressed in a maroon skirt, short, black heels, and a white top. She had her hair pulled back in a maroon bow. She was actually quite pretty, Hannah noticed.

Eva sat across from Hannah. "Thank you for meeting with me," she said.

Hannah was wearing a green cotton dress and sandals. She had worn her hair up in a loose updo and had on the pearl earrings that her dad had given her when she graduated from high school.

"The clam chowder soup is good," Hannah said, by way of hello. She opened her menu and pointed. "I also like the BLTs."

Eva scanned the menu. The waiter came, and they both ordered iced tea.

"I think I'll just have a salad," Eva said when the waiter returned with their drinks. Hannah only ordered a side of fries to pick at. She wasn't feeling very hungry.

After the waiter left, Eva folded her hands on the table in front of her and looked across at Hannah. "I'm sorry," Eva said.

"For what?" Hannah replied. She was going to make her mom work for this.

Eva watched her for a moment. "Everything."

"That covers a lot."

There was an awkward pause. Hannah took a deep breath. She tried to remember what she knew about focus. Chase's words echoed in her head. *Breathe. Be in the moment. Nothing else matters.* She could use that here. Nothing else mattered. Her mom was here, *now*. Focus on that.

"I see you're still into horses," Eva said. "I remember how much you loved them when you were little."

206

Hannah reached into her purse and pulled out the photo from her nightstand, the one with the pony and her very first ribbon.

"See this?"

Eva took it and looked at the photo. "That's your dad with you."

"That's my very first blue ribbon, which you weren't there to see me win."

"I know I wasn't around," Eva said quietly. "I regret that."

Hannah watched her carefully across the table. Eva ran her fingers across the print on the bottom of the frame.

"You're quite competitive," Eva said.

"I'm on my way to the Olympics."

Eva nodded. "I know. I've watched you on TV."

She had? It had never occurred to Hannah that her mom had kept up with them over the years. She had erased her mom from her mind, pretending she didn't care, that she didn't need a mom. Most of the other competitors had always had their parents around when Hannah was younger, and later, their boyfriends, but Hannah had always been alone.

"Your earrings are pretty," her mom said.

"Dad got them for me when I graduated."

Eva nodded, and slid the picture across the table to Hannah. "He's a pretty pony. What's his name?"

"She. Her name was Apples."

"That's cute."

What were they doing here? What did this woman want from her? The small talk was about to kill Hannah.

"Mom, why are you really here?"

Eva looked up at Hannah, and her eyes looked sad. "I've missed you," she said. "I thought maybe we could...you know...start hanging out."

"Hanging out?" Hannah felt the heat rising in her face. "Now that I'm all grown up, you want to hang out? Where were you *then?*" Hannah said, stabbing her finger at the photo of her and the pony. "I needed you when I was little. I needed a mom!"

Eva nodded. "I know."

"I needed you when I was in middle school, and Jacob Wheeler kissed me under the mistletoe at the Christmas dance. He was really cute, but he had braces and bad breath, and I was grossed out instead of excited, and I needed to know if that was okay."

Hannah took a breath.

"And where were you when I got my driver's permit? My nanny took me for that! Oh, and what about on my sixteenth birthday, when I got my driver's license? I was so excited, but my nanny was sick that day and Dad was working so the housekeeper had to take me. The *housekeeper!* She took an extra hour of her day to do that, because I had no one else. Because I didn't have a mom."

Hannah felt all the pain of the years coming back.

"When I was fourteen, I had the chicken pox. Dad was busy. The nanny took me to the doctor and bought me calamine lotion. You know who took me to buy my first bra? The nanny! Oh, and these were different nannies. Not the *same* nanny. The first was a college-aged girl who moved on to raise her *own* family."

Hannah grabbed the picture and stuffed it back in her purse.

"And yes, I've been winning at horse shows. And I have a kick-butt trainer and a routine that will get me to the Olympics. The trials are coming up at Castleby Farm in a few weeks, and I plan to win there. But you know what I would have loved more than any of this? To have my mom out there in the stands cheering me on. To have *anyone* out there in the stands cheering me on that wasn't paid to do so."

Hannah paused when the waiter brought their food.

"What about all the other things a girl needs? When I went to my senior prom, I had a discussion *with my father* about how much cleavage was proper to show. With my father! Where were you then, Mom? Where were you when I had my wisdom teeth pulled, and my best friend in school moved away, and I hit a deer with my car?"

Hannah's heart was pounding. She felt tears coming to her eyes. She didn't remember ever feeling this much pain. Her mind went back to the day she sat on the couch, waiting for her mom to come home. She realized that she had been waiting for fifteen years for her mom to come home. *For fifteen years.* She wanted to go back to her eight-year-old self, put her arms around her, and tell her how much she loved her, like her mom should have done. Her mom should have come home that same day, asked her to forgive her, and promised to never leave her.

"You have something for me?" Hannah said.

"What?" Eva looked up, surprised. Her eyes were shining with tears.

"You said you had something from my grandma."

Eva nodded and dug in her purse. She pulled out a small parcel wrapped in tissue and handed it to Hannah.

"It's your grandma's wedding ring," she said. "I thought, now that you were older, if you ever get married, maybe you'd want to put the stone into your own band."

Hannah looked at the parcel laying between them. She took it and unwrapped it. It was a simple gold band with a small diamond on it. It was pretty, but it held no sentimental meaning to her. For some reason, this made Hannah even sadder.

She pushed it back to her mom. "No, thank you." Then she stood. "I have nothing else to say. Goodbye, Mom."

"Hannah, wait," Eva said, standing. "I want to tell you about my life, about what I've been doing. I know I screwed up, but I'm here now. Can you give me a second chance?"

Hannah looked away. "No," she said. "I can't." She threw a twenty down on the table to cover their bill and walked out to her car. It was parked in front on the curb. She heard Eva's heels clicking behind her.

"Wait," Eva said, and grabbed Hannah's arm. "I want to make up for lost time."

"Mom, I needed you when I was little. I don't need you now. Please go away."

"Give me a second chance," Eva said.

"No."

Hannah jerked her arm out of her mother's grip and got in her Mustang. She put the car in drive and left. In the rearview mirror, she saw her mom standing on the curb, her skirt blowing in the breeze from the lake. She looked very small and alone.

Hannah wiped the tears from her eyes so she could see the road, and turned, heading back toward her farm and her horse.

She had other things to focus on. She hoped Eva would never contact her again.

Chapter Twenty-Four

Hannah was riding terribly. Grace's ears kept flicking back and forth, and even from here, Chase could see the tension in Hannah's shoulders.

"Hannah, can you ride into the center of the ring for a moment?" Chase said.

Hannah did as he requested. The afternoon was hot for September, and both she and the horse already had a light sweat on them.

Chase removed his sunglasses and squinted up at her, waiting until her blue eyes met his. "What's up?"

"What do you mean?" That was Hannah, always in denial.

"You know what I mean. Your riding is awful today. You're upsetting your horse. You were both doing fine this morning. What happened over lunch?"

Hannah let out a long, loud sigh. Although they had been getting along well since their talk a few weeks ago, Chase was prepared for her to go on the defensive and attack him with her words. He was surprised when she said, "Can we go somewhere and talk?"

"Sure," he said.

Hannah hopped off her horse and peeled off her riding gloves. "Can you cool her off?"

"Um...yes," he said, taking the reins from her.

"I'll be at the gazebo down by the lake. You know the one—where I was the morning we first met."

"Okay."

"Thanks."

He watched her as she started walking in that direction. This was weird. Something was definitely wrong.

Chase hosed Grace off and walked her until she was cool. Then he grabbed two chilled water bottles out of the break room in the barn and walked to meet Hannah. He found her sitting in the gazebo, tapping her crop against her foot. She looked up when he arrived.

"Thanks," she said, taking the water bottle.

Chase sat beside her. The lake was dark blue and pretty. They were surrounded by willow trees, and the breeze was cool. They were far enough away from the barns that the only sounds he could hear were the birds and the rustle of leaves.

"It's nice here," he said.

"I come here for lunch a lot. Or I used to. You've kept me too busy lately." She gave a little laugh.

Chase knew from experience with his sister that often the best way to get people to talk was to just wait and listen.

"I usually like to move, to keep busy when I'm upset, or to train hard," Hannah said, still tapping her toe with her crop. "But today I just want to sit. I'm just..." She sighed again and focused on her tapping. She wouldn't meet his eyes.

"I went to meet my mom for lunch," she said.

Ahh, there it was.

"I take it that it didn't go well?" Chase asked gently.

Hannah shook her head. "No. I mean...maybe? I don't know. She was pleasant enough. She just wants to get back in my life. But I'm so *angry.*" She looked at Chase now. "I thought I'd be glad to see her if she ever came back, you know? But instead...I think I hate her." She said the words quietly, as if she was ashamed of them.

"I think that's kind of natural, don't you?" Chase asked. "She really hurt you, and at an age when you couldn't protect yourself. She was supposed to be there, protecting you, but instead, she's the one who hurt you."

Hannah nodded. Her head was down, and she was looking at her boot again. The tapping was getting harder. He saw a few tears slide down her cheeks.

"I think it's probably okay to feel how you're feeling," he said.

She smacked her foot with the crop. It made a loud cracking sound, and he saw her flinch. He reached over, gently took it from her hand, and laid it beside him on the wooden bench.

"Have you told your dad?"

Hannah shook her head. "No. What if he wants to bring her back into her lives? Or he gets angry and forbids me to see her. I mean, she hurt *him* too."

"I suspect she was hurting when she left. Didn't you say your dad was never around?"

Hannah started to cry harder now. "Yes," she said. "I think I'm mad at him too. If he had been a better husband..." her voice trailed off. "Do you think this is his fault?"

"I don't know," Chase said. "But whatever happened in the past, he is trying to make up for it with you now. Maybe your mom is too."

Hannah was still looking down, not wanting to meet his eyes. "While I was waiting for you to cool Grace off, I was sitting here thinking that most women my age would have called their girlfriends and told them about this. They would have had these great conversations and probably shared a tub of ice cream." She gave a little laugh that held no humor. "But I don't have anyone. How pathetic is that?"

"You have me," Chase said.

"But you *have* to listen to me because my dad pays you," Hannah said. "You're my trainer."

Chase put his arm around her shoulders and pulled her against him. She leaned into him, and he felt her shaking from her tears. "Oh Hannah, I'm more than that," he said. "I'm also your friend."

He held her like that for a while and let her cry. It felt so good to have her next to him, so natural. He wished there was something he could do to ease her pain, something he could say. He thought of Marina and how he had had his heart broken. He knew what that kind of pain felt like.

After a while, her crying stopped, and she pulled a tissue out the pocket of her riding breeches and wiped her eyes. But she stayed leaning against him.

"You okay?" he asked gently.

"Let's sit here a little while. I don't want to go back to the house. Or the barn."

"Sure," he said, and kept his arm around her. He remembered the day he'd found out that Marina didn't love him the way he loved her. He wanted Hannah to know the rest of the story.

"I didn't lose the Olympic gold because I was concentrating on my proposal to Marina," Chase said. "I lost it because she broke my heart." He remembered the pain like it was yesterday.

"I had forgotten my riding crop," he said. "I had a few minutes, so I got off Manny and went to get it. When I stepped inside the barn, I saw Marina in the arms of Salvador Burley. They were in quite the passionate kiss. Salvador had come over here with her from her country. Marina loved him. She was only using me for marriage. She wanted to become a US citizen and stay here, so she led me along, hoping I'd ask her to marry me. And I was about to. I knew we had the gold medal, and I thought that right after the Olympic ceremony would be a great time to drop to my knee and propose. But she had played me. I was foolish."

"You found out just before you went in the ring?" Hannah said.

"Yeah. Literally like three minutes before. I was in shock. I was hurt, and I was angry. Manny was a nervous horse, and he used me as his barometer. If I kept calm, he knew everything was okay. But that day I wasn't calm. I was very shaken up. I couldn't get them out of my mind, them kissing. So I forgot my routine, and Manny got upset because he didn't know what to do next. He was supposed to do one thing, and I cued him to do another, and it didn't match the music. After about two minutes into this, a cameraman moved his equipment, Manny shied, my weight shifted, and then he bucked and threw me. End of story."

Hannah was quiet for a long time. Chase wondered if he had said too much.

"So you lost the gold because of a broken heart?" she said finally. "That's kind of romantic, actually. How come you never told anybody?"

"I wanted to protect Marina. She hurt me, yes, but she was trying to make a better life for herself. She had a child to think about."

"She was using you."

"Yes. Plus, it was embarrassing. I was already embarrassed enough."

"What happened in the other shows?"

"I made the mistake of thinking, 'What if I forget the pattern again?'" Chase said. "I was nervous at the next show, and it happened again. It became a psychological thing."

Hannah straightened up, and he removed his arm from her shoulders.

"No one helped you?"

"No," Chase said quietly. He thought about Hannah's mom. No one had helped Hannah either. "Why do *you* think your mom wants to come back into your life?" Chase said. "Is she after your money?"

Hannah shook her head. "No. She said she doesn't want anything. She just wants to be a part of my life."

Chase unscrewed the cap of his water bottle and took a sip. "Are you going to let her?"

Hannah shook her head. "No."

"Why not?"

"She had that chance fifteen years ago."

217

Chase wasn't sure how much to say. He didn't want to push her, but he did want her to know his own struggle.

"I had a choice after Marina left me," he said. "I could blame her for destroying my life, my career, for everything. Or I could pick myself up and carry on."

"You want me to *forgive* my mom?" Hannah asked.

"Maybe not right away," said Chase. "You have a lot to work through. But yes, I think eventually you should."

"I don't think so." Hannah stood, brushed her pants off, and picked up her riding helmet. "Thanks, Chase," she said. She met his eyes. "I'm sorry I fell apart. That's not like me."

He smiled and stood. "No, it's not. But a very smart woman once told me that everyone is allowed to have a bad day."

Hannah laughed.

"You have a lot on your plate. A burden gets lighter if shared. Talk to your dad."

"Okay," she said. "I will."

"Tonight?"

"Are you speaking as my trainer or my friend?"

"Both," Chase said.

"Okay, then," Hannah said. "I'll go do that now, I guess." She stood on tiptoe and gave him a brief kiss on the cheek, then turned and walked away. She didn't look back, and he watched her for a while until her figure grew smaller and disappeared behind the trees.

Then he walked back to the guesthouse alone.

Chapter Twenty-Five

Hannah was mortified. She had never cried in front of a trainer before. Chase had been so comforting and sweet, and it felt so good to be held by him. But what if he realized what a flake she was, and figured she'd never be able to win if she got so emotional? Olympians only cried when they won the gold, right? Tears of joy. She'd have to get a better grip on things, or she would miss out on her dreams.

She showered and changed into fresh clothes, then went down to join her dad for dinner. It was late—after 8 p.m. He had called and said he'd be working later but to wait for him.

Her dad seemed to be in a good mood. He told her a few stories about work and laughed at the antics of a new manager he had hired. She only half listened and pushed her food around her plate. She had made up her mind to tell him about Eva, and her stomach was in knots.

"Hannah, is something wrong?" he asked.

She nodded. She felt like she was going to throw up. Why was it so hard to talk to him about this? She loved him. She trusted him. Well, *now* at least. That was the one good thing about the spiritual "change" he had gone through—she found she could rely on him now.

"Um..." she said, stalling for time.

She looked across the table at her dad. If she brought up the topic of Eva, it would change everything. He'd want to know details. He'd want Eva's business card. He'd look her up, research her, find out where she had been and what she had done. That's who her dad was. He was a man who had to feel like he was in control.

She had just gotten her dad's attention focused on *her.* She didn't want to lose that. He was all she had.

She thought briefly of Chase. She had him, too. At least until the trials. She had to win those trials, so Chase would stay on and continue training her. Otherwise, she might lose him as well.

Winning isn't everything, it's the only thing. She had put that quote on the fridge.

Hannah, what are you doing? she told herself. *You need to focus. Only two more weeks.* That was it. Two more weeks and then she could talk about her mom, about her feelings, and about her life to whoever wanted to talk. But right now, she had to focus on one thing: winning.

"I'm not hungry," she said to her dad and pushed her chair back. "My stomach doesn't feel so well." She put her hand on it. "Cramps." She gave him a small smile.

"Oh." Her dad busied himself buttering a piece of bread. She had learned over the years the easiest ways to escape his scrutiny. Claiming female issues was on the top of the list.

"I think I'm going upstairs to bed," she said.

"Bed? It's not even nine."

"I know," Hannah said. "But I have an early day tomorrow."

Her dad nodded and went back to buttering his bread.

"Good night, Daddy," she said. "I love you."

When she got back to her room, she texted Chase. **I'm sorry for falling apart. I'm better now. Decided not to tell Dad anything. I need to focus on winning. That's all that is important right now.**

Then she forwarded him a screenshot of the home screen of her phone. It was a quote she looked at every day.

Every day is a chance to get better.

She waited for a moment, but he didn't respond. She got dressed for bed and climbed in. She was reading a book about dressage and wanted to get a few more chapters finished.

Just as she opened the book, a text beeped in.

To get better at what?

She laughed.

At what I do. To win.

Winning is your main goal?

Winning is my ONLY goal.

Maybe you have the wrong goal.

She paused her typing. What was he talking about? She typed: **The wrong goal?**

After a moment, her phone rang. It was Chase.

"Hey," she said. "You said there was nothing wrong with wanting to win."

"There is if it's your main goal. Your only goal." His voice was soft, with no hint of accusation. "Hannah, don't you think there's more to life?"

"No," she said.

There was silence on the other end of the phone.

"Hello?" Hannah said after a moment.

"I'm here," Chase said. "I'm just thinking I've done a bad job these past six weeks as your trainer if that's what you believe."

"Isn't that your job? To help me to win?"

"Over everything else?"

"Yes."

"Hannah," Chase said. "What if you fell tomorrow and broke your leg. What if you couldn't ride in the trials? What would happen then?"

"Why would you ever say such a thing?" Hannah said. Was he crazy? Wasn't he supposed to be instilling confidence in her? "Now you have me freaked out."

"Think about it. What if you did? Or what if there was a world pandemic, and all horse shows were cancelled? What would you have then?"

Hannah was silent. What would she have? She'd have her dad. She'd have her horse. And she'd have... She couldn't think of what else she'd have.

Pussy Willow jumped up on the bed. She'd have her cat.

"I have my cat," she said.

Chase laughed. "That's good."

"Hey, what happened to your dog? Didn't you used to have a Jack Russell terrier?"

"Yes," he said. "I did. She got out of the house one morning and got hit by a car."

"Oh no," Hannah said. She couldn't imagine. He used to take that dog everywhere with him.

"When?"

"The same year everything else bad happened."

"Wow."

"Yeah. It was a tough year. But back to my question. I'm waiting for an answer."

Hannah sighed. "I don't want to play this game. I'm getting ready for bed."

"When you're old and a grandma someday, with no broken legs, what are you going to tell your grandkids when they ask what you did with your life?"

"I'm going to tell them I was an Olympic gold medalist," Hannah said. "That's all I've ever wanted to be."

"I see," Chase said. "And if you're not?"

"Failure is not an option." This conversation was making Hannah uncomfortable. "I need to get to bed..."

"And if those grandkids ask about their relatives? About their great-grandma? Do you want to say you had the chance to know her and gave it up?"

"Chase, this is none of your business," Hannah said. She was suddenly very angry. "Your job here is to train me to win. That's it. You're not my counselor or my family. You're my trainer."

"I thought I was also your friend."

"So then be a good one."

There was silence on the phone. She wanted him here now, to hug her again. She needed to feel his arms around her, for him to tell her it was going to be okay, that she wasn't going to break a leg, or lose, or that the world wasn't going to end. She wanted him to tell her all positive things—that she was going to get on the Olympic team, and then they'd go on to the gold, and he'd always be there by her side, cheering her on.

But he didn't.

"This whole thing with your mom is going to screw your head up if you don't deal with it," he said. "Maybe not now, but someday, it'll catch up with you."

"Well, it can wait. I'll have more time to deal with it after the trials. That's the plan. After the trials, Chase. Then I'll deal with it."

"Okay, Hannah," was all he said.

"Good night, Chase," she said, and hung up.

Chase showed up the next morning, full of encouragement and praise, as if nothing had happened yesterday. He didn't ask how she was doing, and he didn't offer comfort. He just got on with their lesson as usual. For that, she was very grateful.

They were able to work hard over the next two weeks without incident. She stopped thinking about her mom and focused on the positive quotes she had plastered around her house. She printed more motivational sayings and put them on her bathroom mirror, in her car, and downloaded them onto her phone. Whenever she was feeling fearful or down, she'd look at them.

With just one week left, Devon came creeping around again. He was always there, but some days, he was more conspicuous than others. Today was one of those days. He had come in behind her while she was putting Grace's saddle away. She smelled his cologne.

"I'm calling in that lunch now," he said. "I have coupons for a free dessert at that place in town that serves the cedar plank salmon."

Hannah knew the restaurant. They did have great food.

"I'm busy," she said.

"Hannah," Devon said. He stepped up behind her and put a hand on her shoulder. They were in the barn, alone in the tack room. She turned so she was looking at him.

"The trials are just a week away," he said. "I'm rooting for you. I think you and Grace will win," he cooed.

"So do I," Hannah said. She lifted her chin a little higher and tried to stand taller.

"I'll put in a good word for you," he said. He moved closer. "When are you ever going to forgive me? I apologized about a hundred times. That woman meant nothing to me. It was all politics. I would never have slept with her out of love. Or passion. You are the only woman for me."

"We were dating at the time."

He had his arm around her waist now. He pulled her closer. Now he was right up against her, and she could feel his breath on her lips. "Remember how good we used to be together?"

She remembered some heavy make outs on their dates. One night, he had tried to put his hand up her shirt. Back then, she had wanted him. She had wanted more, but she had stopped him. They had only been dating a month, and she had learned early on that guys were only after one thing. Or two. Her money made two. So she moved slowly. Always. Trust no one.

"You do still care," Devon said. "I can see it in your eyes."

Hannah had to make a move before he kissed her. She pretended to sneeze, jerking her head sideways and covering her face with her hand. "I'm so sorry," she said.

"Bless you," Devon said. But his eyes narrowed. "Hannah, you do realize how good we'd be together. Me with my training talent, you with your riding talent. We could take over the horse show world, the two of us. Devon and Hannah, the winners extraordinaire." He laughed. "We could have stables full of horses."

"I already have that," Hannah said. She laughed, so it didn't sound so harsh, but he took hold of her wrist.

"You know I love you," he said. "I want you, Hannah. I need you." He pulled her to him and pressed his lips up against hers. She started to struggle but remembered how much power he had. She let him kiss her, and then when he was done, she backed away.

"I make it a point not to date staff," she said, her voice harsh.

"Staff? Is that what you think of me?"

"No," she said. "I mean..." He had her cornered. Not just in the tack room, but in life. She'd never escape the reality that everyone wanted something from her, and the only way to the top was to play the game.

"Sure, Devon, let's do lunch," she said. At least she'd be in public then and not cornered alone in the tack room. "I have some errands to run. I'll meet you at the restaurant. What time?"

Devon smiled. "1 p.m. will work. That'll get us both back in time for afternoon lessons."

"Great," Hannah said. "I'll see you then." She forced a smile.

Devon moved aside and let her pass. She headed home, not looking back, wondering where Chase was. While she wasn't a woman who usually needed saving, it would have been nice if he had been there to step in and throw Devon up against a wall. Sometimes, maybe it would be nice to be saved after all.

Chapter Twenty-Six

Chase's sister drove up for a visit on the weekend before of the trials.

"This is a cool place, Uncle Chase!" Taylor said. He ran around the small guesthouse, checking out the back porch, the kitchen pantry, and finally settling on the porch swing. Chase had bought popsicles for the occasion and brought three out onto the porch. Anika took strawberry, leaving grape for Taylor, and he got stuck with lime.

Anika looked tired from the six-hour commute, but she wasn't one to complain. She sat in the wicker chair and let Chase and Taylor share the swing.

"This is a cute house," she said. "I love it here. And that barn! My goodness! I remember some of the ones you used to ride at, but this one seems to top them all. Somebody has money!"

Chase nodded, opening his lime popsicle. "It's beautiful here," he said. "St. Ives is a sweet town. You'd love it. Oh! I have something for you."

He got up and went inside to get the candle. Camilla, the store owner, had put it in a nice sturdy bag with handles that had the name of her shop on it. It was the sort of thing Anika would like, so Chase left it in the bag.

"Ooh, what's this?" Anika said, taking the bag. She reached in, pulled the candle out, and smelled it. "I love lavender! I'll set this in my bedroom. Thank you!"

"Did you get me anything?" Taylor asked.

"As a matter of fact, I did," Chase said. He pulled a little carved horse out of his pocket. "St. Ives used to be quite the fishing village," he said. "In the wintertime, the fishermen didn't have a lot to do, so they'd carve things out of bone."

"Wow!"

Taylor took the little white horse figurine and examined it closely. "Mom! It's carved out of bone!" He turned to Chase. "What kind of bone?"

Chase shrugged. "Fish bone, I guess."

"Wow!"

Hannah pulled up in front of the house in her Mustang. He had invited her to meet his sister. He wanted Anika to meet Hannah, to show her that Hannah wasn't as bad as her reputation.

Hannah was wearing a pair of blue jean leggings with a soft, gray long-sleeve t-shirt over them. The weather was cooler today than it had been. But not too cool that they couldn't enjoy their popsicles.

Introductions were made, and Hannah chose a chair next to Anika.

"Want a popsicle?" Chase said.

"No thanks," Hannah said. "I just had lunch."

"Where'd you go?"

"This restaurant in town that serves salmon. With Devon."

Chase raised an eyebrow. Hannah rolled her eyes.
"Did it go well?"

"The food was good."

Anika launched into a story about Taylor's school
and a mishap with a teacher and a student that resulted
in the bathroom flooding. Chase was hardly listening.
Hannah was laughing, and he was enjoying this
other new side of her. He hadn't had a chance to see
her interact with anyone whom she didn't consider
competitive or out to get her, or somebody she had
to prove herself to. She was actually enjoying herself
with Anika.

Hannah told Anika a little bit about Grace, and
how hard they had been working.

"Chase swooped in and saved the day,"
Hannah said. "There I was, without a trainer or a
choreographed routine. I didn't even have a song
picked out!"

"Chase is good at saving the day," Anika said.
She lowered her voice. "I don't know if he told you
about my situation."

Taylor had disappeared inside to look for some
books and toys he had brought along.

"No," Hannah said.

"When my boyfriend left Taylor and me behind,
I was desperate for money. So for about a year, I
ended up with a bit of a gambling addiction." She
smiled, a little embarrassed. "Chase is helping me
pay off the debts."

Hannah looked over at Chase. "That's so kind,"
she said sincerely.

"It is," Anika said. "I keep telling him we'll be fine, but he insists. He should be spending that money on himself. He needs to get a horse."

Anika had been telling him that for years. Buy a horse and board it somewhere. Just a nice, riding horse that you can go and visit. The idea appealed to Chase, but it was more than he could afford right now. Horse boarding in their area was nearly as much as Anika paid for her monthly house payment. And there were the vet bills, hoof-trimming, and other expenses that came along with it.

Besides, he wasn't sure he would ever be able to love another horse. Not after Manny.

"He should," Hannah said. "Chase, when is the last time you've ridden?"

"Not since Manny," Anika chimed in.

It was true. Chase hadn't been on a horse since Manny, and he wasn't sure he wanted to ride again. He had too many bad memories tied in with it. His last ride had ended his career and life has he knew it. Maybe someday. Maybe if Hannah won the trials, and he started getting training jobs. Or maybe not. What if he *was* a has-been?

They visited for a while. Hannah kept looking over at him, and he saw her mind working. He wondered what she was thinking.

After Hannah left, he took Anika and Taylor into town to eat at Louie's. Then they walked down to the beach and let Taylor play in the surf.

"I like her," Anika said.

"Hannah?"

"Yeah."

Seagulls screamed overhead. His sister pulled her sweater closer around her from the chill of the evening air. "She's sweet. She's nothing like I thought she would be."

"She can surprise you," Chase said.

"And *you* like *her*," Anika said, elbowing him in the side.

"It's not like that."

"Oh, I think it is."

"She's my student," Chase said. "I've already been warned by her dad. Besides, now isn't the time. She has the trials in less than a week."

Anika nodded. "There will be time afterwards."

Afterwards. Chase wondered what his life would look like a week from now.

Anika drove back home the next day after lunch. It was Sunday, and she had an early shift at the restaurant on Monday morning, and Taylor had to get back to school.

Shortly after they left, Chase got a call from Hannah.

"Come out to the ring for a few minutes," she said. "I want to show you something."

"Show me what?"

"Just come."

"Sunday is our day off," Chase said.

"This isn't work, I promise."

Chase hung up. Curious, he pulled on his boots, grabbed his baseball cap, and headed to the arena.

Hannah was standing in the middle with Grace. The mare was tacked up with Hannah's dressage saddle and bridle. The arena was quiet. No one was out today, as most riders were resting up for the competition next week. Devon never came out on Sundays.

"What's up?" Chase said.

"Get on."

He looked at Grace, then back at Hannah. "What?"

"I thought you might like to ride her."

"Hannah," Chase said. "No. Not this close to the trials. We don't want to confuse her."

Hannah rolled her eyes. "You think Grace is that stupid?"

"No. I mean...that's not what I meant."

Hannah put her hands on her hips. "You're afraid."

"I am not afraid. Not of a horse," Chase said. Or was he? When was the last time he had ridden a horse other than Manny?

"Grace is gentle and wouldn't dream of hurting you," Hannah said.

"I'm not afraid of being hurt. Hannah, this is what I do. I'm a rider."

"Are you?" Her eyes were sparkling. She was teasing him.

He sighed. "I really don't think this is a good idea. What if she gets hurt?"

Hannah laughed. "It's not like you're going to barrel race with her."

She moved Grace over to the mounting block. "I've adjusted the stirrups to your length already, or what I think it is. Go ahead. Get on. You can just walk around a few times. That's all."

Chase looked longingly at the horse. He wanted to ride. He really wanted to.

"Please?" Hannah said. "For me?"

He looked at Hannah. She was doing that thing with her wide eyes and innocent look.

"Oh geez, Hannah, don't play me," he said, but he was laughing.

"Here," Hannah said. She handed him her riding helmet. "I don't have lice. I promise."

He strapped the helmet on. It was a little tight, but it would work. Then, before he could overthink it, he stepped up on the block and climbed on Grace.

The mare turned her head, sniffing at his boot. "Hey, girl," he said, patting her on the neck. "Hi there."

"She hasn't had anybody but me up on her in over four years," Hannah said. She was smiling. She seemed to really be enjoying this. "Let me adjust your stirrups; they still seem a little short." She played with the buckles a little until they were the right length.

Hannah stepped aside, and Chase gathered up the reins.

"Go ahead," Hannah said. "Ride."

Chase started walking around the outside of the arena in a counterclockwise direction. The familiar feel of the horse under him brought back so many memories. He relaxed into Grace's stride and felt the rocking motion of the horse. She had a smooth walk, an elongated step, and her mouth was responsive to his hands on the bit. She had been handled well.

"Can I see a trot?" Hannah asked.

Chase looked at her. "A trot?"

"Yeah. I want to see my horse move under saddle."

He gathered his reins and touched Grace lightly with his calves. She moved right into the trot. It amazed him how after all these years his muscle memory took over. He posted to the trot, rising with each stretch of Grace's outside leg. He did a few circles and figure eights, then asked Grace to extend her trot. As she elongated her stride, he posted higher. She was so smooth that he felt like he was flying. He concentrated on riding, and everything else disappeared.

He did a few more figure eights, then slowed Grace down. Soon, they were trotting in place. He asked for a canter, and, after a few turns, they did a few flying lead changes, a more advanced dressage move.

He forgot where he was. He was lost in the movement of the horse, the power underneath him. Whatever he asked for, Grace responded to. She was enjoying this as much as he was.

Finally, as Grace's breathing (and his) started to pick up, he remembered that he was on a multi-million dollar horse that was headed to the Olympic trials. He slowed her to a walk and gave her her head, letting her stretch her neck down as she cooled off.

He was smiling. He couldn't help it.

"Well, wasn't that fun?" Hannah said. "Look how happy you are!"

It was true. He hadn't felt this happy in years. He leaned forward and patted Grace on the neck.

He walked the mare around the arena a few times, then brought her into the middle and dismounted.

He handed Hannah the reins.

"You looked great out there," Hannah said.

Chase smiled again and took off the helmet, handing it to Hannah. "It felt good," he said. "Thank you."

She smiled at him. "You're welcome. Wasn't this a fun way to spend a Sunday? Now go home. It's your day off. I'm going to hose Grace off and have dinner with my dad."

Chase couldn't quit smiling. He nodded and watched as Hannah walked her horse back to the barn. He wondered if Hannah realized what a great gift she had just given him.

Maybe when he got back to Chicago, he'd try to figure out how to buy a horse after all.

Chapter Twenty-Seven

The trials were at Castleby Farms, a huge riding center near the southside of Chicago, not far from where Chase had told Hannah he lived. There were a variety of classes going on that weekend, with the dressage trials being only one part. There were also hunter-jumper classes and competition for three-day eventing. The best of the best would be there from around the country, competing against each other, some of them Olympic contenders.

Hannah was riding beside Chase in the huge truck that they were using to pull the horse trailer. Devon was following in another truck, pulling several of his pupils's horses. Chase and Hannah were alone.

She leaned forward and turned the radio to a local contemporary pop station. Then she opened her bottle of water and took a sip. She felt relaxed.

Chase seemed anything *but* relaxed. He fiddled with his hands on the steering wheel, played with the bill of his baseball cap, and munched on some nuts he had brought along.

"What's wrong with you?" Hannah asked. She felt playful today. It was just the two of them, with about seven hours of driving ahead of them. Her dad was driving up with Marion.

"Nothing's wrong," Chase said, and gave her what she knew was a fake smile.

"Sure there is. Talk to me."

"Okay. Well, there's going to be a lot of people there that I've been avoiding for years," he said. "There might be some backlash. You need to be prepared for that."

He was trying to act tough, but she knew there was a lot at stake here. He didn't want to let Hannah down. He didn't want to let *himself* down. And he was walking into a circus. She knew there would be people talking and journalists. That's why she had saved the article to read to him now.

Hannah glanced over at him.

"Did you see this month's *Dressage Gold* magazine?" she asked.

He shook his head.

"It came in this morning's mail." She pulled it out of her bag and flipped it open to the page she wanted. "It's about you."

"Me?" Chase looked horrified. He had tried to keep a low profile while training Hannah. It helped that they hadn't had to attend any shows in the short ten weeks they had been working together.

"The headline reads 'Wonder Kid Back in the Saddle?'"

Chase shook his head. "Is thirty still considered a kid? And I'm hardly back in the saddle."

"You were last weekend," Hannah said, smiling.

She remembered how good he had looked on Grace. His muscle memory had taken over, and he had ridden like a champion.

"The article says that you are trying to make a comeback in the sport, as a trainer," she said. "I'll read it to you.

"Former Olympic wonder kid Chase Livingston is back in the game this weekend as a trainer for Olympic potential Hannah Whitney."

She looked over at him and smiled. "That's me. The Olympic Potential." She was so happy she felt like she could burst.

Chase nodded.

"After embarrassing himself during the last games..." she skimmed over that part. He didn't need to hear that.

"Wait," Chase said. "Read it all."

Hannah sighed dramatically. "That part doesn't matter."

"I need to know what I'm up against."

Which was true. Know your enemy, her dad had always said.

"After embarrassing himself during the Olympics and letting his entire team down..." Hannah looked over at him. "Ouch."

"Keep reading."

"...Livingston went on to repeat his mistakes in several follow-up competitions. Finally, being stripped of his horse and his sponsorships, Livingston claimed to have seen an angel and knew that he was on the right path. That path, however, seemed to be a losing one. Livingston went into hiding for several years and hasn't been seen back in the dressage world until now.

"This weekend, as Whitney's last-minute trainer, the two will attempt to capture a place on the US Olympic team with

Sunday's dressage freestyle routine. They haven't been seen competing in public since Livingston came on board, so what they have planned will be a surprise to both judges and contenders.

"'Hannah is good at what she does,' says Fieldcrest Farm trainer Devon Miller. 'She can overcome most odds. I think she'll capture the win.'"

Hannah stopped reading and glanced over at Chase. "So I have to overcome odds?" she said.

"I'm the odds," Chase said. "You know he means me."

Hannah continued. *"Whitney has been through several trainers in the past few years. Her reputation as a difficult student precedes her. Pairing with Livingston may be the only option she has left. It remains to be seen if the two can overcome their troubles to tap into the talent they both obviously possess."*

The article ended there. "Wow. That wasn't the glowing story I had hoped for."

"What else did you expect?" Chase's voice was bitter.

"Hey, it's not just you. I have a bad reputation too."

After a moment, he smiled. "I guess winning will be the best revenge," he said. "We need to show them."

Hannah smiled. "You're right. You're absolutely right. I'm ready!"

They unloaded Grace and got her settled in her stall. Chase stuck close to Hannah, helping her bed the stall and making sure Grace had fresh water and hay. It was normally something the grooms would do, and several had come along in Devon's truck to help the

Fieldstone Farm entrants. But Hannah liked to care for her own horse. Chase admired that about her.

Marcus had supplied plenty of security, so they felt like they could leave and walk around.

Devon stopped them on their way out of the barn. "Hey Wuss, your crazy horse is here."

"Manny?"

Devon smiled. "Yep. He's over in Barn A. Looks like his owner put him in a class. Maybe you'd better go pray for him." Devon winked at Hannah, enjoying his own little joke. Then he brushed past them, bumping Chase on the shoulder.

"Jerk," Hannah mumbled under her breath.

"Manny's *here*," Chase said.

"Let's go see him!" Hannah pulled a map of the farm out of her pocket and unfolded it. "Here," she said, pointing. "Barn A is up this way."

As they approached the barn, Hannah saw a black horse in the arena out front. The rider was having a hard time with him. The horse was hopping, trying to unseat his rider. The man had steady hands and kept saying "Whoa, boy" but the horse was having none of it.

"That's him!" Chase's voice was excited. He jogged over to the railing.

"It seems he still doesn't like other riders," Hannah said.

They stood at the rail, watching. "He's putting too much leg pressure on him," Chase said. "That's the problem. Manny is sensitive to touch."

"Well, look who's here." Hannah turned to look at the man who had come up beside them. It was

Solomon Jr. She recognized Manny's owner from her clippings.

"Your rider is giving him too much leg," Chase said, keeping his voice neutral.

Solomon looked at the horse. "Yeah, well, too bad you're not still on him. I'm sure you have all the answers."

"I'd be happy to talk to your rider," Chase said.

"That isn't going to happen, Livingston. Stay away from my horse."

"I can help."

"You've helped enough. Do you know how long it took us to get another rider to stick on him? This is Debonair Man's debut. Stay out of it."

Hannah saw Chase dig his hands into the wooden fence rail.

Solomon watched the rider for another moment. "If I see you in this barn, Livingston, I'm going to call security."

Chase's jaw tightened. "Come on Hannah. We have work to do."

"I'm sorry," Hannah said as they walked away. "The rider was at least being patient with Manny. He's not being mean to him."

Chase nodded but said nothing.

Hannah's phone beeped, and she looked at it. "Dad wants us to join him and Marion for dinner."

"Sure."

"Are you okay?"

Chase nodded. "There's nothing I can do. I accepted that a long time ago. It's just hard to see him and not be able to...you know."

242

"Yeah," Hannah said. "I know." She thought about the leased horse she had lost with the last trainer.

She texted her dad back.

"I guess some of the grooms are going to join us," she said, reading his reply. "Devon is having dinner with the parents of one of his students, thank goodness."

They went to dinner, and no more was said about Manny. Chase seemed to enjoy himself, laughing and talking with her father. They retired to the hotel early because Hannah wanted to get to bed.

"I'll see you tomorrow," Chase said. He had walked her to her door.

"Okay." Hannah watched him for a moment. This was where the guy usually kissed the girl. But...what was she thinking? She was just lucky to have him here, working with her and Grace. She owed him her gratitude. "Thanks," she said.

"For what?"

"For getting me this far."

Chase smiled. "Now get some rest."

"Yes, trainer." She laughed and went inside, closing the door behind her. She leaned up against it for a moment, wondering if he was still standing outside. Then she sighed. She was here. Her horse was ready. And she had a friend. She realized that she was happy.

Hannah went to bed early. The next day would be a day to warm up, and then Sunday would come. She had to be at the top of her game.

"Are you ready?" Chase asked. They were in the warmup arena, while the shows were going on in another place. Castleby Farms was huge. But there were crowds around the arena already set to watch Hannah.

They had agreed not to do the routine until the show tomorrow. Instead, they were simply going to do warm up exercises to keep both Hannah and Grace supple.

"I'm ready," Hannah said. There were a few TV crews there. "Are *you* ready?"

Chase nodded. "Of course. I have the best horse and rider team here."

Hannah smiled. She rode Grace into the ring, and Chase followed. He gave instructions, and she and Grace performed well. When they finished, she could see the looks of disappointment on the faces of the people who had come to watch the former "wonder kid" make a fool of himself.

"We did good," Hannah said.

"We did," Chase said.

Afterwards, they walked back toward Barn A again to casually see if they could catch sight of Manny, but the horse was gone. Chase had missed Manny perform while he was working with Hannah.

"It's just as well," he told her. "It was hard to see him again after all these years."

Hannah only nodded. She didn't know what to say.

"Now get some rest," Chase said. "Tomorrow's your day."

Sunday dawned cool and crisp—one of those fall days that Hannah used to love as a child. It brought the promise of turning leaves and apple cider. As an adult, she wasn't as thrilled with the cooler weather. It had come to mean eventual snow, and that she'd have to move her riding to the indoor arena.

But it was perfect weather for today.

She breathed in the cool, morning air. It felt good to be alive. She had left the hotel early, before Chase, and was waiting for him in the barn at Grace's stall.

This was the day. *Her* day. The day she had dreamed about for so many years. Today, she and Grace would capture enough points to join the Olympic team, and she'd be on her way to a gold medal. She was sure of it.

She had never felt better about her routine. Chase had come up with something that was beautiful. She had watched the videos that Chase had recorded of her and Grace, and the beauty of Grace's movements had brought tears to her eyes. Before, Hans and her other trainers had always found fault. Fix this. Strengthen that. Don't forget this. But Chase had been so optimistic and encouraging that Hannah now felt she could do the routine blindfolded.

Blindfolded. She laughed out loud. She'd have to try that at home.

"Are you ready, Hannah?" It was Devon. She wouldn't let him ruin her mood.

"I sure am! How about Tiffany?"

"She's all set. She rides in an hour. I need to get over to her, but I thought I'd come by first and wish you good luck."

"Thanks!" Hannah said.

"Afterwards, we'll have to celebrate," Devon said. "I found a great restaurant. Maybe we can go out with your dad and split a bottle of something."

"You think I'll do well?" Hannah asked.

"I know you will. You have the talent. It doesn't matter who your trainer is."

She heard the cutting reference to Chase.

"Thanks. Good luck to your students as well." Hannah didn't want to argue with Devon now, of all times.

"Thank you." Devon nodded and left her.

Grace nuzzled Hannah, and she turned to pet the horse on her soft, velvety nose. Yesterday she had spent hours bathing Grace, polishing her hooves, and brushing out her long, black tail. She had wrapped each of Grace's white legs with ace bandages to keep them clean and shaved the whiskers on her muzzle.

"You're so pretty," Hannah said.

"Good morning!" It was Chase, coming in the barn. He had his chin up and his shoulders back. He seemed much more relaxed than he had yesterday. After their warm-up performance, people had left him alone, for the most part. Old friends were giving him the nod, and people who didn't know him had complimented him on his work. But he still had to prove himself. Hannah had to get this right; not just for herself, but for Chase.

"Hey," she said. They fist-bumped.

"You ready?"

"We are!"

"I saw your dad. He's parking his car."

The morning sped by with preparations. As the time drew near, Hannah dressed in the black and white outfit that she'd show in. She pinned her hair back in a bun so that it was neat and no tendrils hung down. She polished her boots one last time.

Then she and Chase tacked up Grace. She felt the familiar flutter of nerves in her stomach. Someone had once said that if she ever stopped feeling nervous before a competition, she would know it was time to quit. Nerves were there for a reason. They fueled her. She just didn't want them to get the best of her.

She took a slow, deep breath.

Grace was impatient and banged the front of her hoof on her stall door for attention.

"She knows what's up," Chase said.

"She certainly does," Hannah said. "She loves the crowds. She loves to perform. Wait until you see her."

They saddled the horse.

"There's my girl!" Marcus said, striding into the barn. He hugged Hannah and wished her luck. Then he shook Chase's hand.

"I never doubted you," Marcus said to Chase.

"Thank you, sir," Chase said.

Her dad hadn't seen the routine yet. They had made him wait for the trials. Hannah had wanted him to be surprised.

"I'm going to go sit down," he said. "I have a reserved seat."

"He brought Marion," Hannah told Chase after he left.

"Are you okay with that?"

"Yeah. Actually, it was my idea."

Chase smiled. "I'm sure that made his day."

They walked Grace to the warmup arena, and again, Hannah went through only parts of the routine

247

but without music. She didn't want to show anybody ahead of time. She asked Grace to bend her neck to the right and then to the left, stretching out her muscles. Her horse was responsive. As usual, she felt her nerves calm just from being on her horse.

"You've got about fifteen minutes," Chase said, leading Grace back into the barn. "Let's wait in her stall."

"Sure."

She took the reins from Chase and put Grace in her stall. The horse pawed the ground, knowing what was coming. Her hay and water had been removed, so she wouldn't eat or drink right before her performance.

Hannah had watched a few performances earlier in the day and could hear the music to another rider's freestyle routine now.

"I want to look at the arena one last time before I get on Grace," she said.

"Sure thing. I've got your horse," Chase said.

Hannah walked down the long aisleway of the pristine barn. On both sides of her, people were buttoning up riding jackets, pulling on boots, and polishing tack. She loved the energy that surrounded her on show day.

She walked over to the arena and stood beside the entrance. The horse performing now was a bay thoroughbred, and he was dancing to a Bach concerto. He was beautiful. Hannah watched him for a moment, saw his rider pause, reconsider, and then move forward. That was a point off. The judges shouldn't be able to see any cues from the rider.

She scanned the crowd and saw her dad and Marion sitting in the front row, near the middle. Only the best seats for Marcus Whitney. She smiled at that. Marion had on a broad-brimmed hat, looking like she was ready for the Kentucky Derby. She was a fun woman. Very light-hearted. Maybe Hannah should try to get to know her better.

Then she saw somebody waving from far above, near the top of the bleachers. She stared hard at the woman. The woman was waving at *her*.

She blinked and swallowed. She felt her stomach drop to her feet, and a cold fear sneaking up her spine. That wasn't just any woman.

That was her mom.

Chapter Twenty-Eight

"Chase!" Hannah said, running down the aisleway. "Chase, I need to talk to you."

"What?" He said as Hannah opened Grace's stall door and nearly pushed him over.

"Stay inside." She slid the door closed.

"Hannah is everything okay?"

"Stay inside the stall."

Chase was standing beside Grace, holding the reins in his hands. Hannah was wide-eyed and breathing hard.

"She's here. My mom is here," Hannah whispered.

"Your mom?"

"She came to see me perform. I was so stupid. The other day, at lunch, I told her that she hurt me because she had never seen me perform. I spent years...*years*...looking up in the stands, imaging she'd show up some day. I told her that. I always wanted her to show up. But not now!"

"Hannah, you need to take a deep breath."

"I can't handle this, Chase. You need to go and make her leave. *Make her leave!*"

Chase looked at his watch. "Hannah, you are on in seven minutes. We don't have time. We should actually be in the warm-up area now."

"I can't do this," Hannah said. She looked truly frightened. "Why would she show up *today?* My dad is here. He's going to see her and know. He'll know I didn't tell him about her, and they will meet and talk, and Marion is here, and—"

"Hannah, slow down," Chase said. He took both hands and put them on each side of Hannah's face. He could feel the hot flush in her cheeks. Her chest was heaving. Her hands were shaking. She met his eyes.

"Make her leave!" Hannah said. "She had no right to come now. Not now. This is too big of a day. I can't handle this."

"Breathe," Chase said.

"Chase—" Her eyes were starting to tear up.

"Hannah!" He made his voice loud and firm. She jumped. My gosh, she was a nervous wreck. "Listen to me. This is your day. You have to focus. Grace can't perform if you're a wreck. She'll pick up on your fear. You need to focus. Take a deep breath."

Hannah stopped talking and took in a deep breath. "I'm scared."

"What are you scared of?"

"She's watching me."

"So? You're good. You'll make her proud."

"No. I was never good enough. I was never..." Hannah gulped back a sob.

Chase let go of her face and pulled her forward into a hug. "You have to let this go," he said into her ear. "Later, in just twenty minutes, you'll be finished. Then you can think about your mom. But not now.

251

Not here. Do this for Grace. Do this for you. Hannah, you've worked too hard to fall apart now."

He held her tight until he felt her breathing slow. "We have to go. If you're late, they will disqualify you." He pushed her away from him gently, until she was at arm's length, then he let go of her shoulders. She was looking at him with big eyes, but they weren't so frightened now.

He saw her lift her chin. "I can do this," she said.

"You certainly can," Chase said.

Hannah nodded. "I need to focus."

"Don't be like me," Chase said. "Don't throw it all away because one person messes up your day."

He led Grace out of her stall and down the aisleway. By the time they got outside, Hannah's breathing was more normal. He boosted her up.

"You've got this," he said. He put a hand on her knee, and she looked down at him.

"I'm going to be at the end of the arena," he said. "If you need me, just look there. Don't look anywhere else. Just there. But only if you need me. Otherwise, it's just you and Grace. The rest of the world doesn't exist for those five minutes. Okay?"

Hannah nodded. "Okay."

"Your music is you, Hannah. I want to see you be more."

She nodded and picked up her reins. Her hands were still shaking.

"Go get 'em." Chase gave her a soft fist bump on her knee. The judges called her number. She looked at Chase one last time, then turned Grace and rode toward the ring, where she stopped and waited for her music to begin.

The crowd was silent. There was no talking allowed during performances in the dressage ring. The judges needed to be able to hear if the rider gave the horse verbal cues.

As the first bars of her song started playing, Grace's ears pricked forward. She knew what was what coming. Then, right on cue, the judges nodded, and Hannah rode her horse into the ring.

Chase stood there with a death grip on the rails of the arena. As her trainer, he was allowed into the "inner circle," as it was called, where he could see her every move. He glanced twice at the judges and saw them watching Hannah, but other than that, he kept his eyes on his student.

She was flawless.

As Hannah had said, Grace was born to perform. The horse perked right up, and he could tell from her forward ears, swishing tail, and the way she held herself that she knew she was performing. And she loved it.

Hannah came to the most difficult moves. She went through them with the grace of an eagle in flight. Their transitions and Grace's effortless trot were so smooth that it looked like they were indeed flying. The music was uplifting and touching, and he knew that the audience would be moved.

Near the end, she was to perform the pirouette. She slowed, and he saw Grace's muscles prepare. The horse knew what was coming. Hannah had no room for faults. They hadn't left time for a joker line. There was no chance at the end to repeat the move if they failed. Hannah glanced toward the end of the arena and briefly met Chase's eyes. He smiled at her and gave her a slight nod. Then, perfectly, Grace executed the turn on her haunches, her front feet up in the air.

Hannah cued her into a forward canter, circled once, and came into the center. They stopped. As the music ended, Hannah dropped her chin in a nodding salute to the judges, and Grace dropped her knee into a bow.

And then it was over.

Five minutes of the most beautiful performance Chase had ever seen. And he had seen a lot.

"Wow!" he said, clapping his hands as the crowd erupted. He saw several people in the audience wiping tears from their eyes. The judges were smiling and talking to each other as they made marks on their cards.

Hannah rode Grace out of the ring, and Chase went to meet them. Hannah leaned forward and wrapped her arms around Grace's neck, then she straightened up as Chase took her reins.

"We did it," she said, tears now streaming down her face. "We did it!"

"You sure did," Chase said. He couldn't stop smiling. He led Grace over to the railing, where they stood to wait for the numbers.

The sport was rated on a scale of 1–10, and each judge would hold up a card. When competition was this stiff, riders had to hope for high numbers, although not many tens were given. If the score was questionable, around an 8.9 or a 9.4, Hannah could still win, but not necessarily be considered for the

Olympic team. If she scored higher than that, there would be no way they'd turn her down, even if Devon voted against her.

Hannah took in a deep breath.

"I think you got it," Chase whispered.

"I hope so!"

After a few minutes that seemed like an eternity, the judges stood.

"Please hold up your numbers," said the announcer.

One by one, each of the five judges held up their numbers. The first one awarded Hannah a ten. The second one did also. So did the third.

One by one, the other judges held up their score cards. They were all tens. As the last judge turned over her card with a smile, showing a perfect ten, Hannah erupted in a squeal, startling Grace. She jumped off her horse and flung herself at Chase, throwing her arms around him.

"Thank you, thank you, thank you!" Hannah said. He picked her up and twirled her around, laughing. "We did it!" Hannah said. "We did it! I couldn't have done it without you!"

Grace bumped them, and Chase set Hannah down and petted the horse. "We love you too," Chase said. "Extra carrots for you tonight!"

Hannah was laughing and crying at the same time. "I'm so happy!" she said. "I can't believe this!"

As the crowd quieted down for the next rider, Chase led Grace away, with Hannah practically dancing beside them. Outside the arena area, there were several TV crews and journalists. They were snapping photos of Chase, Hannah, and her horse.

"So you're heading to the Olympics!" said one young woman reporter.

"I sure hope so!" Hannah said.

"With a score like that, you don't need to hope!" said another reporter.

"How did you do it? What would you say was the move that sealed the deal for you and Amazing Grace? Was it that pirouette at the end?"

Hannah turned to the crowd. "The best move we made that got us to this point," she said, "was hiring Chase Livingston as our trainer. He's the most talented coach I know. We couldn't have done it without him."

Chase smiled as the attention turned to him. "This isn't my moment," he said, nodding back to Hannah. "It's hers. I can talk to you all later."

He watched as more people asked Hannah questions, and the attention shifted back to her. He stood there quietly, holding on to Grace, and felt a deep sense of joy enveloping him. It was from winning, yes, but it was also because he was back in the game he loved.

And yes, he had to admit, with a *woman* he loved.

Hannah's smile lit up the area. Finally, after answering a lot of questions, she told the reporters that she had to go and cool her horse off and give her some extra treats.

When she and Chase were alone in the barn, she turned to him. "Thank you," she said again. "Thank you so much." She pulled him into another hug. "I'm so grateful."

Then she stepped back and met his eyes. Her hands were on his shoulders. "Chase, there's something I want to tell you..." He felt his body tingle as her lips parted slightly. He could smell her shampoo and the leather on her gloves. He wanted to hold her, to pull her into a kiss. She moved forward, her face coming closer to his. "I wanted to tell you that—"

"Congratulations, honey!" It was Marcus. His voice boomed down the barn aisle. Following him were Marion and Devon, and several barn attendants. They all came rushing forward to congratulate Hannah.

Had she been about to kiss him? Chase sighed inwardly and tuned to face the crowd of friends who had arrived. "Thank you everybody!" Hannah said. "Daddy, I'm so glad you're here!"

Then her eyes moved beyond him to someone else. A woman was walking down the aisleway, her blonde hair pulled up into a short bun. She looked a lot like Hannah, only older.

Hannah froze, and Chase saw her face turn pale, and then red.

"What?" Marcus said, seeing his daughter's sudden change. "What is it?

"It's..." Hannah said. She swallowed, and just as her dad turned around to look, she said, "It's Mom, Daddy. She's here."

"What?" Marcus said, and Chase heard him exclaim, "*Eva?*"

"Please not now," Hannah said under her breath. "Please Mom, don't ruin this for me."

Eva was walking down the aisleway toward them, waving, as if she belonged there, as if she hadn't disappeared for the past fifteen years.

"Eva?" Marcus said again, and his voice sounded weak.

Hannah grabbed Chase's arm. "Do something," she said. He looked at her, and her eyes were pleading.

"Here." He handed her Grace's reins and stepped out of the stall.

"Hannah, did you know about this?" Marcus said, turning back to look at Hannah. Chase grasped his shoulder tightly and looked him in the eye. "Your daughter needs you now, Marcus," he said. "I'll handle Eva."

"But what...I don't understand." The poor man looked dumbfounded. He had turned very white.

"Just be with Hannah. Congratulate her. She needs you." Chase let go of Marcus and walked quickly in Eva's direction. When he reached her, he put his arm around her shoulders and gently turned her around.

"I'm Hannah's trainer," he said, "and now is simply not a good time to meet the family."

"But she's my daughter," Eva started to protest.

"Then if you love her, leave her alone right now," Chase said. "There will be time to talk later."

"I don't get it," Eva said.

"Let me explain."

He steered her out of the barn and away from Hannah and her father. It was the least he could do. This was Hannah's moment, and he wasn't going to let anyone ruin it. Not even her long lost mother.

Chapter Twenty-Nine

"Hannah?" Marcus said. He had turned from pale to a deep shade of red. "I need to speak with you. Alone." He glanced at the others, and they scattered. Marion gave him a quick peck on the cheek and left.

Hannah stepped out of the stall.

"Did you know she was coming?'

"No," Hannah said. "I told her not to show up anymore." She knew it was too late now, she'd have to tell her dad she had visited with her mom. Twice.

"Anymore?"

"Dad, she came to visit about two weeks ago and said she wanted to be part of my life."

"I don't understand," her dad said. He put his hand on his chest.

"Dad? Are you okay?"

"I think I should sit down."

Hannah saw Devon standing a little bit away from them.

"Devon! Can you finish Grace for me?

Devon nodded and walked toward them. Once he was in Grace's stall, Hannah took her dad's elbow and walked him toward the snack area she had seen at the end of the barn. They went in and sat down at a table.

"She's back?" her dad asked.

"She came back a few weeks ago. She surprised me, and we did a brief luncheon at Louie's. She wants to be back in my life. I told her now wasn't a good time. I guess she didn't listen."

"Eva's back," her dad said. She had never seen him like this. He rubbed his chest again.

"Are you okay?" Hannah asked again.

"Yes," he said. He took a few deep breaths, and she saw him gathering his thoughts. Then he sat up a little straighter, pulling his shoulders back.

"I could use some water," he said.

There were cold bottles of water in a nearby cooler. She wasn't sure who they belonged to, but she gave one to her dad. He opened it and took a long drink. His face started to return to its normal color.

"When did you first see her?"

Here it goes, Hannah thought. She started with the first time Eva had visited, and then told him about their luncheon at Louie's.

"I hoped she'd go away and never come back," Hannah said.

"Why *is* she back?"

Hannah shrugged. "Just to see me, I guess."

"I see," her dad nodded. He looked more like the man she knew now that the initial shock was over. He was starting to take charge, to figure out how he would handle this, and what needed to be done.

"Why didn't you tell me?"

"I don't know," Hannah said. She was starting to feel chilly. She had worked up a sweat in the show ring, and her clothes were damp. She really wanted to change. Or maybe just find a heavier jacket.

She thought again about the high scores she and Grace had been given. Devon would be heading over to vote with the committee in about an hour, after all the riders were through. Hannah checked an app on her phone that she had been given to keep track of the event. So far, she was still the top rider in her division.

"I think you do know," her dad said.

She looked across the little table at him. He had been so happy just a few minutes ago. Now his face looked tired again, worn and drawn.

"I was afraid I'd lose you," Hannah said.

"*Lose* me?"

"Yes," she said. She had her riding gloves in her hand, and she played with the finger of one. She couldn't look at him. "I just got you, Dad. After all these years, you've finally been paying attention to me. I know that sounds childish, but I've missed you. All my life, I've missed you, and then a year ago when you had that conversion, or whatever you call it, you finally saw me. I love our dinners together. I love that you remembered my birthday and baked a cake for me all by yourself last year, even though it was lopsided." She laughed at the memory. "I loved that cake. It was my favorite cake of all of them. Because *you* made it."

Her dad smiled. "I love you, Hannah," he said. "I know I messed up, and I can never fix your childhood, but I'm trying to be there for you now."

"You're doing a fantastic job, Dad."

"If it isn't too late."

"It's not too late," Hannah said. She reached across the table and took his hand. She squeezed it. It felt strange to hold her Dad's hand. He had never been a physical man, and physical affection was something that didn't happen in their house. But it felt right now.

"I love you, and I was afraid that if Mom came back in the picture, I'd lose you."

"Oh, Hannah," her dad said. He took her hand in his and patted it. "You'll never lose me. Not again. I plan to be here for you as long as the Lord gives me life."

Hannah felt tears come to her eyes.

"I was so proud of you today," her dad said. "You and Grace looked beautiful out there. I'm just sorry I missed so many years. I should have been here cheering you on."

They were silent for a moment. Hannah thought about Eva, waving from the stands, running down the barn aisleway to congratulate her.

"Maybe that's how Mom feels," she said quietly.

She looked up at her dad. He patted her hand. "Maybe it is," he said.

There was a slight knock on the door frame of the little break room. Hannah looked up. It was Devon.

"Grace is all set," he said. "I've got to go vote. I'll see you in the winner's circle." He winked at her.

Hannah felt a surge of joy rise through her. For now, at least, she'd push her mom aside and enjoy this moment. This was *her* moment. As Chase said, it didn't matter what Devon thought of her now. He'd never be able to keep her off the Olympic team with the scores she had received in her routine. She was in. She knew she was.

"I made it," she said to her dad. "I really made it."

He nodded, smiling. When he was truly happy, the smile traveled across his whole face, filling him with joy. She loved that look.

"I can't believe it!" Hannah stood and came around the table. She leaned down and hugged her dad. "Thank you, Daddy. Thank you for all the years you have supported me with horses. I know I haven't said it much, but I really appreciate it. I appreciate you."

She hugged him hard.

"Hey." It was Chase. "I'm back. Eva's on her way home. She apologizes for shocking everybody. She said she was so excited about seeing Hannah's show that she didn't think of the consequences of showing up unannounced. She'll give you a call tomorrow, if that's okay."

"Thank you, son," Marcus said. Then he turned to his daughter. "Hannah, here's the man you should thank."

"She already thanked me," Chase said. "And I want to thank the both of you. For this chance."

Marcus stood. "Let's get everybody together before the announcement. Devon says they'll name the team members shortly. Then we'll all go out to dinner. My treat."

Hannah felt light as air. She practically skipped out of the room.

"You look cold," Chase said and draped his jacket over her shoulders. She hugged it to her.

As she waited for her win to be announced, she heard her dad and Chase talking about horses and her show. There they were, the two men she loved most in all the world.

Love. As she said the words in her head, she knew it was true. She loved Chase Livingston. A part of her always had. But now, here he was, here with her. She'd ask her dad to hire him permanently to take her through the Olympics. And maybe, just maybe, Chase would agree and move into their little guesthouse. She couldn't be more thrilled.

The announcement came while Hannah was standing in the ring, holding her first place blue ribbon. First, they had named the winners in her division. Then, they would announce the members who would be joining the United States Dressage Team for the upcoming Olympics.

The sun was low in the sky, and the evening lights were coming on. She still had Chase's jacket on, and it felt good against the chill in the air. She listened as they played the National Anthem, as her flag flew up high, because she had beaten the Germans, the French, and the Canadians who had come to Castleby to compete. They, too, would be using this show to pick the members for their own dressage teams.

She looked around the edge of the arena, searching for Chase. She found him, standing by her dad. Their eyes met. "I'm proud of you," he mouthed. She smiled. She was looking at him when her name was announced, when she heard the words that she had waited her whole life to hear.

"Joining next year's Olympic Dressage Team is Hannah Whitney of St. Ives, Michigan."

The crowd cheered. Chase had a huge smile, and she knew he wasn't just smiling because he, too, had accomplished a dream. He was smiling for her, because that was the kind of man he was.

Dinner was at Venturo's Italian restaurant. Marion, Chase, Devon, and a few staff form Fieldcrest joined them. Hannah sat by Chase. She couldn't stop smiling. She had never been happier.

"I still can't believe it," she said to him.

"But you were always so sure you were going to the Olympics," he said.

"I was never as sure as I acted."

The waiter brought out drinks, along with salad and rolls. Hannah's dad stood and raised his glass. "I'd like to toast my favorite daughter," he said.

"Dad, I'm your only daughter," Hannah laughed.

"She's always been a champion in my eyes," Marcus said. "Congratulations, honey."

Everybody shouted "here, here!" and took a sip of their drink.

"And I'd like to toast her trainer," her dad said. He raised his glass in Chase's direction. "For a job well done, and if you're willing, I'd like to hire you to take my daughter on to the Olympics."

Hannah looked at Chase, and he had a huge smile on his face.

"I'd love to, sir," he said. Everybody cheered. Hannah glanced at Devon and saw a glint in his eyes that she didn't like. Well, she didn't need him anymore. She was on the team.

She reached under the table, grabbed Chase's hand, and gave it a squeeze. He squeezed it back. Life couldn't get any better.

Chapter Thirty

They came back home Monday morning. Chase kept glancing over at Hannah. She was smiling and couldn't seem to stop.

"Thank you," she said, for what must have been the hundredth time. "Did you see how Grace perked up when I asked her for that extended trot? And she knew she had the pirouette down. She *knew!*"

For the past several hours, Hannah kept reliving every moment in the ring. Her mom was never mentioned. Chase decided to let it go. Hannah would tell him if Eva tried to contact her. Or maybe she wouldn't. Either way, Hannah was happy, and that made him feel good.

He thought about the long weeks—months actually—of getting her though the winter, training, and preparing for next summer's Olympics. He was thrilled that he was "back" in his sport, that Marcus Whitney was giving him this second chance. They had talked, and Marcus wanted him to stay in the guesthouse for the foreseeable future. Chase would tell his sister, and make arrangements to go back to Chicago and pack up his things. His lease was almost up on his apartment, so now was a great time to move. It was all coming together.

But he had other reasons to feel this happy. He was in love with Hannah Whitney. It had been growing in his heart for weeks now, but he knew it for sure that moment she was in the ring and she had looked for him. That last few seconds of her ride, she had sought him out. And then again, when her name was announced for the team, she had met his eyes. She had wanted to share the moment with him. And he knew then that loved her.

He hadn't acted on it yet, but he was pretty sure she felt the same way. Hadn't she been about to kiss him when her dad had interrupted them in the stall right after her ride? Or was that just the excitement of the win, pumping them both up?

She had been looking at him like that for a while now.

But he was her *trainer.* He remembered Marcus's firm words about keeping their relationship strictly to business.

Chase sighed. They'd cross that bridge when they came to it.

"Heavy sigh?" Hannah said.

"Just thinking," he said. "I have a lot to do. I need to pack my things and get ready to move here."

Hannah smiled again. "I'm so happy you agreed to stay on as my trainer."

"Just ten weeks ago, you were trying to get rid of me. You fired me at least twice that I can remember."

"I was a different woman then," she said, teasing him.

When they arrived back to the farm, they unloaded the horses and settled Grace in her stall.

"I want to go check on Pussy Willow," Hannah said. "He hates when I leave him."

"Sure," Chase said. "Are we going to take tomorrow off then?"

"What? No way!" Hannah said. "We need to get started!"

Chase laughed and shook his head. "Go and get some rest then."

Hannah ran off to the house like an excited child.

Chase was leaving the barn when Devon stepped out of the tack room in front of him.

"Stay away from her," Devon said. "Don't mess with what doesn't belong to you."

The drive home with the horses had been long, and Chase was tired. He didn't want to deal with this right now.

"She's not mine," Chase said. "Nor is she yours. You need to let Hannah choose her own way."

"I should be her trainer," Devon growled. "Among other things."

"But you're not," Chase said. He'd had it with this man. Chase was tired of everybody always talking down to him. Hadn't he proved himself? Did he really need to put up with this?

But it wasn't his place to tell Devon to take a hike. He'd leave that pleasure for Hannah.

"I want you gone," Devon said. "Tomorrow, you need to tell Marcus you changed your mind, that you want to go home, that your sister needs you. You won't train Hannah anymore."

Chase snorted. "Or what?"

"Or I'll get rid of you my own way."

"Is that a threat?" Chase said.

"It is indeed."

The two men stood and looked at each other for a moment.

"I know exactly how to get rid of someone like you," Devon said. "You have no right to waltz in here and take what's mine."

Chase laughed. "Devon, none of this is yours. It all belongs to Marcus. Including his daughter!"

Devon laughed. "That's what you think. I have history with Hannah." He turned to walk away, then stopped and looked over his shoulder. "We'll see who wins."

Chase watched him walk out of the barn. "I wasn't aware it was a contest!" he called out after Devon.

Chase ran his hands through his hair. It had been a long day, and all he wanted to do was go home, take a long, hot shower, and fix himself a nice meal. Maybe he'd watch TV while he ate.

By the time he sat down to dinner, he had almost forgotten Devon's threat.

Lord, he prayed. *Give me wisdom. Help me to live my life for You. And please protect Hannah.*

He'd leave it in the Lord's hands.

Chase and Hannah started working first thing Tuesday morning. She was full of energy, and Grace seemed to be enjoying her workout as well. The morning went well, then Chase proposed something different for their evening lesson.

"Take her on a trail ride," he said.

"A trail ride?" Hannah looked confused. She was astride her horse, all ready to start working.

"Yeah. Don't you sometimes ride her down by the pond? That's where you were the day I met you."

Hannah grinned. "I'm not supposed to. She's too expensive."

"She'll be fine. She needs a day off. Not everything you do should be goal oriented. Take her out. Have some fun with her."

Hannah thought for a moment. "We have another horse. His name is Percy, and Dad bought him last year when he thought he might learn to ride. He never did, so one of our staff exercises him. He's not a show horse anymore, he's retired. But he's a great ride. Why don't you join us?"

"Me?"

Hannah laughed. "Of course. You need to have some fun too!"

Chase agreed, and Hannah texted one of the stable hands to ready the horse. Ten minutes later, the stable hand led a bay gelding out to the arena.

"Here you go, Mr. Livingston."

"Thank you." Chase mounted the horse, and the two of them started down the winding path toward the pond.

The ride was beautiful. They saw a family of sandhill cranes, the two babies almost as big as their parents now. A flock of birds covered one of the pastures. They looked like starlings, gathering for fall.

A few leaves had fallen, and the horses' hooves crunched them as they walked.

It felt good to be back on a horse. Chase would definitely have to buy himself a horse soon. As if reading his thoughts, Hannah spoke up.

"You can ride Percy any time you want."

"Shouldn't I ask your dad?"

"No. He won't care. He leaves me in charge of the horses."

When they returned back to the barns, the sun was setting. Marcus was standing in the circle drive, his hands on his hips. He had his car with him.

"Hannah, I need for you to come to the house," he said.

"What's wrong?"

"Your mom is here. She wants to talk to both of us together."

"Dad..."

"Hannah, don't argue with me. Let's do this. Let's get it out of the way. Give Chase your horse and come on."

Chase saw her face fall. "It'll be okay, he said. "I'll take care of Grace."

They dismounted, and Hannah handed Grace's reins to Chase. "Can you handle both horses?" she asked. It was late and the stable help had gone home.

"I'll be fine," Chase said. "They're both well behaved."

"Thanks." Hannah got in the car with her dad, and he drove them the short distance up to the house. Chase turned to take both horses into the barn, praying for Hannah and Marcus while he worked.

Chapter Thirty-One

Eva was sitting on the sofa in the living room. She had a cup of tea in her hand. She was dressed casually, in jeans and a green sweater. Again, Hannah saw how pretty she was under the worry lines.

"Hannah, I'm so proud of you!" Eva said, the moment she saw her.

Hannah hung behind Marcus, in the doorway. She nodded.

"Eva and I have been talking," Marcus said. "She has some things she needs to say to you. Then we have to figure out how to move forward. She's asking us for forgiveness."

"And you've forgiven her?" Hannah said. Her voice sounded harsh. She cleared her throat.

"I'm willing to try," Marcus said. "She wants a chance to explain."

"I don't want to hear it," Hannah said.

"I think you do."

Marcus sat down in a wing-back chair, across from where Eva was sitting. Hannah remained standing by the doorway to the living room.

"Hannah, won't you come and sit down?" Eva asked. She nodded to another wing-back chair next to Marcus.

"I'm fine standing," Hannah said. She crossed her arms over her chest.

Eva took a sip of her tea. "I wasn't in my right mind when I left," she said. "I was lonely and had been for a long time. Your dad"—she briefly looked at Marcus, then returned her gaze to Hannah—"your dad was never home. I saw him about once a week for dinner, and you and I always had to go to events by ourselves. You remember the Thanksgiving dinners, and even that Christmas morning, that he worked? He was always on the phone, or in his car or his plane, going off somewhere. Anyway, I was lonely. And I got depressed. One morning I got up after a sleepless night. Packing your lunch, making your breakfast, sending you to school, and then facing another day alone seemed like too much. I just couldn't do it anymore. So I wrote your dad a note. At first I thought I'd just go away for a couple of days, maybe a week."

"You didn't take anything with you."

"Only my purse," Eva said. "Like I told you, I wasn't thinking clearly. I was exhausted and depressed. So I started driving and the next thing I knew I was in California. It felt good to be out on my own. I drew enough money out of our savings to support me until I could find a job, and I changed my name."

"That's why dad couldn't find you."

Eva's eyes shot briefly to Marcus's, and then she looked away, but Hannah caught it.

"What?" Hannah faced her father. "You couldn't find her. That's what you told me."

Marcus cleared his throat. "I found her once," he said. "At the beginning. I begged her to come home."

"You told me you couldn't find her. You told me you had no idea where she went."

"Hannah, she was drawing money out of our account. Of course I tracked her down." Marcus sounded angry. Hannah wondered what he and Eva had been talking about while she was out for her ride.

"Why didn't you tell me?" Hannah asked. She remembered wondering if her mom was even alive.

"Because she didn't want to come home," Marcus said. "Even for you. I was trying to protect you. I figured the less you knew, the better. You were only eight years old."

So he had lied to her.

"Hannah, I loved you, you have to believe that," Eva said. "I know I messed up. I regretted it almost immediately. But I couldn't come home. The longer I stayed away, the more ashamed I was. I changed my name and decided to start over."

"Start over?"

Eva nodded. She glanced at Marcus again.

"She has a family in Grand Rapids. Her husband has two children from a previous marriage. One of them has a baby. Your mom is a grandma."

Hannah suddenly felt the room tilt. She leaned back against the wall. Her heart was hammering in her chest, and she tried breathing deeply to steady it. For a moment, she was on Grace, with Chase's voice in her head. *Breathe, Hannah. Focus.*

When she felt like she could stand without falling, she opened her eyes again.

"You have other kids," Hannah said.

Eva nodded. "Step-kids."

Hannah swallowed. "How long have you been married?"

Eva set her teacup down on the coffee table. Hannah wanted to tell her to put it on a coaster or she'd wreck the wood.

"Twelve years."

Hannah's head jerked up. *"Twelve years?"*

Eva nodded.

"So you've raised someone else's kids?"

Eva looked down at her hands, folded in her lap. "He's a good man," she said. "He's very caring and attentive, and we've been happy."

"You've been happy," Hannah said, her voice flat. She looked at her father. "She has been happy, Dad. Did you hear that?"

Marcus leaned back in his chair. "Yes, I did." He was watching Hannah intently. "Are you okay?"

Hannah laughed, but there was no humor in it. "No. I'm not okay at all. I want her to leave." She choked on the last word. She felt like her heart was going to burst. All these years she had been yearning for her mother, her mother had been living another life, giving attention to other kids.

Her dad rose and came toward her, but she took a step back. He stopped.

"You need to realize that a lot of this is my fault," he said. "I was never a good husband to her. I didn't give her the support she needed, and I expected her to not only raise you alone, but to take care of that big house we were living in and to attend luncheons and business dinners with me, supporting me. But I did nothing to support *her*. In ten years of marriage,

I did nothing for her, Hannah. I didn't give her any part of me."

"You gave her money," Hannah said. "That's more than she apparently has now." She knew it was a cheap shot, but she didn't care. She was hurting.

Eva self-consciously ran her hand over the front of her sweater. "It's true. We don't have much. Barry is a teacher. I do some interior design work for a small company in my hometown."

Her hometown. She had a hometown.

"We don't make much, but we're happy," Eva said. "I've never quit thinking about you, Hannah. I just had to see you. I was hoping that now that you're an adult, you can find it in your heart to forgive me. We can start over. I want to be part of your life. I want to be there when you get married and when you have children. I want to be at your horse shows. I am asking, no I am *begging*, for you to try to forgive me. Just give me a chance. Please."

Hannah shook her head.

"Get out," she said. "Get out of our house. You don't belong here."

Marcus put his arms out, as if to hug her. "Hannah."

"No," Hannah said. She marched over to the front door and swung it wide open. "Get out."

Eva glanced at Marcus, and he nodded slightly. She stood, picked up her purse, and walked to the front door. Before she left, she turned to Hannah. "I love you, Pussy Willow," she said.

Suddenly Hannah remembered. Pussy Willow. Her mom had nicknamed her that from the book. The book was about a little gray cat who couldn't find a home. Then one day, he found the perfect place to live, with a little girl who had loved him more than all the world. When Hannah got her cat a few years ago, she had named him Pussy Willow, thinking of the little girl in the book.

"You've found a home with someone who loves you more than all the world," she had said to him.

But it wasn't the cat her mom had been talking about back then. It was Hannah. She remembered her mom's words to her every night after they read the book. "Hannah, you're my Pussy Willow. You've found a home with someone who loves you more than all the world. Your momma." And then Eva would pull the covers up around her and kiss her goodnight.

Hannah felt a lump forming in her throat. She was about to cry, and there was no way Eva would be there to see it.

"Get out," she said again, this time through gritted teeth.

Eva nodded and stepped outside. Hannah slammed the door behind her.

"Hannah," her dad said.

"I don't want to hear it," Hannah said. "Good night." She ran up the stairs without kissing her father. She slammed her bedroom door and buried her face in her pillow, where she cried for a very long time.

Hannah couldn't sleep. Her dad had never been one to pursue people when they were hurting, so she hadn't expected him to come and knock on her door to try to make her feel better. Nor had she wanted to.

She had put her pajamas on, climbed into bed, and had been laying there for six hours, thinking. It was now 2 a.m.

She turned over and adjusted her pillow for the thousandth time. She should get up and do something. Maybe read a book. But she kept thinking about Eva having kids and wondering what their lives had been like.

Had Eva attended their games? Had she made them cupcakes to take to school on their birthdays? Had she been there when they had fevers, or did they too have to rely on a nanny to take care of them?

Not a nanny. Eva wasn't rich.

But maybe grandparents. Did these kids have grandparents? Maybe Eva's husband had parents who doted on them. She imagined Eva and her husband going out to dinner, leaving the kids with their grandparents for the evening. They got special snacks and lots of hugs and did whatever grandparents did with their kids. She had no idea what that was. She had never experienced it. Her dad's parents hadn't been around.

She sat up. There was no reason to lay here and imagine what could have been.

She really wanted to call Chase. He'd know what to say. But it sounded pathetic to say, "Mom never loved me. What do I do now?"

He'd be asleep, dreaming good dreams. They'd had a good day. She didn't want to ruin it for him.

She turned on her phone just to see if maybe he had texted her while she'd had it on Do Not Disturb. Her latest motivational quote popped up: *The harder you work for something, the greater you'll feel when you achieve it.*

Of course. She should be focused on the fact that she had made the Olympic team. It was her lifelong dream, after all. And here she was, goal acquired. So why wasn't she happy?

She swung her feet off the bed and stood up. She'd go see Grace. Maybe she'd even ride. Why not? The indoor arena had lights. But poor Grace was sleeping. She'd just hug her. The world would feel right then. She pulled on jeans, a pair of heavy socks, and layered a sweatshirt over a t-shirt. Pussy Willow had been sleeping on her bed. He stood up, stretched, and yawned.

"Go back to sleep, Puss," she said. She quietly went downstairs.

The barn was quiet and dark. She loved coming here after everyone was gone, and it was just her and the horses. She heard a bucket clank, and a horse snorted somewhere down the aisle. She left the lights off and made her way down the familiar passage. There was enough light from the full moon outside.

"Hey, Gracie," she said quietly, using her dad's nickname for the horse. She didn't hear the usual nicker. Grace must be sleeping. But something seemed off. She saw a big, dark, shape up ahead of her, near the feed room. It looked like a horse. But in the aisleway?

Hannah backtracked and turned on the light. She shielded her eyes against the sudden brightness, but after a moment, they adjusted, and she saw what the shape had been. It was Grace, and she had her nose stuck in a bag of grain.

"Grace, no!" Hannah said, panic setting in. She ran down the aisle, tripping once and almost falling, until she got to her horse. She yanked on Grace's mane, trying to raise her head, then instead, grabbed the bag. It was nearly empty.

"Oh Grace," she said. She ran for Grace's halter, put it on her horse, and led her back inside her stall. The stall door looked fine. It had simply been left unlocked.

But now Hannah was panicked. Horses, like dogs, would eat themselves to death. Because they couldn't vomit, once the food went in, there was no way to get it back out. If a horse ate too much, it could founder, or worse, colic and die.

"Oh no," Hannah said, and put her hand to her face. What should she do next? In a panic, she grabbed her phone and dialed her vet. She got his answering machine and paged him. While she waited for her vet to return her call, she dialed Chase's number. On the third ring, he answered, his voice thick with sleep.

"Hello?"

"Chase, I'm in the barn. I need you. Hurry."

She hung up and ran back to Grace. Quickly, she searched on her phone "What to do when your horse eats a bag of grain." About a hundred articles popped up.

"Oh no," Hannah said. She felt like she was going to throw up. She looked at Grace. The mare's head was hanging low, and she looked sick. But she wasn't trying to roll or lay down, so her stomach didn't hurt. Yet.

Chase showed up, breathing hard. He had thrown on jeans and a t-shirt. His hair was disheveled.

"Grace just ate a whole bag of grain!" Hannah said.

"What? How?"

"I don't know. I have a call in to the vet." Hannah noticed her hands were shaking. She pulled open Grace's stall door and felt her feet. They were warm, a sign that founder was setting in from the rich food. If Grace foundered, if the fever in her feet was severe enough, she might never recover. Ever. Hannah came out and slid the door closed again.

Chase walked to where the grain was kept and picked up the empty bag. There was another bag next to it, partially eaten.

"I think she tore into this one, too."

"Oh my gosh," Hannah put her face in her hands.

"How did she get out?" Chase walked over to the stall.

"It looks like the stall door was left open," Hannah said. "Someone must have forgotten to latch it. But I'm the only one who ever handles Grace."

Her eyes met Chase's as she spoke, because she suddenly remembered. "Wait. I had to go to the house to see my mom. You were the last one to lock Grace up."

Chase raised his hands. "I locked it. I swear."

"How do you know?"

"I remember."

"Do you? Because we were both pretty distracted."

Just then, Hannah's phone rang. "It's the vet." She answered it, spoke with him briefly, and hung up. "He's on his way."

"Maybe we should call your dad," Chase said. He was inspecting the stall door.

"No. I don't want to deal with him right now. The vet will be here in ten minutes."

What a night! Hannah was exhausted from the lack of sleep and the fight with her parents. And now Grace! She went into her horse's stall again and wrapped her arms around Grace's neck. The mare turned to nuzzle her. "Please don't die," Hannah whispered.

Chase came over to the stall. "What can I do?"

Hannah shook her head. "Nothing. Just wait here with me."

It seemed like forever before the vet arrived. He listened to Grace's stomach and ran his hand down her legs.

"Her pulse is high, and her hooves are hot," he said.

"I know," Hannah said weakly.

"She's definitely in trouble." He straightened up and looked at Hannah and Chase. "As you know, a sudden diet this rich causes founder. That's when the laminae, which connects the hoof wall to the coffin bone, separates. The next few hours will tell how bad off she is. It's possible she could recover. Fully."

"What if it's bad?" Hannah said.

"If it's bad enough, and her coffin bone turns downward, it's best to euthanize. But we aren't there yet."

"Oh my gosh," Hannah said. She felt Chase put his arm around her shoulders.

The vet gave Grace a shot to make her more comfortable, and another shot for something Hannah didn't quite understand.

"You need to walk her to keep things moving," he said. "We don't want colic on top of this."

Hannah nodded and took the lead rope from the vet. "Thank you, doctor."

He looked at his watch. "It's 3:30 am. I'll be back out around nine to check on her again."

"Okay." Hannah watched him leave, then she took the lead rope and asked Grace to walk. Her horse obediently followed.

"I'll walk her around the arena," Hannah said. "Can you go turn the lights on? They're right inside the door."

"Sure."

As Chase went ahead of her to turn the arena lights on, she thought about how Grace could have gotten out. And why hadn't the grain been put away? The barn had a rule about not leaving horse food out for this exact reason. She felt a hot flush of anger.

Chase had been the last one with her horse. He had forgotten to lock the stall. He had been handling two horses at the time, by himself, and had been distracted by all the excitement of the weekend. He had gotten careless.

Chase turned the lights on and opened the gate as she led Grace in past him.

She walked Grace slowly around the arena. Her mom had other children. Her dad had lied to her about not ever seeing her mom again. Chase had let her horse get foundered.

What if Grace didn't get better? Was this the end to her Olympic dreams? What did she have left?

"She doesn't look so good," Chase said.

"It's your fault." The words were out before she could stop them.

"What?"

284

"It's your fault. You left the stall door open. You know how bad founder is. What if I can never ride Grace again? What if she dies?"

"Let's not go there," Chase said. "Hannah, I locked that stall door, I swear. I always double check these things. Believe me, after a lifetime of being around horses, I know what kinds of trouble they can get into. I would never get so distracted as to forget."

"You can't be sure."

"I can."

She glared at him from across the arena.

"You're really blaming me for this?" Chase asked.

"Who else could it be? Why would anyone else be at the barn, messing with my horse?"

"What about Devon?"

"You think Devon did this? What would he gain?"

"What would he not lose?" Chase said. "He's probably on his way out of a job here, and he knows it. Your dad just hired me as a full-time trainer. And he sees how you feel about me."

Her head shot up, just in time to see Chase turn red.

"Which is what?" Hannah asked. Her voice was icy.

"Never mind. That's not what I meant. He's very protective of you. He thinks he owns you. He told me that I needed to quit, to resign, because he should rightfully be your trainer. And more. He wants to be *more* than just your trainer."

"He never said that."

"He did."

Hannah looked at Chase. He seemed sincere, but she was hurting and scared and she needed to lash out at somebody.

"You're just jealous," she said. "You can't stand that someone is interested in me."

"Hannah, he's a jerk!"

"Well, he didn't let my horse out to get sick. You did! Chase, after all this time...you still let me down. I thought I could trust you." As Hannah spoke, she felt the emotion rising in her. There was literally no one she could trust. Not her mom. Not her Dad. Not Devon.

Not Chase.

She glanced at Chase again. She knew in her heart that most, if not all, of what Chase was saying was true about Devon. Hadn't she planned to ask her dad to fire that jerk after the trials? Once she got on the team?

"You can trust me," Chase said.

"I can't. You're just like the rest of them."

"Hannah, you're tired. Let me walk your horse."

"Don't you touch my horse!" Hannah said. She was shouting now. Grace jerked her head up, and she felt bad that she had frightened her. "Go away."

"No. I'm not leaving you."

Chase pulled his phone out of his pocket and dialed.

"Who are you calling?" Hannah snapped.

"I'm calling your dad."

"Don't you dare."

But it was too late. Chase was already talking to him. After a moment, he put his phone back in his pocket. "He'll be right down," Chase said. "I think you need him."

Hannah had never been so angry. It was going to be a long morning before the vet arrived.

The vet showed up promptly at 9 a.m. Hannah had refused to leave Grace all night. She was so tired that the world was swaying.

Chase hadn't left her side. She refused to talk to him, and when she did, she snapped at him. Same thing with her dad. She hated everybody.

The vet took some x-rays, and Hannah waited, biting her nails, to hear the results. When he emerged from his fancy trailer-lab, he looked grim.

"It doesn't look good," he said. "The cannon bone has separated from the hoof wall. I'm not sure she's going to recover."

Hannah felt her knees go weak. Before she knew it, she had sunk to the ground. The only thing holding her up was Chase's arms.

"We don't know for sure," the vet said. "I'm going to give Grace something to help her sleep. Hannah, you need to get some rest. Grace is going to need you if she's going to make a recovery, and you're no good to her like this."

Hannah was only vaguely aware of the vet sedating her horse, and of Chase putting Grace in her stall.

"Go get some rest," Chase said gently. "I'll stay with Grace."

She let her dad lead her up to the house. Anastasia had a plate of eggs and toast waiting, and she sat with Hannah, making sure she ate every bite.

"Take this," Anastasia said, handing her a pill.

"What is it?"

"It's a mild sedative. Your dad wanted me to give it to you."

"I don't take drugs."

"Take it, Hannah. Please."

What did it matter? Hannah's life had just ended. She didn't need to take care of her athletic body anymore. Those days were finished. Hannah grabbed the pill and swallowed.

Then Anastasia walked Hannah upstairs and tucked her in as if she were a little girl.

"It'll all work out," Anastasia said. "It always does."

She closed the door quietly as she left.

Hannah drifted off into a deep, dreamless sleep.

Chapter Thirty-Two

Chase sat on a bale of hay, thinking. He was sure he had locked the stall door. He remembered Hannah asking someone to put the bags of grain away yesterday. Jared. The stable boy was a little slow to get his work done and was always distracted with his headphones on, bopping to music.

But the stall door was another matter. Chase was sure Devon had opened it. But what would his motive be to make Grace sick? He wanted Hannah. He wanted "in" to the world of the Whitneys. He would never risk hurting Hannah's horse.

But if Hannah couldn't go to the Olympics, there would be no reason to keep Chase around.

I know exactly how to get rid of someone like you. Devon's words echoed in his ears. That was it. That was his motive. If Hannah was out of the Olympics, he'd be her rescuer. And Chase would be gone.

As if on cue, Devon came into the barn. It was late morning, and he was here for a lesson.

"Wuss Livingston," he said, sauntering over. "I heard what you did to Hannah's horse. She'll hate you forever. Pity."

Devon gave Chase his wolfish grin. For a moment, Chase thought about punching those pearly white teeth down his throat. But he had a better idea. If he could prove that this was Devon's fault, Devon would not only be fired but probably prosecuted.

"I don't think it's going to happen that way," Chase said. "We all know who let that horse out."

"You think it was me?" Devon laughed. "What is my motive? You can't prove that."

"I can," Chase said. He got up and walked out of the barn, leaving Devon to ponder his words.

He didn't see Hannah until the next day. The vet came out for a second visit, and the news was grim. Grace would live but would probably never show again. The resulting founder from the fever in her hooves would cause her problems for the rest of her life. With care, she'd be ridable, but she'd never be able to perform to the extent she always had. Her life as a show horse was over. The Olympics were a lost dream.

If Hannah was devastated by the news, she didn't show it. She took it quietly, and then led her horse away to her stall.

Marcus rubbed his face with his hands. He had been off work the past two days, splitting his time between the barn and the house. Hannah still wasn't speaking to him, from what Chase could tell. He looked like a man who had been beaten.

The barn staff went back to work. Devon was out in the ring giving a lesson.

"What happened?"

Chase turned to see Marcus looking at him. "What?"

"I want to know how this happened. I know it wasn't you. People make mistakes, but I just know in my gut that this isn't your fault."

Chase felt a profound sense of relief. So far, every finger had been pointing to him. Hannah still wouldn't speak to him either.

"I think it was Devon," he said.

"So do I."

"Do you have security cameras in the barn?"

Marcus shook his head. "No. Just outside."

Chase thought about it. "Well, he had to get here somehow. Would they catch him driving in? Or walking?"

Marcus thought about it. "I know. Come with me!"

Chase followed Marcus back to the house and into his study. Marcus booted up his computer.

"I have cameras on the arenas."

"You do?"

"Yes. We've used them to record the students training. A few months ago, just before you came, we had a stable boy who was stealing silver off the saddles. He was sneaking it out with the golf cart, past these two arenas. I decided to leave the cameras on all night and caught him, and I never turned them off."

He clicked a few buttons and found the night that Grace was attacked. They watched slowly. The black and white image was blurry, but they saw a figure come around the arena. He had snuck in between the bushes in the back.

"It's Devon," Marcus said. "He didn't know about those cameras. I'll bet he parked out on the road and came in this way. He knows the codes, so he probably turned the electric fencing off that night before he left and came in this back way. That way, the cameras at the gates wouldn't catch him, and neither would the cameras outside of the barn." Marcus smiled. "Gotcha."

Chase was with Marcus and Hannah when the police officer showed up at the farm thirty minutes later. Devon had just finished a lesson with a student.

"What's up?" Devon asked, his eyes darting to the police officer, and then to Chase.

Hannah's eyes were shooting daggers at Devon. She walked up to him, close enough so their faces were almost touching.

"I knew you were a snake," she said. "But I never thought you'd go this low to get your way. You've been playing a game with me for the past two years. But you know what, Devon? You just lost."

"Hannah, what are you talking about?" Devon said, but Chase saw him grow a shade paler.

"You're under arrest," the officer said.

"I didn't do anything!" Devon said. He turned to Hannah. "Hannah, tell them. I'd never hurt a horse!"

"Nobody said anything about hurting a horse," Marcus said. "Sounds like you just confessed."

Devon shot a look at Chase and pointed. "He did it!"

"Did what?" Marcus said.

Devon turned red, realizing he had just incriminated himself.

"We caught you on camera sneaking into the barn," Marcus said. "You let Grace out. You hurt our horse and my daughter. I'll prosecute you to the fullest extent of the law."

Marcus stood there, talking with the officer. Hannah's dad was wearing khakis and a sweater, not his usual business attire, but he was still an imposing sight. Chase watched Devon squirm.

"Hannah, please!" Devon pleaded. "You know I did all of this for you."

"Ruining my dreams?" she said.

Chase had the immense satisfaction of watching the officer put handcuffs on Devon.

"That horse is worth at least a million dollars," Chase said. "I believe that's going to be some serious time behind bars."

The three of them watched the police car drive Devon away. Then Chase looked over at Hannah, hoping she'd talk to him now that she knew it wasn't his fault. But she simply turned and walked back to the house.

"Give her some time," Marcus said. "She's been through a lot." Marcus put his hand on Chase's shoulder. "Why don't you go home for a few days, son? Check on your apartment back in Chicago. Come back on Monday."

Chase nodded. Then, so Marcus wouldn't see the tears in his eyes, he turned and made his way back to the barn.

But it didn't feel right to pack his bags and leave. Hadn't he promised Hannah he wouldn't leave her?

He laid in bed that night, thinking. As soon as morning came, he had a plan.

Chase sat at the piano in the Whitney's conservatory. It was just before noon. He had called Marcus that morning and told him what he wanted to do. Marcus had agreed.

Chase picked out a few notes with one finger. It had been a long time since he'd played. A piano didn't fit in his apartment at home, and he didn't make it over to his mom's enough to get much practice in. Still, the music was in him, just like the riding. Muscle memory was a great thing.

He felt strangely calm. He had been praying last night, and a peace had come over him. And by morning, he had known what he needed to do. What he needed to say.

He heard footsteps coming down the stairs and knew that it would be Hannah.

"Dad?" she said. "Why did you want me to meet you in the conservatory?" She stopped short when she saw Chase. "Where's my dad?"

"I'm here," Marcus said, stepping out into the room from the corner. "Now that you're here, you two need to talk."

"Dad. You set me up."

"Hannah, you need to work this out."

Marcus walked out of the conservatory and closed the door behind them. They were alone.

Hannah's hair was unbrushed and hanging down on her shoulders, and she didn't have any makeup on. She was wearing leggings and a sweater, with baggy socks on her feet. It was the first time he had seen her this unkempt, and yet she looked even more beautiful to him than ever.

"I never told you the story behind the hymn that your horse is named after," Chase said. "Amazing Grace." Without waiting for Hannah to respond, he started to play the song. The music was powerful, and beautiful, and always moved him. He played two stanzas, and then stopped. Hannah was standing beside the door, her arms crossed, but she hadn't left yet. That was a good sign.

She took in a deep breath, and her eyes filled with tears. "Do you hate me?" she asked.

Chase shook his head. "I could never hate you."

"I knew it wasn't you, and even if it had been, it wouldn't have mattered. I just needed somebody to blame."

"You needed to leave me before I left you," Chase said.

More tears. "Yes."

"I told you I wouldn't," he said.

"But why not? I don't have a horse to show anymore. There's no reason for you to stay."

Chase turned back to the piano and played another stanza of Amazing Grace. When he was finished, he said, "Do you know the words?"

"No. I was always going to look them up, but never did."

"John Newton, the writer, lived a hard life." Chase said. Hannah was still by the door. "His mother was a Christian who taught him about Jesus. But she died two weeks before his seventh birthday, so he was raised without her. His father was a stern boat captain and took John to sea with him at age eleven. So he didn't have a lot of nurturing."

Hannah uncrossed her arms.

"Newton mocked God, partied too much, and eventually wound up on a slave ship as a slave trader. He was a bad man. Then one day, a storm blew up, and a crew member was washed overboard. Newton tried all night to keep the ship from sinking. He was sure he was a goner and wondered what would happen when he came face to face with God. After all, he hated God; he was rude, profane, and cruel to people, and mocked the gospel. Then he recalled what his mother had taught him, that God was merciful and forgiving. And Newton knew then that he had a chance. So he began to pray, and God forgave him. Newton turned his life around, and later became one of the men who helped abolish slavery and the slave trade."

Chase played another verse. "It's a beautiful song. He wrote it out of appreciation that God could take a man like him and make him a child of God. It's about God's incredible, *unconditional* love and grace. Amazing grace."

Hannah came further into the room and sat down on a couch next to the piano.

"Newton didn't have to prove himself to God," Chase said. "All he had to do to be in God's family, was ask."

"What are the words to the song?"

Chase opened up the hymnal that Marcus had given him, and read.

"Amazing grace, how sweet the sound
That saved a wretch like me!
I once was lost, but now I'm found,
Was blind, but now I see."

The tears in Hannah's eyes had escaped down her cheeks. "I feel so lost," she said. "Like John did."

"You aren't, Hannah," Chase said softly. "God knows right where you are. He created you. He knows your heart and He loves you."

Chase looked down at the hymnal and read more of the lyrics:

"Twas grace that taught my heart to fear,
And grace my fears relieved,
How precious did that grace appear,
The hour I first believed."

He looked at Hannah. She was listening.

"Through many dangers, toils and snares,
I have already come.
'Twas grace hath brought me safe thus far,
And grace will lead me home."

He closed the book.

"So what does that mean?" Hannah said. "I don't see how that can fix my life. I'm ruined, Chase. For my entire life, my only goal has been to get to the

Olympics. And now that isn't going to happen. I didn't go to college. I don't have any friends, any connections. I'm nothing."

"Hannah, you are so much more than nothing. You're incredible."

"My mother had other children. The man she married had two kids, and she helped raise them. She had another life. She didn't want me. And Grace. Grace is my best friend and now she's..." Hannah put her head in her hands, hiding her face. "Oh Chase, what am I going to do now?"

Chase got up and went to sit beside her on the couch.

"Hannah, when I felt like my life was over, it took God to make me realize that it wasn't. All the things I had been chasing were just that—*things*. I didn't need a gold medal to make me somebody. I didn't need Marina, or another partner, to make me whole. And all those people who were mocking me and making fun of me, I didn't need their approval. I was okay because *God said I was*. Broken and incomplete, I was okay in God's eyes. And you're okay too, because He says you are."

"I'm not," Hannah said.

"Look at me," Chase said. Gently, he pulled her hands from her face. He reached over and wiped the tears from her cheeks with the back of his hand. "God loves you, Hannah."

"I'm not good enough, Chase," Hannah said. "I'll never be good enough. I'm not like you. Look at you! You help your sister with her debts and her child. You've hung in there with me despite my awful temper. You didn't even pound Devon's head in when

298

he deserved it. You're so good. Me? I'm awful. I could never earn God's love."

"You don't have to earn it, Hannah. We never could. And we don't deserve it. I certainly don't. John Newton, the slave trader, didn't. That's why it's called grace. Amazing grace."

She was looking at him now, really listening.

"There's a verse in the Bible. In the book of Romans. It says that it's by grace we are we saved through faith. Not of works. It is a gift of God. Not of ourselves, so that no one can boast. You see, Hannah, God's love and mercy are gifts. You don't have to earn them. All you have to do is ask."

"How do I do that?" Hannah said.

"You just realize that you need Him and believe that Jesus died for your sins."

Hannah sniffed and gave a little laugh. "So I have to believe in Jesus?"

"Yes."

"I'm not sure I can."

"You only have to have a tiny bit of faith. Just as big as a mustard seed."

Hannah reached her hand out to Chase. He took it. "Tell me how," she said. "I want to know."

"Pray with me," he said, and began to recite the prayer he himself had prayed one night, several years ago. The same prayer her father had prayed when Julius Bloom came to visit him.

"Jesus, I am not perfect," Hannah said, repeating after him. "And I know you died for my sins. I want to accept your gift of grace. Please forgive me and make me whole. Please become Lord of my life."

After they said "Amen," she looked over at Chase. "Is that it?"

"That's it," Chase said. "Welcome to the family of God!"

Chapter Thirty-Three

Six weeks later, Hannah was sitting in the gazebo eating her lunch. Grace was beside her. The horse was doing a lot better, and Hannah had led her down the long, winding path. Chase was busy training a student, so she was alone with her horse. He had been so kind and patient with her and her questions about his faith.

Hannah's dad had been thrilled that Hannah had decided to trust Jesus as her Lord and Savior. He had actually cried when she told him. She had never seen her dad cry before, not even when her mom had left them.

Her mom was the reason she and Grace were here at the gazebo. She was waiting for Eva. Chase had told her to try to have grace with her mom. Not the horse but the concept. "It'll give you peace," he said. "Let go of the anger and offer her grace."

She saw Eva driving her compact sedan up the winding path toward them. There was a small hole in the muffler, and it made a lot of noise as she drove. She parked and got out.

"Thank you for agreeing to see me again," she said.

"Thank you for driving all this way from Grand Rapids."

Hannah motioned for Eva to sit down on the little wooden bench across from her. Grace had her eyes closed and was sleeping on her feet. There was a brisk breeze. It was early November, and it would have probably been more practical to meet in the house, but this gave them more privacy. It was a beautiful, sunny day, and still warm for this time of year.

"Mom," Hannah said, "you hurt me deeply."

"I know," Eva said. "All I can ask is that you forgive me."

"I'm going to try," Hannah said. "I can't make any promises, but I'm going to try. I think we should try talking on a regular basis. Maybe I could meet your stepchildren. I guess they're adults now, so step-adults or whatever they call them."

Eva nodded. Hannah saw tears in her eyes.

"I will try to be open," Hannah said. "I want to hear more about your life, and I can tell you more about mine."

Silent tears ran down Eva's face.

"I don't make any promises," Hannah said. "But I've made my share of mistakes in life. And if I ever do marry and have kids, it might be kind of nice if they could meet their grandma."

Eva put her hand to her mouth. "I don't deserve this," she whispered.

"No, you don't," Hannah said. "But that's not for me to decide. My job is to forgive you and let God take care of the rest."

Eva nodded. "Thank you for giving me a second chance," she said.

Hannah reached into her bag and pulled out the banana bread that Anastasia had made that morning. She had brought two thick slices.

"You want a piece?"

"Yes, I'd like that."

"It's your recipe," Hannah said. "I found it many years ago in your recipe box. Anastasia—she's our housekeeper now—does a great job making it."

"I still bake this," Eva said. "My kids..." She stopped, aware of her mistake.

"They like it?" Hannah said.

Eva nodded.

"They have good taste then," Hannah said.

It was hard, talking to her mom. And awkward. And she still felt stirrings of anger. Chase had told her that the feelings didn't always go away, but if her heart was in the right place, she'd get there. Over the past weeks, she had noticed a relief from the anger and fear that had been her companion her entire life. The need to live up to expectations was slowly disappearing, and she was growing more comfortable in her new skin. She was no longer an Olympic-bound woman, and yet her dad still loved her, her mom still wanted to be a part of her life, and Chase hadn't left her. And God...God had accepted her as-is. Maybe she was worthy of love after all.

"How's Grace?" her mom asked. "Your dad told me what happened."

"She's doing great," Hannah said. "The vet took more x-rays yesterday and said she might fully recover, but we won't know until spring. We're not going to be able to show next year, and the Olympics are out, but there may be hope for the future of her show career. It's hard to tell."

"I'm sorry, Hannah, I know how much being in the Olympics meant to you."

"It's okay," Hannah said. With each day that passed, she was realizing that maybe it actually was okay after all. She would love to win a gold medal and go along for the exciting ride of being an Olympic athlete. But if that never happened, she still had a lot to be grateful for.

"That's great that she might recover," Eva said.

Hannah nodded. Tomorrow would be the first day that the vet said it would be okay to ride Grace. Hannah had made plans with Chase to go out for a trail ride in the evening when their lessons were over.

"It's not so bad, just hanging out with her," Hannah said. She glanced at her horse, who was contentedly sleeping on her feet. Grace looked relaxed and happy. Her whiskers were growing out on her muzzle.

"What's going to happen to that man who hurt Grace?"

"Devon?" Hannah said. "He's out on bail. We will, of course, press charges." Just thinking about what Devon had done to her horse upset her. She took a deep, calming breath.

"I hope you win in court," Eva said.

Hannah let the anger she felt rise to the surface and then dissipate. She was getting better at letting go.

"I want to hate him," Hannah said. "But perhaps I should try to forgive him."

Eva broke off another piece of bread, and looked up, holding it between her fingers. "Does he deserve that?

Hannah shrugged. "Is what *he* did to me any worse than what *you* did to me?" She regretted the harsh words as soon as she said them.

"No," Eva said quietly. She looked down.

Hannah had talked at length with Chase and her dad about the situation. About what would happen to Devon.

"I don't really think it's our place to choose who is deserving and who is not," Hannah said. "God offers forgiveness to everyone who asks. Maybe I need to do the same."

Chase had told her that forgiving people didn't mean becoming a doormat to be walked all over, or letting people like Devon hurt her. It meant letting it go and turning it over to God. There was something freeing about that.

The two women were quiet for a moment, lost in their own thoughts. Finally, Eva broke the silence.

"So how are things going with your man, *Chase?*" Eva said his name like he was famous.

"Oh, we're just friends," Hannah said.

She wished they were more. She wanted more. But Chase kept his space, always the gentleman, never asking her for anything. She wanted to grab him and kiss him, but a tiny part of her was afraid he didn't feel the same way she did.

And she was still afraid, on some days, that she'd lose him if she pushed him too far.

"Oh, I think he wants more than that," Eva said. "Your dad, he was crazy about me when we first met. I can still remember the look he used to get in his eyes whenever he saw me. Chase gets that look when he sees you. I knew the moment I saw him that he loved you."

Hannah thought about that. She thought about the time she had almost kissed him after the trials. And how he looked at her when he thought she wasn't watching him.

"Maybe," she said.

Her mom stood and looked at her watch. "I need to go. It's a long drive home, and I don't want to get stuck in rush hour traffic."

"Okay."

"Can I see you again?"

"Yes," Hannah said. "Let's try to meet once a month. I can come out your way next time."

"I'd love that," Eva said. "I can show you my garden. Remember the little fairy gardens I used to make with you? I have one of those in my own garden. It has a little gray cat figurine in it, like in the book I used to read to you."

"Pussy Willow," Hannah said.

"Yes."

They didn't hug. Hannah wasn't ready for that. Eva waved, and Hannah watched her mom's car drive off until it turned and was lost behind the trees. *Her mom.* It sounded funny to say the words. Her mom had found her. Had sought her out. Had wanted to be in her life. It was late, some might say too late, but Hannah knew that she had a whole lifetime ahead of her to decide that.

She looked at the time on her phone. She had to get back to the house. She had something else she needed to do now.

Chapter Thirty-Four

Chase woke up the next morning to his phone ringing.

"Happy birthday!" It was Hannah.

He looked at his watch. It was only 7 a.m. Today was his day off.

"How'd you know it was my birthday?"

"I peeked in our employee records."

"I'm pretty sure that's illegal."

"Maybe. But I think you'll change your mind when you see your birthday gift."

"You got me a gift?" Chase sat up and the covers slid to the floor. The day was gray outside and cold. He wanted to crawl back into bed.

"I did. And it's a big one. You need to come up to the barn to get it."

"Now?"

"Yes. Hurry!" She sounded as excited as a child.

"Okay. Let me get dressed."

Chase brushed his teeth and pulled on his clothes. Then he put his coat on and walked up to the barn.

Hannah and her dad were waiting for him at the door.

"What's this about?" Chase said.

"Come and see!" Hannah said. She was so excited he thought she might burst. He wished he had grabbed a coffee.

"Your present came early this morning," Hannah said.

"We had it delivered while you were still asleep," Marcus said.

Grace peeked her head over her stall door and nickered at them. The stall door next to her had a big bow tied to the front of it in the green and white colors of the farm. A banner was strung above the stall door that said, "Happy Birthday, Chase!"

"What on earth?" Chase said.

Then he heard something shuffle in the bedding, and he saw a horse look out over the door. It took a moment for it to register—the black coat, the tiny pin-point ears, the familiar face. The horse saw him and nickered a warm, low greeting.

"Manny," he whispered.

"Yes!" Hannah said and bounced on her toes.

"But how? He wasn't for sale."

"Everything is for sale if the price is right, son," Marcus said.

"I found his owner and talked to him, and Dad paid for him," Hannah said. "He's yours, Chase. We had the papers put in your name."

"Manny," Chase whispered again. He walked forward, and Manny—*his* horse—greeted him with another nicker. "How are you doing, boy?" The horse nuzzled Chase and pushed his forehead up against him. Then he playfully bumped him with his nose. Chase opened the stall door, went inside, and put his arms around his horse's neck. "You're home, Manny," he said. "You're home."

He stood there, letting the tears run freely down his cheeks.

"You're quite something," Chase said to Hannah later. They were sitting on a hay bale across from their horses' stalls, watching Manny and Grace munch on their hay. *His horse.* He still couldn't get over that he owned Manny. It was too extravagant of a gift to accept from the Whitneys, he knew that. And yet he had. Marcus was adamant, and Hannah was so happy, he just had to. He would find a way to repay them. Somehow. Someday. But for now, he finally had his horse.

"I am," Hannah said. "I'm something pretty special."

"And not a bit conceited," Chase said.

"Not a bit."

He turned to look at her. Her blue eyes were shining. Despite all that she had been through, she looked happier than he had ever seen her. Things were looking up. She and her mom were starting to establish a relationship, and Grace was doing better. Today, they were going to go for a ride together. He had planned to ride Percy, but now he was going to ride his own horse.

His horse.

He smiled. Hannah smiled back.

"I love you." He said the words. He had felt it for a long time, and he couldn't hold it back anymore. His heart hammered as he waited for her response.

"You do?" She didn't seem surprised. He saw her grin widen. "I'm pretty into you too. You saw my scrapbook."

He laughed. "But your dad...well...I'm your *trainer.*"

"Technically, you're *not* my trainer at the moment. The way I see it, if you start to train me again in the spring when Grace is ready, well, by that time, it will be too late for Dad to complain. Meanwhile, I am not your student."

Chase moved closer to her. "So maybe it's okay if I kiss you then?"

"I'm pretty sure it is, and just so you know, Dad loves you too. Not in the same way as I do."

"I hope not."

"But he loves you. And my mother approves of you."

Chase smiled and put his hand on Hannah's face, cupping her cheek. Her skin was so soft, and her hair was loose around her shoulders. He smelled her shampoo, a scent that had grown familiar to him. Everything about her was familiar to him, like he had finally found what he had always been searching for.

He leaned in until his lips met hers, and he felt her melt into him, pulling him closer.

"I love you, Chase Livingston," she whispered into his ear.

"I love you too, Hannah Whitney."

They kissed, there on the bale of hay, in the barn where it had all started. And although he had his eyes closed, when he heard the whinny, he knew that it was Manny talking to him.

"Somebody's jealous," Hannah said.

"He'll just have to get used to it. I plan on doing this for a long time to come."

He leaned forward again to kiss the woman he loved.

The End

Read more books in the *Horses and Hearts Inspirational Romance* series. In *Finding Hope*, Tori Reynolds' life as a horse trainer and owner of a historic B&B on the shores of Lake Michigan is perfect—until a visit to New York changes everything. When Tori steps into the Manhattan art show of handsome, nationally-known artist Matt Cheval, she unexpectedly finds herself, and her horse, in his paintings. Angry and frightened, she is faced with a memory—and a man—she has spent years trying to forget.

Turn the page to start reading…

Finding Hope

Chapter One

"I don't understand," said Victoria Jones. "*Who* is this guy?"

She adjusted the Bluetooth speaker in her ear so she could hear her friend Emma better. They were talking about tonight's dinner in New York, and she could have sworn Emma just set her up.

"Relax, Tori," said Emma. "He's just my husband's co-worker."

Tori flipped open the carry-on suitcase that was on her bed and tossed in a few pairs of socks. She was packing light since the trip was short. She'd arrive this evening, Friday, and return on Sunday morning. She was flying to New York to promote her new book on horse training and give a live performance at an indoor arena.

"I've set up some fun things for us to do," said Emma.

"I'm only there for one full day," said Tori. "And I have to work all day on Saturday."

"I know," said Emma, "but you'll be here early evening tomorrow, which is why we're going out for dinner."

"With the *co-worker*," said Tori, hoping the dread came across in her voice. "What's his name?"

"Colton."

"Sounds stuffy."

Emma laughed. "Colton Rausch, and he's a banker, like my hubby." Then she sighed. "Tori, it has been *four years*."

"I know," Tori said quietly. She opened her drawer to look at her t-shirts.

"Oh, and wear something nice. For dinner with Colton and for earlier tonight. I found something fun to keep us busy until the men are off work."

Emma was Tori's best friend. They had bonded during freshman year of high school when they were partnered together to dissect a frog, and Emma had thrown up on Tori's textbook. Then, after graduation, they had shared an apartment briefly before Tori married Tim. Emma was more like a sister to her than best friend.

"You mean, like a *dress?*" Tori moaned.

"Just something *nice*. Then on Sunday you can come to church with us and we'll go out for brunch before you catch your plane"

"Okay. Look, I need to go pack. I'll see you tonight. You're picking me up at the airport, right?"

"I'll be there!"

Tori hung up the phone and turned back to her suitcase. Simon, her orange cat, had crawled inside and was already asleep.

"Oh *no*," Tori said, but she stroked his head. He cracked open an eye to peek at her. "So, since you're in the middle of this, what do *you* think I should wear this weekend?" She walked over and pulled open another drawer. "Blue jeans? Or…blue jeans?"

Simon answered with a yawn.

Packing was usually easy. She didn't need to be stylish for horse seminars. As a professional horse trainer and nationally known author, she was well respected and well known in her field. She used to train horses for shows, but her techniques were so well received that people started asking her to give demonstrations. The seminars paid better, beat the everyday back-breaking work of training show horses, and gave her a chance to see the country. She had seminars booked for the next year and a half, plus her fourth book at a publishing house ready to be put into hardcover.

"Meow." Simon climbed out of the suitcase and walked across the bed to demand petting. She obliged, scratching him behind the ears. Then she tossed two pairs of jeans, three fresh t-shirts, and some underwear into her suitcase. She threw in an aqua colored sundress that would accentuate her hazel eyes, and a pair of white, strappy sandals with low heels. She grabbed her bag of toiletries that she always kept filled and ready, threw in the book she was reading, and zipped up the suitcase.

She was wearing a soft blue cotton dress that hung just past her knees, and decided to pair her western boots with it, because she'd need them for the horse-training seminar anyway. It was easier to wear them on the plane then pack them. She'd maybe change into the sandals later, depending on Emma's choice of restaurant.

She ran the brush through her brunette hair. It framed her fair complexion, hanging about halfway down her back. She'd leave it lose today.

"I guess I'm ready," she said to Simon. He curled around her leg, pressing up against her in a cat hug. "I'll miss you too, boy."

She had a few minutes left, and she had already said goodbye to the horses and given the housekeeper and the barn assistant directions. So, she opened her bedroom window and climbed out onto the roof.

Hopeful Farm—*her* farm—stood on the shores of Lake Michigan, just north of Ludington, about mid-way up the mitten state. It overlooked the Great Lake and its swelling waves that rolled in just beneath the sand dunes on top of which her house, now a popular bed and breakfast, sat.

She stood on the widow's walk, which offered an incredible view of the mighty lake. The small walkway, about three-feet wide, ran the length of the roof along of her two-story house. The piece of architecture got its name from history; the wives of sea captains stood on it to watch for the safe return of their lovers. The tall mast of a ship, which could be spotted at a great distance, was a sign of rejoicing and welcome. Its absence could mean many things. That was how the widow's walk got its name.

She came here often to reflect and to gaze out over the vast acreage of shoreline she owned. The wind caught her hair, blowing it out behind her. She wrapped her hands around the weathered railing and breathed in the fresh lake-tinged air, much as other women had done over the years. Many of the older homes that faced the Great Lakes had similar widow's walks.

"Tori, you're going to be late!" a voice called to her. Tori turned to see her housekeeper and cook, Phyllis, peeking her graying head out of the window. "Let's go!"

Tori nodded and climbed back through her window, grabbed her suitcase and followed Phyllis out to their car. A few of their guests waved at her as she passed. As usual, they had all five guest rooms filled this weekend.

She saw Hope, her horse, grazing in the front pasture.

"Bye, Hope!" she called, waving her hand in the air. The mare lifted her head and gave a joyous whinny.

"She thinks your bringing carrots," Phyllis said.

"She's going to be disappointed," said Tori. She climbed in the passenger side of the car and watched Hope until they turned off the driveway onto the dirt road, where large beech trees blocked her view. Then she turned to face ahead. She believed in always looking forward. New York and a fun time with Emma (minus the date she was going to try to get out of) awaited her.

Emma rushed forward, squealing, to embrace Tori. She hugged her so hard that Tori nearly lost her balance.

"I missed you too!" Tori said, laughing. They hadn't seen each other in over six months, when

Emma came to the farm to stay a long weekend last winter. But they talked several times a week on the phone. They knew every detail of each other's lives. Or, almost every detail.

"This is going to be such a fun weekend!" said Emma. "Oh, and I made reservations tonight night at the Opal."

"About that," said Tori.

"But *first*," said Emma, "I have found something for us to do that you will *love*."

Emma was always so energetic. Sometimes it was draining. What Tori loved was curling up with a good book someplace quiet.

"What?" Tori asked. "Please tell me before I die of anticipation."

"An art show," said Emma.

Now *that* was different. They had attended author events (they read books together), plays, and movies, yes… but an *art show?* They had never done that before.

"Yay!" said Tori, trying to sound more excited than she felt. She thought longingly of her book.

"Don't get all poo-pooey on me," said Emma. "You'll *love* this. He's a *horse* artist. He paints pictures of horses, and he has this very popular series of paintings which I heard advertised on the radio. I guess he's really famous. I've never heard of him, but I figured if it had horses it *had* to be good. Right?"

A horse artist. Well at least it wasn't nudes or abstract. "What's his name?"

"The artist? Let me see." Emma rifled through her purse as they walked out of the airport toward the parking lot. "I have a brochure in here somewhere…" After a moment, she gave up. "I have no idea. Let's

319

just go. They have champagne and cheese and a showing, then we can go out to dinner and meet Brian and Colton. I made reservations for that as well."

"So you said. At the Opal."

"They serve seafood."

The showing started at 4 p.m. and it was nearly 6 p.m. "It only lasts until eight, so we need to go straight there," said Emma, clicking away on her high heels. "We can just throw your things in the trunk." She turned to Tori. "And you look *adorable!*" She grabbed Tori's hands and squeezed them, then used her keys to pop the trunk of her car.

The art gallery was about twenty miles away from the airport, and it took them over forty-five minutes in traffic to get there. Emma found a parking place on the street, grabbing a spot as an older gentlemen pulled out. She looked at her watch. "We still have over an hour before they close. Let's go!"

They were in the meat packing district of Manhattan, not far from where Emma lived with her banker husband. Emma didn't work at a paying job. Instead, she filled her hours doing charity events in Manhattan and hosting dinner parties for Brian's work. She loved every minute of it.

The art gallery looked like it was a former warehouse but had been warmed up with drywall and fancy lighting. They walked through the front doors and were greeted with servers in black aprons carrying trays.

"Champagne?" offered the first server they saw.

"Um, I could use some water," said Tori. The plane had been dry. She was thirsty.

"Water?" Emma whispered, grabbing a champagne flute. "*Really?* Oh, hon I never thought to offer you a bottle in the car. I'm such a dunce! Oh, look!" Emma pointed. There was a poster on a wall in front of them. It read, *Matt Cheval. Presenting 'The Woman and the Horse series.'*

"Look! There's a picture of him!" said Emma. "Oh, he's *cute!*"

But Tori wasn't looking. She was enthralled by a painting of a black Arabian stallion that was nearly as tall as her and sitting on an easel to her left. She walked over to see the painting closer.

Tori hadn't had much interest in dating since her husband had died four years ago. Emma had let her grieve for two years, then started gently prodding her to get back out. Tori was trying to at least *look* at men. Emma reminded her regularly that she wanted kids and she was already twenty-nine. Her clock was ticking.

They walked around the wall to see the display room. Several paintings hung from panels coated in black cloth. These didn't seem to be a part of the series. There was a landscape. A painting of one of the Great Lakes that Tori found soothing. But no horses other than the stallion out front.

"Let's get to the good stuff first," said Emma, grabbing her hand. A sign pointed back deeper into the gallery, and she pulled Tori around another wall. They came to a different room, and here apparently, was the series "The Woman and the Horse."

The room was filled with people, so it was hard to see the paintings. Tori counted nearly a dozen paintings, at least. Most were big canvases, about 3 x

5 feet. There were a few smaller 8 x 10s. They hung on panels much like the ones in the previous room, only these panels had royal blue clothes on them. Each painting had its own light shining down on it. It was all very fancy.

"Here," said Emma, and pulled her in between a middle-age couple and a group of women in business attire. They found themselves facing a painting of a field of lavender flowers, with a tree line in the background. Sitting on a tree stump in the field was a woman, her back to them, her head tilted slightly so you could just see her cheek. Her long, dark hair trailed down her back from under a wide-brimmed straw hat.

"That looks like a hat you own," mused Emma, quietly, almost to herself.

But Tori was looking at the horse. The white mare was standing near the woman, her head down, her muzzle near the woman's shoulder. The mare's long white mane hung down her neckline, but it didn't conceal the marking on her shoulder. The red, distinctive marking that Tori had memorized, had traced with her fingers over the smooth hair so many times.

"That's Hope," Tori said.

"What?" Emma turned her eyes to the horse. "*Hope?* But how...?" Emma stared. "That can't be right. It must be a coincidence."

Emma grabbed her hand. They pushed their way through the crowd to the next painting. This one had the backdrop of a shoreline. It looked like Lake Michigan with its characteristic dunes and grass. On the beach, the same mare walked quietly behind a woman. The only disturbance in the picture was the wind, whipping the mare's white mane and tail behind her, and the woman's long, dark hair. The woman was barefoot, wearing a flowing white dress, her shoulders bare. In her hand, she carried the wide-brimmed straw hat.

The horse had a distinctive marking on its shoulder. Almost like blood. But exactly like Hope's.

"Emma," Tori said, and reached for her friend's hand.

"Come on," said Emma.

She pulled her to the next painting. Same horse. Same woman. The woman's face was never shown. Only her dark hair, and often just a glimpse of her cheek or her nose.

But the horse. The horse was Hope.

Emma turned to look at Tori. Tori's heart pounded. This was creepy. More than creepy. She had books out about the horse, yes. So, Hope wasn't unknown. But these paintings were so…personal. The white dress was one that she owned. The hat was at home hanging on the hook by her back door. The hair… that was *her* hair.

"Where is this creep?" Tori said, probably a little too loudly.

They went to the next painting. It was quieter, calmer than the ones with the wind, a painting of the same woman standing at a stall door, the barnwood weathered gray. Her back was to them, her hair down. There was no hat in sight, and she was wearing jeans and a faded yellow t-shirt. Tori noticed, absurdly, the incredible lighting in the folds of the material.

The mare had her head over the stall door, her neck arched around the woman, and the woman's hand was on the horse's neck. The picture was one full of emotion, and the love between the woman and the mare was evident.

The stall door was low enough to reveal the marking on the mare's shoulder. It was Hope. And there was no mistaking, that was Hope's stall door.

"*Where is he?*" Tori said louder. She was clenching her teeth, a habit it had taken her years to break after Tim's death.

"Ma'am? Can I help you?" said a short woman wearing a tight suit and skirt combo.

"Yes, I need to see…" Tori cast her eyes around for the man's name but couldn't see the sign at they had passed at the entrance or read it on his paintings. "The artist. *Now.*"

"Can I tell him your name?"

"Oh, he *knows* me," Tori said. She glared down at the woman, and her anger must have shown through, because the woman said, "Just a moment. He's just coming back from an early dinner," and hustled off.

"Oh my gosh," said Emma. "Tori. What on earth…? I mean…?" Emma was, for once, speechless.

A moment later a man entered the room.

"That's him," whispered Emma. "He's wearing the same shirt as in the photo. Tacky."

He wore sunglasses, faded blue jeans, cowboy boots, and a black Stetson hat.

He followed the woman further into the room to where Tori and Emma were standing, and the crowded parted for them, people eyeing him reverently.

He had a smile for the cameras, for the people, but when he saw Tori, he stopped so suddenly that a waiter bumped into him and spilled some champagne on the dark burgundy carpet.

He kept his sunglasses on, but his face seemed familiar. Where had she seen it before? She cast her mind about to the many events she attended over the years. She could have met him anywhere.

"*What is this?*" she said. The room had grown quiet. "What are these paintings? Why have you painted my horse?"

"And Tori," said Emma. "Why have you painted Tori? That's just…creepy."

"Way to give him my name, Em," Tori hissed.

The man looked at a loss for words. Tori wasn't sure if she wanted to hit him or run from him. She had a million questions going through her head.

The man gathered his composure and turned to the woman in the pants suit. "Allison, please bring these two women to my office. I'd love to speak with them."

"I'd love to speak to you right here," said Tori, keeping her voice low.

"I think we should have some privacy," he said. He glanced around. Tori followed his eyes. People had started to take their phones out and were snapping photos of her. Because no photos were allowed in the gallery, security started ushering people out and threatening to take phones.

"Is it *her?*" someone said.

"I think it is. It's the woman in the paintings! Look at her hair!"

325

Voices went from whispers to murmurs. Tori felt her anger turning a little bit to fear. This whole problem was getting worse.

"Okay," she said. "Let's go talk."

She looked at Emma for support. Her friend nodded and put on her "tough face." Emma's "tough face" consisted of a frown that didn't do much to make her slightly round five-foot-three-inch frame look stronger. Her blonde bob swung as she turned. Tori followed. She had to know why *her* horse—and *her* clothes—were on canvases for the entire world to see.

To continue reading *Finding Hope: A Horses and Hearts Inspirational Romance*, visit PamelaGossiaux.com..

Acknowledgments

A special thank you to my readers for taking the time to read my books when there are so many out there to choose from. I love hearing from you, and I am grateful from the bottom of my heart for each and every one of you. This series has all the things I love: Lake Michigan, a small town, faith, family, horses, and of course, a love story. I believe that all things are possible through love and the grace of God, and it's my hope that my books offer you not only a few hours of enjoyment and escape, but a sense of comfort, like a warm blanket on a cold night.

Thank you to my beta readers, who get the roughest of drafts and don't complain: Peggy, Anna B., and Sheila C., and of course to the gals in my writer's critique group: Xanthe, Other Pam, and Anna. What would I do without you? You all have not only suffered through my rewrites, but have listened to my endless horse stories without rolling your eyes.

I spent many years in the horse show world, thanks to my parents and some very good friends. Thank you Mom and Dad, for giving me the opportunity to get started, and thank you Duane, for helping me continue. And of course, thank you to my boys, Zack and Logan. You are the light that keeps me going.

And finally, to Jesus, my Lord and Savior. I humbly write because of you. To God be the Glory. Always.

Note from the Author

(Note: May contain spoilers!)

Horse showing is a world I'm familiar with, and a world I love. That being said, I have taken some liberties in the writing of this book.

First, many of the people portrayed in this novel are selfish and focused on winning and the money it brings. I've found the opposite to be true in real life. While there are some obnoxious people in equestrian sports, most horse people are kind and friendly, willing to help out a fellow horse person.

Secondly, qualifying for the Olympics is a long and complex journey. I've shortened the process and added a few liberties for the flow of the story.

The rest of the book is hopefully accurate. I have spent most of my life around horses, and dressage is one of my favorite equestrian sports. All of the horse and dressage facts should be correct. I hope that if you have never watched the dressage freestyle event, Hannah and Grace's story will encourage you to check out a few routines on the internet. I don't think you'll be disappointed.

Other Books by Pamela Gossiaux

A sweet romantic comedy!

Meet Amy Summers, a big-hearted heroine whose simple life gets turned upside down when she finds a winning lottery ticket worth millions…but should she cash it?

Amy Summers has it all: the world's best job, an awesome boyfriend, and a happily-ever-after in sight. Then, in one very bad day that involves burnt toast and a police arrest, she loses everything – except for a winning lottery ticket her ex left behind.

Afraid to cash it, she decides to give up men and become a Bohemian novelist. She takes her laptop to Starbucks and literally bumps into caffeine-free, easy-going Josh Gray, a life coach and very handsome man. (Not that she's noticing.) When he offers to help Amy get back on her feet, she decides to hire him.

Her heart is telling her that he's the man for her, but Josh is big on honesty and Amy has a huge secret that could push him away if he ever finds out.

"Richly meaningful while wildly entertaining, GOOD ENOUGH is a major new book by an exceptionally talented author."
– Grady Harp, Amazon Hall of Fame Top 100 Reviewer

"This story is such a fun read, it is impossible once you have opened it not to be thoroughly captivated by Amy's escapades."
– Susan Keefe, *Midwest Book Review*

"GOOD ENOUGH touches a nerve every woman faces. Are we ever going to be good enough? Gossiaux has written a funny, revenge romance that will have you cheering on the heroine, Amy, until the very end."
—Diana Lesire Brandmeyer, author of CBA Best Seller *Mind of Her Own*

Available at PamelaGossiaux.com

About the Author

Pamela Gossiaux is the international bestselling author of the *Horses and Hearts Inspirational Romance* series, the *Russo Romantic Mystery* series, the romantic comedy *Good Enough*, the YA book *Ordinary Girl*, and the inspirational books *Why Is There a Lemon in My Fruit Salad?* and *A Kid at Heart*. She is also a keynote speaker, freelance writer, and teaches writing workshops. She lives and writes at her horse farm in Michigan, where she resides with her family and an assortment of pets. Visit her website at PamelaGossiaux.com. Follow her on Instagram, Facebook, Twitter, and BookBub. To receive updates, news, and special offers, sign up for her newsletter.

www.ingramcontent.com/pod-product-compliance
Lightning Source LLC
Chambersburg PA
CBHW071154100726
47908CB00002B/378